OUT
OF
A
SEASON

OUT
OF
A
SEASON

Gabriella Kramer Mautner

Originally published by Thomas Y. Crowell Company

Copyright © 1968, 2011 by Gabriella Mautner

ISBN: 978-1-5040-3703-7

Distributed in 2016 by Open Road Distribution
180 Maiden Lane
New York, NY 10038
www.openroadmedia.com

To my mother

As every blossom fades and all youth sinks
into old age, so every life's design,
each flower of wisdom, every good, attains
its prime and cannot last for ever.
At life's each call the heart must be prepared
to take its leave and to commence afresh,
courageously and with no hint of grief
submit itself to other, newer ties.
A magic dwells in each beginning and
protecting us it tells us how to live.

—*Hermann Hesse*

ONE

The dream world of my adolescence was scarcely more unreal than the unreality of those three Italian summers. Then, everything was magnified. I still remember the noise, the crowds, the pink gaping watermelon rinds spilled like jellyfish on the shore; those long sleepless nights torn by the early-morning cries of vendors; the honey-trickle of love songs pouring from invisible gramophones; and the fantastic glow of picture-postcard sunsets. Now those memories stand out in clear relief, no longer dimmed with closeness. Not only because of Dario. He blends into the landscape and atmosphere; he was for me the vital center of it all. Yet regardless of Dario, my love for Italy and its people began, I believe, with one incident, and from there on, it grew and spread into an ever-widening tapestry.

In the Piedmont mountains, in the hamlet outside of Turin where we spent our first September, there was a priest by the name of Father Giacomo. A tall, lean ascetic, he was severe and dry with coal-black eyes sunk deep in their sockets and an enormous hairless skull. Mother sent Maxine and me to his barren room twice a week for Italian lessons. We both feared this man's austerity and would sigh with relief when he dismissed us at the end of the hour.

The day my sister was stricken with scarlet fever we rushed back to Turin in a hired cab. We saw Father Giacomo on the mountain road, and briefly stopped to tell him what had happened. We found him in front of Maxine's hospital room the day she died. He said he had some business in town and wished to inquire about her health on his way back. When Mother told him in a broken voice that the doctors had given up hope, he looked at her in consternation. His big hands stretched out toward her in a helpless gesture; then he seized my arm as he stood there above me, weeping. The religious words of comfort he said later meant nothing to me.

As I write this down, I wonder if Father Giacomo's tears were really the beginning of it all. Where does anything begin? And where does it end? We always put up defenses against what we don't understand. Or we look for the incident that will define for us the abstract and the intangible.

I can no longer loaf or rest on beaches. I shun the midday heat, the sight of white flesh exposed, the vulgar voices of summer crowds. The sense of tension, anguish, and longing that those early summers seem to have injected into my blood is quite irrational. Now I flee all such places where once Dario and I could never be alone and undisturbed, where we could never be by ourselves in a cool and private silence. Perhaps I don't want to be reminded of the repetitive circles of our living, which stifle all poetry within us as if it were secret and shameful. How then can I yearn for what never really was? If not for the dreams in which I can no longer believe?

Mother and I met Dario near Lake Como when I was thirteen. It was the beginning of my first summer vacation in Italy after Maxine's death, the end of a year's convent school in Turin. On leaving those monastic walls for the independence of carefree days at my mother's side, I felt like one restored to life. We were two friends, she the younger, I the older. It seemed to me that I was burdened with a more ancient blood, weighted by the darkness of my appearance. I was supposed to be my father's image. I had inherited his black hair and his straight high forehead. I wasn't sure if this included his sullen bearing. People used to say that my father was a handsome man while they spoke of my mother as charming. Yet how I wished her Titian hair and light blue eyes that never lost their childlike gleam and her stately nose slightly curved at the tip had not been passed on only to Maxine.

Oh, Maxine! How I loved you and cried for you and how I regretted our childish quarrels. . . . It was only a year since she had died. Father had flown back from Zurich just in time for the funeral. Mother had not wanted me to go to the cemetery. She had returned with a blind and bloated face, and had paid no heed to me in her grief. "Now you are the only thing I have left in the world, my one and only comfort," she had said to me later. I did not like to be just a comfort. I wished I had died instead of Maxine. She was only two years older than I, and we had been steady companions in a nomadic life as we moved from one country to another: from the States, where we were born, to France, where my mother's family lived; and from France to England; then to Switzerland, and finally to Italy. Always foreigners, wherever we would settle, Maxine and I had been a stronghold for each other; we had teamed up against the maids and governesses in whose care we had frequently been left.

On that warm June afternoon when we met Dario, the motorboat cut leisurely across Lake Como. The sun had

3

wandered around the hills, and the green garlands of vineyards on the slopes turned purple. In the distance, at the other end of the lake, the tongue of land that was part of the town of Bellagio formed a sharp triangle of light. Areas dipped in shade seemed to grow silent, deserted, as if hushed by the withdrawal of the sun. There was about an hour left until dusk.

Mother and I stepped ashore, then walked slowly along a road lined with cypress trees. The road was narrow and short, and the tops of the trees glowed golden in the sun. Visitors streamed out of the gate as we entered the park. Soon the warbling summer voices were drowned in the rattle of the motorboat making ready for another crossing.

I was glad we had come late. Now Mother and the park belonged all to me. The long summer ahead belonged to me, too. I could do with it as I pleased. For a moment I thought of my father, who would join us a month later at the seaside, in Rimini; but the weight of his shadow could be pushed back. A month was a long time.

Hand in hand, we strolled on the winding paths under huge eucalyptus trees, beside exotic plants and rampant shrubs and flowers. We must have been walking for an hour or so when Mother stopped near a couple of American tourists to admire a white orchid. They said something to us, as they heard us speak English, and Mother, seeing fellow Americans, began to talk to them in her outgoing way. I must have grown bored with the chatter of the grown-ups. I remember moving toward a white wooden bridge that took me across a dried-out river bed. Below the bridge orchids grew in abundance among the climbing plants and tall fern.

I walked on quickly, half frightened, half lost in dreams. This must be some enchanted wood, full of

4

insects with silken, variegated wings building their homes in those little orchidboots, spear-shaped dragonflies, and iridescent beetles. Once or twice I heard a voice but in my absorption paid no attention to its sound. Unaware of whether I was walking or standing still, I came awake at the touch of a breeze and looked up to see that the park had grown quiet and empty. Now I remembered the voice calling in the distance. I ran back in the direction I thought my mother must be, but the more I ran the more lost I became. The shadows grew deeper, and no living soul crossed my way.

At last I found myself near the white bridge again. My eyes avoided the frightening wilderness below. An evil spell seemed to have spread over the park. I called for Mother, but my voice was soundless. A gust of wind blew over the fern, bending and spreading it with a fanning motion. I took a deep breath and called as loudly as I could. In response I heard nothing but eerie laughter that seemed to rise from the thicket. I ran on blindly, in zig-zags and circles until, after what seemed an eternity, I found myself once more at the same spot.

Trees, bushes, plants closed in on me. Now the laughter rose again, scornful at first, then threatening and wild. I closed my eyes. Beyond the walls of my lids, trees and plants smiled like Halloween masks. Encircled by stampeding crowds, I could hear the clash of cymbals, the gold sounds of trumpets. There were fat piggish snouts of *papier-mâché*, evil flashing eyes, paper snakes, and confetti raining down on me. It brought back some early memory of a carnival in a strange town when I was torn from the anchor of my mother's hand.

I compelled myself to remain calm; then I opened my eyes. Before me stood a bush in golden bloom. For a moment I was convinced that nothing is, nothing was, nothing would be but an illusion. I reached out for the golden dots and stroked a few of the bush's delicate leaves. They shrank from my touch. Surely my imagination was playing tricks on me. Once more I brushed over the tiny fans, but they contracted, withdrawing from my caress. If I was lost before, I was now rejected, cast out by nature itself. I knew that I would not find my way back to a life full of order and clarity, but would die in the midst of this entanglement. Mother would lose me as she had lost Maxine, but I was too anxious for tears.

Then Dario found me, to lead me out of one thicket into another.

When I heard steps approaching, I instinctively sought protection behind the mimosa bush. My hair tangled with the twigs. I made myself quite small. Through a branch I caught sight of a stranger's white-trousered legs as he stopped, and then of a dark-blue linen jacket. He remained standing on the path a few feet away from me. Then he talked in Italian to me, in a deep and reassuring voice.

At last I stepped out of my hiding place and saw that his face was not frightening. He smiled, his dark eyes gleaming, and brushed some yellow dust off my shoulder. "Come, I'll help you find your way," he said reassuringly. At a slight turn of his head I noticed the deep scar under his left eye. When he smiled, he seemed very young and handsome, hardly more than twenty, but now he appeared to be old and almost ugly. We walked on in silence. Sometimes he turned to me with a smile that erased the scar. He asked no questions, and I was grateful.

Mother was standing guard at the main gate. I ran to her and threw my arms around her. For a moment she scolded me in angry English that extinguished my happiness. When she calmed down, she noticed the stranger. He inclined his head toward her with his charming smile and explained how he had found me lost and frightened.

"My name is Dario Ventura," he said. He put his hand into the inner pocket of his jacket and slowly pulled out a white card and handed it to Mother ceremoniously. His lips were thin when he did not smile.

"I am Clarisse Steiner," Mother said, glancing at the card; she put it into her bag. "And this is my daughter, Nicole."

The sun was setting over the lake as I squatted in the motorboat, listening with my head averted to my mother's and the stranger's conversation. He had grown talkative and, like so many Italians, was obviously fascinated by the color of Mother's hair and her linguistic slips. Once he turned to me and said he had thought I was an Italian because of my looks, and Mother answered proudly that I spoke the language fluently because I had been with nuns in a convent school this past year.

"Did you like it there?" he asked. I shook my head. "I was brought up by priests," he told me, "and it didn't do me too much harm. I managed to keep my wickedness intact. You still look a bit sheepish, but one gets over it fast enough."

Then Mother told him how the sisters had made me study an endless poem by heart, and bragged of how I had recited it to her fluently and without mistakes.

I looked at the stranger. The light of the sunset was on his face, softening its colors and contours. He was really no stranger at all.

"What poem was it?" he asked. I blushed.

"What poem was it, Nicole?" Mother asked.

7

" 'Davanti a San Guido'," I said so softly that they made me repeat it.

"Carducci," he said. "That's long enough even for an Italian."

"Nicole is going to write poems, too," Mother said indulgently. I bit into the flesh of my cheeks and looked at the lights on shore. The vine-grown fields were covered by a mantle of dark-brown shadows. All at once, as I felt the stranger's eyes on my face, I was glad that Maxine was not with us. I thought how much he would have been impressed with her lovely blue eyes, her golden-reddish hair, and her fair complexion. I just could not help rejoicing.

It was dusk when we stepped ashore. The young man accompanied us to our inn where we stopped under the colonnade to say good-bye. As Mother thanked him again for having brought me back to her, my mind was full of questions I dared not ask. I was afraid he might walk out of my life.

"I hope we shall meet again," he said, bowing to Mother and smiling at me.

"That would be nice," Mother answered in the same polite tone of voice, "but we are leaving the day after tomorrow."

"So am I," he said. "I've come here from Milano for only a couple of days between exams." As Mother walked ahead into our hotel, he turned to me and whispered, "Perhaps I shall see you tomorrow, Nicole?"

I nodded shyly.

"You aren't afraid of me any more?"

I shook my head. "*Arrivederci*," I murmured.

"*Addio, piccola mimosa.*"

He walked away slowly under the *portici*, past chairs and white metal tables, once waving his hand with a backward motion, without turning his head. Then,

8

before stepping out of the arcades, he halted, faced me, and waved again.

"He has a crown on his card," Mother said, as we sat down for dinner. "Count Dario Ventura. I doubt that it's authentic."

"He does look aristocratic," I said.

Mother took back the card, put in into her purse, and said, "Paper is patient, Nicole. You mustn't believe everything a stranger tells you. Especially an Italian."

Italians for me were the fat and kindly market queens enthroned behind their mountains of greens, tomatoes, garlic strings, fish, rabbits, or fowl; the tram conductors; the chestnut vendors with their frostbitten fingers whose flesh-cushioned tips burst from black knitted gloves like the hot starchy fruits cracking their shells; the brown-cowled Capuchin monks on the hills with their noses in their prayer books; the self-effacing black-clad nuns in my school, always on their knees praying or scrubbing floors and turning their Madonna smiles on you as you passed; my exquisite and adored teacher, Madame Marie Thérèse; and Zita, our gay, snub-nosed, blabber-mouthed maid with her trail of admiring soldiers. . . .

The next morning, I looked in vain for Dario Ventura, in the street at first, and later in the open-air swimming pool. Mother napped after lunch, and I sat in front of our hotel reading and watching the passersby. Mother came down refreshed, and suggested we walk to the hills. I was tired and bored, hating the drudgery of climbing the dusty mountain road. The only pleasant diversion occurred on the way down when a friendly farmer offered us brown earthenware cups filled with homemade red wine across a hedge of wild roses. My steps turned into hiccups as I leaned upon Mother and stumbled down the cobblestoned paths. I felt numbly aware of the idiotic grin on my face. When we returned to our hotel room I fell face down on my bed, oblivious to the dirt on my shoes.

It was dark when I awoke. Mother's laughter spilled over my face along with the water of a dripping sponge.

"Quit it!" I cried.

"Dinner time, you drunkard!" I opened one eye and saw that she looked radiant in my favorite dress, a low-cut light-blue chiffon with wide long sleeves. I inhaled the heady fragrance of her perfume. She went to the tall cupboard and returned with a white organdy dress, which she put at the foot of my bed. In spite of her protests, I drew her close to me. It was good to feel the softness of her full body, which seemed to say pleasure for its own sake. After a moment, she tore herself out of my clutches and pulled me to my feet.

"What's for dinner?" I became fully awake. How starved I was!

We went down, ate an ample meal, then took our coffee at an open-air table in front of the hotel. Mother had taught me the rules of chess. We played a few games, and I was proud of my progress. I had just succeeded in rescuing my queen from danger when I felt two hands on my shoulders and saw Mother looking up above my head.

"I passed by this afternoon," Dario said.

"We had gone for a walk. Won't you join us, Signor Ventura?"

He drew a chair to the table and sat down between us. "You have an ambitious daughter, signora," he said, pointing at the board.

"Do you play?" she asked. He nodded. I offered him my chair.

Mother took a white pawn into her right hand and a black one into her left, changed them under the table, then stretched her two fists toward him. He hesitated. "What lovely hands!" he whispered, as he touched her left one softly. She flung it open with a challenging glance at his face.

"White for me. I'll be starting the battle," he said, returning her gaze.

He set up the figures. His hands were coarser than I had expected, rather large and broad, with well-groomed round fingernails. They were in striking contrast to his gaunt and handsome profile. His good side was toward me as he played, the one without the scar. I became aware of the exquisite shell of his ear. I have never come across more delicately shaped ears than Dario's. They were small and close to his head.

I paid some attention to the game, but whenever it was Dario's turn to move, I continued with my secret scrutiny. His fine brown hair was straight and full, brushed back without a part; his bushy brows were traced in full curves above the large brown deep-set eyes. He snapped his fingers at a passing waiter, and, after we had declined his offer for pastries and drinks, asked him to bring him an espresso and a shot of cognac. I was impressed by his worldly ease and the perfect poise of his manner. His suntanned appearance did not fit my picture of students as starving creatures in sunless attics, with rounded backs and glasses on their noses.

Later on, when he sipped his coffee, I noticed that he stretched his little finger away from the others. Mother had once told me that this was a mannerism uneducated people considered refined. It did not match his lofty brow and the sweeping curve of his hair. I watched carefully the next time he lifted his cup from the saucer. To my relief, he did not repeat the gesture. I was now convinced that Dario must indeed be a count.

They played two games, and Mother won them both. Dario sighed with a comically unhappy expression, and said that I would probably be a better partner for him. I would have liked to play, but Mother remembered that it was past my bedtime, since we had to rise early the next morning for our trip to Rimini.

"Rimini?" Dario said. "I'm going there in August. Will you still be there?"

"We have rented a house for the summer on Viale Dardanelli," Mother said.

"What a coincidence! That's where I'm going. I have an idea," he said. "Since I must leave tomorrow, too, I might as well take the early train with you, and then we can play chess all the way to Milano."

"Very good," Mother said, and then she turned to me. "Go ahead, darling. I'll be up in a few minutes."

The next day, however, Dario was not on the bus to Como. After the trip, winding around the cliffs of the lake, I still hoped to see him at the station.

"I warned you not to believe strangers," Mother remarked as we settled in the compartment of a coach.

I said that he might have hired a cab and might now be somewhere on the train. But Mother was doubtful and added, "I wonder why he made up that story about Rimini and Viale Dardanelli. . . ."

As the train moved out of Como, I stepped into the corridor and looked out the window. From time to time, I glanced toward the far end of the narrow passageway. I felt a mingled sadness—a sadness of loss, of regret, and a sense of void following his unkept promise. Mother was right, I told myself, though still refusing to give up hope. I would probably never see Dario Ventura again.

♣ ♣

A few months earlier, that previous winter, Zita came to our house in Turin for the first time. We had just moved from the furnished apartment near the River Po to a fine and roomy flat on Corso Galileo Ferraris. It was February, and our furniture had arrived from Zurich along with my father. Mother was napping while I piled books onto the shelves of a case in the bright square hall next to the entrance door, which we had converted into a library. I can still hear the elevator humming and stopping outside. A moment later an ash-blond-haired girl with a skittish air stood before me and wished to know if the job for a cook and general assistant was still available. At the words "general assistant" her face swelled with pompousness, and I pretended to sneeze as I burst out laughing. Her short hair was tight and frizzy with a new permanent, and she smelled like a beauty parlor, but she looked fresh and pretty with her ruddy, Slavic cheeks, her upturned nose, and her green, narrow, cat-like eyes.

I asked her to come in and offered her a seat, after clearing Schiller's collected dramas from a soft brown velvety chair. She sat on the edge, not from shyness, but as if she wanted to impress me with her gentility, but I only feared her bottom might slide onto the floor at any instant. I was amused by the touch of insolence which denied her studied behavior.

She introduced herself as "Zita." I looked at her for a moment, and she repeated proudly, "Zita, like the Austrian empress." Then she asked my name, and when I told her, she remarked that Steiner was a German name.

I said that my father was Swiss, but that we were really Americans. "Marco Polo was my mother's great-grandfather," I added importantly.

"Oh," she said.

I went into the long narrow hall. At the other end Mother came out of her room, tousled and groggy. One of her cheeks showed the imprint of the initials embroidered on her pillow case. I told her Zita, "like the empress," had come to see her about the ad.

Was she nice? Mother wanted to know, and I followed her to the bathroom and watched her comb her hair and pat the paler cheek until it took on the pinkness of the other, without the imprint. "You should sleep on the other side for an hour now," I said. "She's pretty."

Mother walked through the hall, and I followed just in time to see Zita who had sunk comfortably into an armchair rise with a start. Mother made her sit down again, then settled herself in another chair, facing her across a low table.

I went on stacking books, every now and then glancing at Zita's even teeth and watching her coy manner. She was of Austrian origin, she said, and she knew a good many Viennese recipes. This information took my mother's heart by storm. Soon they were delighting each other with descriptions of imaginary doughs and strudels and puddings, and I found my mouth watering. First I listened with growing interest that gradually turned into irritation when Mother began to expose our family history. Within five minutes, Zita knew of her French-American background, of Maxine's death and Father's export business, of my grandmother in Paris and my convent school in the hills across the river.

I can remember Mother's confiding familiarity with amusement now, although at the time it used to vex me to the point of shame. Yet her childlike candor took the edge off my annoyance. Italians were especially receptive to her openness. They rewarded her in trains, waiting rooms, and other public places by entrusting her with their life stories.

At last Zita left to get her belongings, and by the time Father came back for dinner that evening she had not only helped us to arrange, clean, and fix our rooms but prepared her first tasty meal as well. The dishes washed, we could hear her talking from the kitchen balcony with other maids across the courtyard.

There seemed to be a link between her tremendous efficiency and her talkativeness, as though her entire machinery was set in motion only by her mouth. Wherever her foot trod, cobwebs disappeared, door knobs sparkled, floors turned into slippery mirrors while the white walls echoed the shrillness of her chants, her chatting, and her giggles.

And now, when we arrived in Rimini, hot and tired from the trip, she awaited us in the cool, scrubbed summer house on Viale Dardanelli. We were subjected to a tour of inspection. With each turn of her head, each motion of her buttocks, shoulders, and hands, Zita was saying that if it weren't for her it would not be fit for living. In the end, she led us to the windows in triumph, as if she were a museum director unveiling his most precious treasure. We had no idea how filthy they had been!

"You didn't clean them, Zita. You broke them!" I said. She looked at me, aghast.

I raced toward a window as if I meant to stick my fist right through it, but she held me back in panic and cried, "No, don't do that!"

After dinner I went to my cubicle of a room and undressed for the night. And then Zita came in without knocking and sat down on the edge of my bed.

She asked me how I had enjoyed my stay at Lake Como. As usual, she did not wait for my answer, but began to tell me the life history of a neighbor's maid, Maria, a nice little girl, you know, but ignorant. After all, what could one expect from a peasant? I watched Zita's large mouth talking, and wondered whether it would ever stop. I felt tired from the trip. I longed to talk about Dario Ventura, and for a moment wondered whether I should tell her of our encounter.

Did I know, Zita was saying, that she had met the most handsome sailor the other night? I nodded, thinking, *No, I can't mention anything about him to her.* She wanted to know who had told me of her sailor and I said, "You did." Ah, she said, laughing good-naturedly, would I ever stop teasing her! At least it showed that I was happy. I would have another three months before having to go back to that awful convent school, she added. But Mother had promised me that I needn't go back there at all, I reassured her, and I would be sent to a regular school this fall.

"*Bene, bene!* You didn't like those nuns on the hills, *nè?*" she asked with the Piedmontese inflection she had recently acquired.

"Some of them, yes."

"So you think they are good and saintly, better than real people, let's say, like us?"

I thought of our Latin and Roman history teacher, Madame Marie Thérèse, so angelic in spite of her sternness, and of pimply Madame Joseph Marie, who used to turn her eyes heavenward while letting the girls know that in the future life would offer us a choice between taking the veil or becoming "good mothers," *buone madri di famiglia.*

Zita's sly, doubting face bent over mine as she whispered, "I've never said this before, but now that you won't go back there again, you should know a few things . . . just between the two of us . . ."

"Know what, Zita?"

"Promise not to tell?" I nodded numbly. "Cross your heart and hope to die?" I put my hand on my heart.

16

"You don't know lots of things because you are still a child."

I saw her knowing slant-eyes narrowing. For a moment she looked like a snake. I became bewildered and apprehensive. "You know, there are several cloisters on the hills." She hesitated. "*Ebbene* . . . the monks and nuns secretly meet in those dark tunnels."

"How do you mean, tunnels?" I asked, my heart missing a beat.

"They lead from convent to convent, underground."

"Are you sure?"

"Positive. The janitress told me all about it, and she knows."

"Is it always dark down there?" I asked. She nodded. "And what do they do when they meet?"

"Oh, you are too young to understand!"

"Tell me!"

"No, no. But I assure you it isn't nice at all. And then they go to holy Mass and confess and pray and have a lot of fine words for you."

I tried to see the monks and nuns doing something hideous in those tunnels, but the darkness was so great, and I could not really imagine what Zita meant. Later after she had turned off the light and left me, I tried to picture Madame Joseph Marie with her yellow buckteeth and black moustache doing evil things in such a tunnel. Then I thought of Madame Marie Thérèse with her white, ethereal features and her dark, all-seeing eyes. I could imagine her only in the park, or in sunny classrooms, or in the chapel. My mind refused to see her go down subterranean corridors, to see her do anything that could not face the light.

I drifted into restless sleep and dreamed that as I walked along Viale Dardanelli I saw Dario's face looking at me from the second-story windows of each house. As I passed door after door, his face changed into the faces of grinning maids who shook their dusty rags above my head with scornful laughter. Then I was back in the corridor of the train, waiting for him to come walking toward me from the other end of the coach. All at once he was there, his back turned to me. I reached out for the sleeve of his linen jacket, trying to make my presence known to him, but he paid no attention and moved away. I followed him slowly, calling his name with a soundless voice, but he receded farther and farther. I groped in utter darkness along the wet wall of a tunnel, trying to find my way out. I could feel a monk's presence, darker than the darkness, closing in on me, like a pinpoint in the distance, growing larger and larger and larger. . . . Frantic with fear, I tried to retreat, but felt walled in from all sides. As I recognized the sweep of the tall monk's head and saw the scar pulling down his eye, I broke out in sweat and screamed a soundless scream and woke sitting up in bed, gasping.

TWO

That summer in Rimini is painted like a fresco on my memory. The days moved slowly, week after week. Like the white, triangular spot of a sailboat on the horizon that at times is the only visible break between the endless azure and quiescent expanse of sea and sky, Dario's image rose in the distance, and then grew paler and paler with the passing of time. Every now and then I would sneak out of my room after sunrise and run down to the water and be back for breakfast before anyone had noticed my absence. In the early morning the sea exuded a strong, tangy odor. Before the blazing sun turned it to its orthodox sparkling blue it was covered by a milky sheen, a silver layer of mother-of-pearl. I felt at one with the silence of the sea. Chatting women and noisy children would soon tear the stillness with the cacophony of their strident voices.

There would be the brown, tattooed attendants opening the large umbrellas and multicolored lounging chairs, untying the white canvases that were bound to poles at night, preparing the boats for rowing. Fat black-haired women would settle in their beach chairs and knit, knit, knit, silver needles pressed tight under wet armpits, their mouths chatting the morning away in competition with their rapid work. Red, blue, white, green, and yellow balls that were the bathing-capped heads of swimmers would float on the water. Along the shore, children would build forts of sand; barking dogs would chase after waves, toddlers, and each other; nursemaids would tend crying or cooing babies.

Cesare, Lilliana, and Augusto were native Italians of my own age I had met on the beach. We used to play marbles in the sand every day for hours, between the cabins. Big, pretty Lilliana always won. She could throw five marbles into the air and catch them all at once on the back of her doughy hand between her fingers. Gradually, the sun baked us all from a rosy red to a fine milk-chocolate brown.

Mother would have to call me to get ready for a swim, a call to which I was never deaf, and I would happily run and plunge into the water.

Augusto would always be at my side, a mute, handsome shadow. If I swam fast, he would accelerate his speed, then dive and swim at a lower level so that I could see his shape like a fish under my body. If I would lie on my back, watching the sky, he would float at my side, watching me. His constant, silent attention weighed heavily upon me, and his boundless devotion challenged my dormant cruelty.

This devotion was utterly passive, almost morose. I teased him to see him flare at me in anger, but his life-less, handsome face would never change its exasperatingly patient and adoring expression. Afternoons, he sometimes took me for a ride on his bicycle. He would let me sit on the rod between the handle bars and the saddle, whispering songs into my hair or saying dull, timid words. He taught me how to ride, running near me for long stretches along the promenade. Perspiring, breathless, like a faithful dog, he was always ready to catch me if I should fall.

Each morning I would recognize the stubborn pace of his legs among the crowds of legs in front of the sea as he approached our tent awning. If I was absorbed in a book and annoyed at his coming, I would run toward the promenade and hide between the rows of cabanas. There I would watch him greet my mother and then move away a few steps and look about searchingly, his protruding ears listening in all directions. He knew I was hiding from him, but he kept coming and coming, even if it was merely to sit at my feet while I read as he let the sand slowly run through his thin brown fingers.

Mother said, "Why are you so mean to Augusto? He's a very nice boy," and I answered that I liked him, but could not help it if he bored me to death. Mother nodded absent-mindedly. She was busy preparing a list of foods Zita was to buy for my father's arrival.

Father, who had been traveling in England, Switzerland, and France on business, joined us in Rimini at the end of July. I used to think fondly of him from a distance and was glad to see him come home.

"Here is something for you," he said, as I joined him in his bedroom before dinner. He handed me a book for young girls I had read two years before.

"Thank you very much," I said politely.

"And here, some chocolates."

I thanked him again and lightly kissed his cheek.

"That's all right." He squeezed my shoulder with a stiff hand.

After Maxine died, he had drawn me to him awkwardly and then had turned away with a dry and helpless sob. Now he sat down on the edge of his bed, patting

21

the mattress all over in order to test its firmness, and asked, "How was school, Nicole? Have you learned a great deal?"

"I suppose so."

"Did you catch up with your Latin?"

"Not quite." He had found a bump in the mattress and was shaking his head disapprovingly. "I'm sure I'll catch up next term," I said.

"That's what I thought!" he exclaimed, annoyed.

"I couldn't do it all at once, Father!" I pled.

"It's a rotten mattress!" he said. "I'm sure I won't be able to sleep a wink in this bed. How's the beach? Noisy, eh?"

"Well . . ."

"I'm not sure your mother made a good choice with this place. They tell me Rimini has a lot of fleas."

"You get used to them after a while."

"*A tavola!*" Zita yelled from the terrace.

At first Father liked the terrace and the garden and eating at home again. But the next morning he joined us at breakfast in a sullen mood, complaining about the bed and the noise in the street. A big woman vendor with a wheelbarrow filled with apricots and peaches had screamed about the excellence of her wares as early as six o'clock.

"I'll switch rooms with you," Mother said.

She had appropriated the nicest place in the house, facing the garden. I saw that she did not cherish the prospect, but still preferred a bumpy mattress to my father's grumblings. It did not occur to me then that she might have reserved the best room for her hard-working husband of her own accord. In my eyes, Mother could do no wrong. I accepted her actions unquestioningly.

Until he met the matrons from the Kursaal garden, the crowds on the beach were even more troublesome to

my father. The two elderly ladies owned a small pharmacy where Father bought some linden-blossom tea for
his nightcaps. Each morning they would leave the shop
in the care of a young man and spend a few hours near
the sea. When they sighted us there a few days later, they
struck up a conversation, complimenting my father on
his daughter's good looks. Italians always compli-
mented parents on their children, and I was more bored
than pleased since I did not believe in their sincerity.
After that Father would chat with them for a while
every day, enjoying the undivided attention they paid
his tales, in contrast to my mother's obvious boredom.

"Ah, *la signorina* Nicole!" they said. "Isn't she her
father's image?"

He smiled proudly. In spite of my vexation I tried to
see my father with the ladies' eyes. He was indeed a dis-
tinguished-looking gentleman, imposing even in his bathing trunks. At that time I did not understand what made
me resent our similarity. I did not dare admit to myself to what extent I felt alien to him.

At sunset we would often wander to the pier, my
father's hand resting on the nape of my neck. He would
tell me episodes from his childhood that I had heard
before, or give me detailed descriptions of something
that had impressed him on his trips. I did not mind his
repetitions as long as there were no quarrels and everything was in harmony. I hardly listened to what he said,
but enjoyed the rhythm of his pleasant voice as I gazed
dreamily at the rows and rows of cabins, stretching along
the wide beach all the way to the mole, and at the Adria-
tic Sea in its immense blue repose.

Peace never lasted long. It was a respite I had learned
to enjoy between storms and clashes. About two weeks
after my father's arrival, I recognized the signs of an
approaching tempest. From day to day his complaints

about the noise, the food, the climate, the international situation, and his sleeplessness increased, until they grew into angry invectives. This usually happened at about the same time his stomach was beginning to be upset by the excessive amount of fruit he ate.

One morning I found him at the breakfast table gloomily spooning a bowl of oatmeal. Mother watched him sullenly at the other end. My heart sank. I brushed his gray, unshaven cheek with my lips for the good-morning ritual. Mother was oblivious to my presence. There followed one of those familiar, trifling arguments over nothing that grew out of proportion and left everybody miserable.

According to my father, Zita had put vinegar instead of lemon juice in his salad dressing the previous night. Didn't Mother know that vinegar upset his entire system? Mother grew indignant at his accusation, and said that she had personally supervised Zita squeezing the lemons. Father retorted that she was lying. Mother's eyes turned green with anger as she shouted at him in turn and accused him of eating too greedily.

I felt weak in my knees, sick in my stomach, and sick in my heart. Mother was right, but she had put herself in the wrong with her shouting. I was unable to grasp why grown-ups could get excited about such trifles. I tried not to listen any longer and slipped away at the first opportunity.

On the beach the children were playing in the shade between the cabanas. I joined them reluctantly. My head felt light and giddy. It was windy, and the sea was choppy and turbid. Mother settled down near the water with a book on her lap. I went in for a swim with her before lunch; then we dressed in silence and just as silently went home.

Mother sat down at the dining table at once, but I felt it a duty to inquire about Father's health. I knocked at his door and peeped in. He was lying in bed, his face turned toward the wall.

"Hello, Father," I said shyly. He answered with a grunt. "Are you feeling better?" He turned round on his back in silence, and without looking at me, showed me his suffering face. "Is there anything I can do for you or bring you?" I asked.

His lips moved soundlessly, indicating that there was nothing anyone could do for him.

"Well," I said, "I'll let you rest."

He joined us at dinner that evening, punishing himself in angry silence with another bowl of porridge. I always sided with my mother because he only seemed to bring friction into our lives. My father sensed this hostility, and responded with unkindness. He did not speak to us for several days. I would sit uneasily between my parents at mealtime, unable to eat. I had heard about Trappist cloisters in which silence was observed, but that kind of silence, I thought, must surely be more enjoyable than this. If Father had to communicate something to Mother, he did so indirectly, telling Zita what was on his mind. Gradually he would grow tired of this situation, and work toward a truce by first speaking to me. It did not matter what method either of them used to bring these hostilities to an end. Sooner or later things always got straightened out, and I sighed with relief to see our lives restored to a friendlier atmosphere.

It was almost the end of August, and there was still no sign of Dario. Only the street signs of Viale Dardanelli brought back a vague memory of his dark eyes, or his smile, or the sweeping fullness of his hair.

We used to eat on the back porch facing the wilderness

of a neglected garden. Large plane trees hid the house and yard to our right. The neighbors on our left, a middle-aged couple with two young children and their maid, were separated from us by a low green wooden fence. Sometimes we used to stop at the fence and exchange a few friendly words with Signora Bontempi.

One afternoon in early September, I sat reading under the vine-colored trellis near the fence in the back of our garden. From time to time my eyes strayed from the book on my lap and wandered to the tight clusters of grapes above my head. Some were full and golden-yellow from the ripeness of the summer sun; others, forgotten in the shade, were still tiny and opaque.

I was about to pluck the most luscious bunch when I heard someone call my name. I turned my head toward the voice and saw Dario leaning over the fence. I leaped from my seat, my book sliding to the ground, and after a moment's hesitation went up to him.

He was wearing the same immaculate white trousers and blue linen summer jacket. "How are you, *piccola mimosa*?" he said. "So we are neighbors!" Signora Bontempi, it turned out, was his aunt. . . .

The sun shone through the foliage of a tree above our heads. Rays of light played with his long black lashes, danced over his tanned cheeks, and our hands were pressed together in greeting.

"Why didn't I see you before?" I asked.

"Because I only arrived last night."

"I didn't think you would come."

"Why? Didn't you believe me?"

"You weren't on the train either," I said, holding on to the wooden spikes of the fence.

"That's because I overslept. Oh, I was furious!"

"I thought you had forgotten," I said, relieved.

"Forgotten! Do you think one finds little girls under

mimosa bushes every day? Especially one who is going to be a poet?" he added softly, patting my head.

I recoiled. "I'm no poet," I said almost angrily. I didn't like to talk about it.

"Now what have I said wrong? I wasn't making fun of you, Nicole." I looked at his serious face. "I said it because I, too, want to write more than anything in the world."

"Poetry?"

"No, not poetry; drama. Plays. Do you like to go to the theater?"

"I have only seen *Weihnachtsmaerchen* in Zurich," I said.

"What's that?"

"Christmas fairy tales. Kid stuff."

"Maybe we can see a real play together some day." In turn, he held on to the fence, putting his hands next to mine. "In what language do you write, Nicole?"

"I'm not writing anything," I said.

He thought for a moment, then sized me up. "Do you know that you have grown tremendously?" he said. "Are you a good swimmer?"

"Oh, yes!" I said.

He smiled. "I'll test you tomorrow. What a tan you've got! Like a mulatto girl. Nice enough to paint."

Under his scrutiny I felt self-conscious in my white shorts, and began to play with a red button on my white sleeveless blouse. "How's your mother?" he asked.

"Fine. They are resting now—my parents, I mean—but they'll soon come down."

"I'd like to meet your father," he said. "Tell me, Nicole, did you ever think of me in these past two months?"

I hesitated, then looked down at his hands. "Sometimes," I said. "When I go through Viale Dardanelli."

"So, if you had moved to some other street, you would

27

have forgotten me entirely." I said nothing. He turned my shoulder toward him so I would look into his eyes: "Nicole?"

"Yes?"

"I would like you to stay the way you are now, just as honest and sincere." He looked at me gravely.

"What do you mean?" I was flustered.

"It's easy now," he said, "but it's going to be harder as you grow older. Society will spoil you. I'm looking for the perfect liar—he's an artist too, you know—or the perfectly honest person. I'll make the perfectly honest person out of you."

"You can't make me," I said. "Either I am, or I'm not."

He shook his head. "To be or not to be is not the question here. It's an art, you will find out." As he spoke, he glanced beyond me, toward the terrace of our house.

"Are you trying to use my daughter for some kind of wicked experiment?" I heard my mother's voice behind me.

I moved aside as Dario stretched out his hand across the fence and said how glad he was to see her again, and how becoming the summer had been to us both. He looked at her warmly. I liked to watch his thin lips grow full when he smiled.

Mother inquired about Dario's exams, and he said he had passed them well, but was glad this was not his last year at the university yet. It would push away serious thoughts about life for a little longer.

"And what are you trying to make out of Nicole?" Mother wanted to know.

He said that he had merely told me to remain as sincere as I was now. "Would you call that wicked?" he asked with an innocent air.

Mother replied that it all depended on what he meant by sincerity, especially if he intended to cultivate it artificially. "You may be like that spirit who always wants the good and always creates evil," she added.

I heard Father clearing his throat as he came down the steps from the porch. We waited for him, and then Mother made the introductions. The two men shook hands across the fence. Father's engaging smile showed me that he enjoyed the new acquaintance.

"Are you going to the beach?" Dario inquired, and Father nodded. "Let's all ride down in a carriage!" Dario suggested. My parents protested, but he said, "Please, let me invite you," and left to fetch a horse and wagon from the Corso.

Three minutes later we could hear the clatter of hoofs, and then we saw Dario riding next to the sleepy-eyed coachman. He leaped down nimbly and made us comfortable in the upholstered seats. I watched Dario's long, lean torso next to the old driver's broad and round back. I leaned back, enjoying the breeze and the clip-clop of the hoofs on the asphalt and the green dome of leaves gliding away above our heads. We rushed all too swiftly toward the open sea.

Stepping out of the carriage, Father and Dario were caught in a noble debate about who was going to pay for the ride. In the end, Father laughed, pushed Dario aside, and handed the coachman the money.

"But this was my treat!" Dario protested with a mock-crushed look on his face.

"Don't accept any bills from this young man!" Father said. "They are counterfeit!"

He obviously enjoyed his victory while Dario shrugged his shoulders, trying to look humble, and Mother nudged me, whispering, "I bet our friend doesn't have a lira in his pocket. . . ."

♣ ♣

The glaring, noisy days were gone, and so were most

of the vacationers. The colors deepened in September; the sand lost its burning heat; and the weeks that followed were a gentle reverberation of summer's beauty without its blindness and clamor.

Day after day Dario joined us under our umbrella at the beach. As soon as he came my father would appropriate him. He would read to him from a Swiss paper and then, with a strategic finger, would clarify the international situation. He would use periods of history to explain his point, tracing comparisons with what had happened centuries ago and must consequently happen again.

"Mark my word, Signor Ventura, it won't be long before there will be another war. Why, it's enough to read *Mein Kampf*. The man's a maniac, and he means what he says! Have you read *Mein Kampf*, Signor Ventura?"

"No," Dario said. "I can't stand the style. It's so vulgar."

"But you should read it. We all should know what sooner or later we shall have to face."

"You are probably right, Mr. Steiner. This is the age of vulgarity, and we might as well imbue ourselves with it."

"My dear young man, how old are you?"

"Twenty-five," Dario said.

"Then it should concern you especially. You will be called to arms, or have you completed your military service?

"I haven't even begun," Dario said.

"And you do, as I understand," Father went on, "belong to the nobility?"

"In name only, sir. I know we are dying out, but I do so want to die beautifully." Dario sighed, stretched himself on the sand and bedded his head on my mother's rubber pillow.

Mother and I exchanged quick smiles. I could see princes and noblewomen charmingly swoon all over the beach, and thought if nobility were like Dario it would indeed be a pity if it was to come to an end.

"This is no trifling matter." My father shook his head disapprovingly. "We are heading for a world catastrophe."

Dario had noticed that Father's outlook on the future became particularly gloomy when he hadn't slept well, which caused an exacerbation of his inborn pessimism, and pessimists, in the long run, Dario had said, are always right.

My mother would rob Father of our friend for a game of chess or tennis across the promenade, and I was left with the crumbs from the rich man's table: a quick, understanding glance, a remark every now and then, or a plunge into the water where Dario chased after me as I swam away. Father used to dip his feet carefully, then wet his arms and chest, then disappear up to his knees, then wet himself some more and sink down inch by inch. Mother swam slowly and evenly, like a contented duck, her face held stiff above the water.

Their nap time was my favorite hour. Then Dario would call me at the garden gate and lift me over his fence, and we would play games of patience, checkers, or chess, and talk to each other alone.

"Tell me, Nicole," he said to me one day, interrupting a game of cards in which neither of us was interested, "how did you feel about convent school? Did they torture you with religion?"

I nodded. "Especially when they knew I'm not a Catholic."

"Oh? What are you?"

"Protestant, I suppose." I could not explain to Dario that my religious background was as much of a potpourri as my secular one: part Quaker and Jewish, part Calvinist and Huguenot. . . .

"Did they make you kneel down and pray?" he asked.

"Not really," I said. "The first day of school was very strange."

"Strange in what way?"

I was silent for a moment, remembering how Madame Joseph Marie had said, "Children, I want you to be kind to Nicole. She just lost her only sister." Paula, the girl who shared my bench, had glanced at me to see if I was crying. The white collar on my black dress was too tight. My legs had itched unbearably, but I dared not scratch.

"At the end of our lesson the girls all cowered to the ground," I told Dario, "and I couldn't see a single head above the desks."

"What did you do?"

"I was nailed to the spot," I said, "neither standing nor kneeling . . . like a pocketknife that hasn't snapped closed."

He threw back his head and laughed, his shoulders dancing up and down. I noticed his Adam's apple.

"My grandmother laughs like that," I said. "Only she doesn't have such a funny thing in her throat."

My remark made him stop for an instant. Then he burst out once more, reaching for my hand as if to reassure me that he wasn't laughing at me. He grew serious again and said, "Sorry, Nicole. I didn't mean to interrupt you. Please tell me more. Tell me all about your life in school."

"Do you really want to know?"

He looked straight at me and said, "It's you I want to know, Nicole."

I felt happy for being able to amuse as well as move him and eager to share an experience I had never told anyone. I let him stride with me over the flagstones of the gloomy corridor to my classroom, let him glimpse behind the mask of secrecy children are so unwilling to set aside, let him guess at my adoration for Madame Marie Thérèse. I still remember her face and hands after all these years, which were paler than the whiteness of her habit, and the sight of her face throughout the monotonous declining of verbs.

As I spoke of her, I began to realize that Dario had taken the place of her image. It had seemed to me, whenever I ventured a timid glance at the perfect symmetry of her profile, that her beauty had an unearthly quality which did not allow even an emotion such as admiration. In the presence of her spiritual austerity my heart would freeze midway in its outgoing of tenderness.

Now I could tell him how sometimes, when I would weep in bewilderment, Madame Joseph Marie would admonish the children to be kind to me because I had lost my sister. I could laugh now, as I mentioned it, like a soldier relating the misadventures of past army life, when all the suffering, madness, and frustration had been distilled into humor. Yet my laughter served to cover the fear of having exposed myself, and I grew silent, shrinking from the scrutiny of his eyes.

"But you did love her, your sister?"

"Yes."

"You must miss her very much." I said nothing, lowering my eyes. "Was she as pretty as you?"

"Much prettier," I said happily.

"Prettier, perhaps. But there's only one Nicole," he said softly. "And did you make friends with the girls?"

"One. Her name was Paula. I was nasty to her."

"Nasty? Why?"

"I don't know."

But I did know. It had happened the day Madame Joseph Marie read to the class from a book about China, and we gathered around her at the desk in order to look at the pictures. The Chinese, our teacher said, were a good people with an infinite patience and capacity for suffering, but they were also a lost people, since many of them believed in Buddha and therefore lacked the blessings of the one and only Holy Catholic Church. No sooner had she said it than the heads of the girls turned simultaneously to me, and their faces told me that I, too, was lost. I moved away from the desk to my bench in humiliation, tears that I fought to repress falling burningly down my cheeks. The hour ended and everyone knelt for prayers as I stood proudly erect but with my head bent to hide my tears. After the class dispersed, Paula put her arm around me, but I pushed her away. She went out, showing that I had hurt her. I wanted Paula for a friend more than anyone else, and I pushed her away because I wanted her too much.

"They always gave me a golden cord on Saturday mornings," I said.

"What was that for?"

I told him that the entire school gathered in the reception room of the Mother Superior. The girls, in black dresses, sat in straight rows along three walls. The nuns, in their flowing white garments, formed a semicircle along the fourth, with the Mother Superior in their midst. Each class was called in turn to stand in front of the sisters. The Mother Superior would then read aloud our record for the week. If we had fewer than three marks of bad conduct we were given a tasseled cord of golden silk to wind about our waists.

Week after week I remember moving toward the Mother Superior with lowered eyes and taking from her with a deep curtsy, as I kissed her outstretched hand, the golden symbol of good behavior and the yellow smile of her praise. Later Mother and I used to wander up to Monte Cappuccino, from where we looked across the city of Turin with its match-box houses, its toy trolleys and cars, its streets ribbons stretching in symmetrical lines toward the mountain ranges. In clear weather we would sometimes catch a glimpse of the chains of Alps in the distance. Peaked by snow-topped Monte Rosa in their midst, they reminded me of the Mother Superior among her flock of white nuns.

"On week ends I used my cord for a skipping rope," I said.

"You mean on Saturday afternoons you shed your piousness like an uncomfortable dress that you put on again on Monday morning?" Dario asked.

Each day after the midday meal Dario would wait for me at the fence. Sometimes he would join me under the trellis in our yard, and we would set the chessmen up on the board, begin to play, and at some point forget to go on with the game. Once he read to me from a slim volume of poetry by Rilke, and although I was too young to understand the full meaning of the words, I drank the love they expressed and stored it in the cells of my being. I began to feel, as I relived the fragments of the past year, that all the lonely contemplation had merely been preparation for this new relationship.

Perhaps during those quiet afternoons in school I had waited for something like this. When everyone went for prayer in the chapel and I remained alone in the deserted classroom, listening to the parting footsteps of the girls, it had been the prelude to what was now taking place. The ringing of the bell from the chapel at the extreme end of the building touched the air with a gentle summons to gathering and devotion. Each chiming stroke echoed in my heart like a rippling wave.

"Did those sisters seriously try to convert you?" Dario once asked me, and I said yes, remembering how I had politely refused to go down to the chapel. My fear of an uncertain mystic attraction had been stronger than the worry of seeming unkind. Each time I felt tempted to kneel down at prayers, or drawn to set foot in the chapel, I would feel a sense of failure and betrayal, as though I were violating the core of my being, some inner direction that was not yet shaped clearly but of which I felt the first stirring roots.

"For a while I was tempted to become a Catholic," I said.

"And what prevented you?" Dario asked, furrowing his brow and looking at me with interest.

"It sounds silly, but I saw myself sitting on our dining-room rug in Paris, at my father's feet," I said, trying to explain the odd experience to myself. "I must have been quite small. My father was hidden behind a newspaper. He was smoking a big cigar and paid no attention to me."

"Go on," Dario said, bending toward me and leaning his elbows on the garden table, right on top of the chess-board.

"I watched the ashes grow longer. His fingers looked just like that cigar. Different in color, but stiff and wooden. That was all." As I spoke, I stared at Dario's tanned, muscular arms. "I was alone in the class, looking out the window. Then I said, 'Dear God, I shall be faithful to you.' After that I never worried about going to church any more."

"That's odd indeed," Dario said. "It sounds like a dream, don't you think?"

"Yes," I said. "But it wasn't."

"You and your father," Dario said, shaking his head, as if wondering to himself, "you are like strangers. Is that why you feel so close to your mother? You are unusually close to her, aren't you?"

I nodded, embarrassed.

36

"It must be nice to have a mother like that." After a moment of silence, "The cigar and the newspaper, it's wonderful!" he exclaimed. "You couldn't have summed up the typical German husband and father any better."

"Swiss," I said, somewhat hurt, "not German."

"German, Swiss. What difference does it make?"

"*Auslandsschweizer* makes a difference," I said defensively.

"What's that?"

"Foreign Swiss. Swiss people living in foreign countries. Like American expatriates. We are a little of that, too."

"You are a little *Ausländer* all right," he said patting my hand. "But I shall make you a citizen of my world, if you like."

"When? How?"

"Right now." He took a pawn from the chessboard and handed it to me as a pledge. "Repeat after me," he said, half jocosely, half in earnest: "I, Nicole Steiner, an *Ausländer* in and out of lands, declare to have become a citizen of Ventura . . ."

"Of Ventura," I repeated playfully.

"And shall never . . ." he said, looking deeply into my eyes.

"And shall never . . ." I said, trying to break the spell of his gaze.

"Forsake it . . ."

"Forsake it."

"To the end . . ." he admonished, putting his hand on mine.

"To the end," I whispered, my heart beating faster.

"Of my days . . ."

"Of my days." I began to laugh nervously. I tried to pull my hand out of his. But he held on to it firmly.

"And I swear . . ." he said, his voice an octave lower.

"And I swear," I repeated in a whisper.

"Holy secrecy." He sealed his lips with his free index finger.

"Holy secrecy."

We shook hands and looked at each other. His face was still serious while I smiled as I put the pawn back on the board. It was I, the smiling one, who played the game in dead earnest.

Summer drew to its close. The games of marbles and the company of my contemporaries had lost all attraction for me. I joined them only for moments when I could not be with Dario.

Sometimes Augusto sat by the shore and looked at me gloomily as I ran past him into the water, followed by Dario. It was as though he kept an eye on me from a distance, waiting with patience, waiting in vain. I made no bones about my indifference. Had not Dario wanted to make me perfectly sincere? I simply showed Augusto how I felt.

On the eve of our departure I sat for the last time on the rod between Augusto's saddle and handlebars as he took me down to the Kursaal garden to say good-bye to my father's matronly friends. Both of them smacked powder-scented kisses on my cheeks.

"Oh," Augusto whispered into my hair, as we glided home across the dark bicycle path, "I wish I were a girl."

"Why do you want to be a girl, Augusto?" I asked, amused.

"Because then I, too, could kiss you good-bye."

It did not occur to me that this might be a timid request. I laughed. "But then you wouldn't enjoy it!"

"I shall never enjoy it now."

"Augusto, what are you talking about?"

"Don't you know?"

"No."

"Now I see what it means when they talk about fickle women."

I leaped off the bicycle and said, "You know something? You are a real bore."

"Of course. I'm only a barber's son and not good enough for you. If it were another boy, I could fight, but a man, what can I do against a man!" he cried out unhappily.

"Come, Augusto," I said, "we are just friends!"

"Just friends," he repeated doubtfully, pushing his bicycle along the path in the dark at my side. "Nicole, will you come back next year?" he asked.

"Maybe."

"If I write you, will you answer me?"

"Ouch!" I cried. He had accidentally hit my calf with his pedal.

"Sorry. Will you?"

"I can't promise," I said, rubbing my leg as I walked.

"If *he* wrote, you would answer, wouldn't you?"

"I don't know," I lied. We had reached our house.

"Well, good-bye," he said abruptly.

"Are you angry?"

"No. One can't get angry at you, really."

"Good-bye, Augusto. Thanks for the ride."

"I'll see you off at the station tomorrow," he called into the darkness, riding away.

As I opened the garden gate I heard my parents' voices in our neighbors' yard. They were probably taking leave of Dario's relatives.

I climbed over the fence and joined them all on the back porch under the dim light of a lantern. Dario stood in their midst with his little cousins leaning against him, and Zita was talking to their maid. I looked up at Dario. He was watching me.

I turned away and shook his aunt's hand and his

uncle's hand, and little Gianna's hand. Politely, I returned their good wishes, and in shaking their hands I felt I was taking leave of summer itself.

The next morning Dario stood at the fence for the last time, saying good-bye. The carriage was outside, our baggage piled on the driver's seat. Father, Mother, and Zita stepped through the gate while Dario drew me back for another moment.

The horse was pawing the ground while I looked into the tenderness of Dario's eyes and listened to him, saying, "We are friends now, *piccola mimosa*, and you won't forget me again."

"No," I said gravely.

"Nicole, hurry up!" I heard my father's impatient command.

"I won't come to the station, this time," Dario whispered, "but I'll come to Turin and visit you soon, soon."

"Right away!" I called; and, "How soon?" I asked.

"Sooner than you think," he said.

"Nicole, what are you doing! Come on!"

"Go now, *piccola, addio*. Go. I will write you a letter."

I felt the pebbles under my shoes on my way to the gate where I turned around once more to see him smile. Though wistful and sad about another leave-taking, this time I was filled with hope that dispelled the sorrow of separation.

All the way to the station I looked up at the sky while the hoofs of the horse and the creaking wheels repeated:

"He's my friend, he's coming, soon . . . he's my friend, soon, soon . . ."

THREE

The drizzling rain was like fog dissolving and penetrating everywhere. Drunk with sleepiness, I reeled to the window on my bare feet and peeped gloomily through the Venetian blinds, then threw myself back into the warmth of my bed.

The church bell had rung from Corso Orbassano: nine strokes at first—nine o'clock; then nine strokes and dingdong—a quarter past nine; then nine strokes again and dingdong, dingdong—half past nine. Zita had carefully opened my door to see if I was still asleep. I had dug my head into the pillow, for I had no desire to talk to her or ever to get out of bed again.

This was the eleventh of November, my birthday as well as King Umberto's birthday and Armistice Day, which meant a holiday from school. My father was traveling in Scotland, and ten days before Mother had been unexpectedly summoned away from Turin to my grandmother's sickbed in Paris. She had returned to Milan a week later and telephoned to tell me that some friends had invited her to stay there with them for two or three days. I did not understand what could be important enough to keep her away from me on my birthday.

"Good morning, and many happy returns of the day!" Zita opened the door with this singsong, balancing a breakfast tray. "A special birthday present to you from Zita."

"Now, don't sulk," she said as I thanked her half-heartedly, "the day's only starting. Look what came in the mail just now. By special delivery."

She put the white tray on my night table and tossed a small parcel onto my bed. Then she sat down next to me, ogling the parcel with curiosity. "It's from that Ventura, all right."

"How does he know it's my birthday?" I asked myself aloud, tearing impatiently at the string.

"Didn't you tell him last time he was here?" I shook my head. "Maybe your mother did. Maybe *la Mamma* is with him in Milano and told him."

"Maybe," I said uneasily, opening the box, which contained a miniature old-fashioned fountain pen and pencil. "Oh, how lovely! Look, Zita!" I exclaimed, holding the pen up to her, opening and closing it. "It's all gold, real gold!"

Zita said contemptuously that one could get these things cheap nowadays. The janitor's wife had one just like it, and it cost her husband only fifty lire.

"But that's a lot! Don't you like it?"

"Not bad," she admitted with the supercilious air she took on about all matters concerning Dario.

"You don't like Dario, do you, Zita?" I asked.

"Like him!" she shouted. Her eyes narrowed, and her big hand kept hitting my blue blanket excitedly. "And why should I like him, will you tell me, after what he did? Treating me like dirt, just because he can't get from me what he wants? I'm a decent girl, I am, I told him, and he laughs at me. Now do you think that's a way to act?"

"Zita, when . . . ?"

". . . *il signor Conte!* Mr. Count! Is that what I should call him? And bake and cook and wash his dirty socks when he comes here to visit? I know his number all right. So his father was a count, some adventurer who seduced a poor girl like your Zita, and then ran off somewhere to Africa. His parents were divorced when he was quite small, his aunt's maid told me in Rimini, and maybe this isn't true, who knows, and perhaps they weren't even married! I bet you he's *un bastardo, ecco tutto*, and his old mother's supposed to live right here in Torino, and I wouldn't be surprised if he pretended she's dead. So he takes me out to dance, and he puts his hand right here." Zita's face was red. She had talked herself into a steam, and now she placed her hand on her breast to show me. "But I says I'm not that kind of a girl, *Signor Conte*, says I, and he leaves me there, doesn't even bother to take me back home after the dance!"

"When was that, Zita?" I asked, half amused, half bewildered. I had learned to take her stories with a grain of salt.

"Last summer. To think he's younger than me, and I'm supposed to respect him like an older gentleman! The nerve!" She snorted the last words through her nose.

"But he is older, Zita. He's twenty-five."

"Is that what he told you? Why, the liar!" Zita threw her head back with a shrill, false laugh. "He told me himself he was twenty-two last spring, if you want to know the truth!"

"But why should he want to make himself older?" I asked her, accustomed by this time to her exaggerations.

"You are such a gullible little girl!" Zita cried out. " 'Why,' she asks me, 'why?' Because he wants older women to take him seriously, that's why!" She looked shrewdly at me, inclining her head to one side. "I'm not naming any names, but if you had eyes in your head, you'd know what I'm talking about!"

I did not want to know what she was trying to tell me, but I knew I could bear her presence no longer. I wished she would leave me in peace so that I could read the card I had just found in the silky white paper in which the gold pen and pencil had been wrapped.

"I think I heard the doorbell," I said, raising a finger as if listening.

"Didn't hear a thing," Zita said.

"You'd better check who it is," I insisted. As soon as she was gone, I took out the card, and my eyes devoured the words in feverish excitement.

"To Nicole on her fourteenth birthday," he had written, followed by a poem.

Compleanno festeggiato	(Every birthday celebration
È una vita che si avvanza,	Marks advancing life and age,
È una tappa del passato	Opens future expectation,
Del futuro una speranza.	Closes of our past a stage.
Quel terribile cinista	(We are wont to call our Fate
Che destin si fa chiamare	That most awful Cynicus,
Che sorride all'ottimista	Who us optimists must hate
Per poterlo rovinare:	Since he plots to ruin us:
Possa sempre Nicolita,	(Would that he, my dear Nicole,
Questo giudice spietato	Cruel judge that he may be,
Darti dolce e bella vita,	Give you life but good and whole,
Avvenire fortunato.	Happy future, joy and glee.)

Dario.

"You must have heard a ghost," Zita said, returning. The shadow her words had cast was dispersed by my joy. "Go on, eat, before your breakfast gets cold."

I took a sip of *caffé-latte*, and then said, "It's nice of you to serve me in bed, Zita. Thanks."

"That's quite all right on your birthday. I have a little something for you, too."

"Really? How nice! Let me see!"

She went out to fetch her gift, and I drew the card out from under my pillow and read Dario's poem again.

"It's nothing much," Zita said, returning. "Only a handkerchief I embroidered for you."

"It's very pretty. Thank you so much," I said, and I felt how insincere my smile was. I put my presents on the night table and began to eat, secretly touching the card from time to time.

When Zita left me alone so that I might dress, for we planned to watch the king's birthday parade, I took a key from my purse and a small wooden box that I kept hidden in a drawer of my cupboard, unlocked it, and put the card inside my diary, along with two letters from Dario. As I was about to push the locked box back into the drawer, I glanced at a letter Augusto had written me a few days after we left Rimini. I took the letter out of the drawer. The boy's tall, awkward writing now touched me with the same silent reproach as his plaintive presence:

". . . almost choked when the train was gone . . . kept standing there, forgetting everything about me, and almost left my bicycle at the station, my dear, dear bicycle that carried you so many times. . . . Come back, will you? next summer. I can't stop thinking of you. . . ."

I had laughed at his long sentimental letter and had read it aloud to Zita in the kitchen, and Zita had gloated over it with vulgar bursts of laughter until I snatched it from her angrily. Each time I looked at it I was overcome with shame and displeasure at myself. I had never answered it, and Augusto had not written again.

♣ ♣

The tinny sounds of a military march could be heard through the bleak November air, through the houses that seemed to have turned porous from the drizzle. I tried to think of the life within all this death, of the lusty green leaves that would sprout forth again from the barren, ghostly trees, of the candles that would pour blossoms over the Corso, the sticky buds, the green, fat porcupines of chestnut skins bursting as they bounced on the ground.

Watching the parade, my feet had grown wet and cold. I felt full of self-pity, but Zita was only beginning to enjoy herself as she waved her handkerchief at the short, dark infantrymen.

"Let's go," I begged for the third time.

"Just a few more minutes," Zita said. "I'll take you to the cinema this afternoon, all right?"

"Yes," I said. "You stay for a while. I'm going home."

She hardly heard what I said. I moved away slowly under the naked branches of horse chestnut trees, like spectres made of *papier-mâché*. On the Corso, to my left, two rows of *bersaglieri* in rich plumed hats swished past on bicycles. I began to compose the first two lines of an Italian poem; they rose in my mind of their own accord, keeping pace with my steps.

When I reached our apartment building, I ran up the flight of stairs. The key wouldn't turn in the lock fast enough. I flew through the corridor into my room, took paper and pencil, and then quickly wrote out a draft of my poem before I lost its pattern.

On reading the words over, I found them shallow and far from expressing the intensity of my thoughts and emotions. With this sense of failure, the spur of feeling left me, and I put down my pencil and stepped out on the balcony.

I heard the sound of steps at the far end of the hall.

It must be Zita coming home, I thought, wiping her feet carefully, then like a bird shaking its feathers, jolting the drops from her umbrella. I hoped she would leave me alone for a while, but soon afterward I heard the door of my room open and a voice say, "No, she isn't here either. . . ."

I stepped back through the glass door. Mother was about to leave my room, obviously looking for me. "*Mammina!*" I called, and she turned around. With a joyous start I flung myself on her. "I'm so happy you have come! But why didn't you let me know?"

"It's good to see you, my darling! All my best wishes and may all your dreams come true," she said, kissing me. "I didn't let you know because we thought it would be a lovely surprise."

"We?" I asked, and looking up from her shoulder, I saw Dario right behind her, framed by the doorway.

"Happy birthday, *piccola*," he said, walking up to me. He brushed my forehead with his lips. He looked elegant in his tan trench coat, but then Dario looked well in everything he wore. "I told Mammina it would be nice to surprise you."

"Well," I said, "I wish you had surprised me last night."

He did not answer, but bent over the table and read the verses I had written in my notebook. "Did you compose this just now?" he asked.

"Yes," I said, quickly closing the notebook.

"And do you always keep on coat and hood when writing poetry?"

"Sometimes I wear a spring hat," I said. "What about you?"

"I can only write in my bathing suit with a pair of gloves, a top hat, and a cigar in my mouth."

"You forgot the boots," I added, laughing. "Dario,

47

thank you so much for your lovely present and poem!"

He pressed my hand tightly, holding it for a long moment.

Zita came home a few minutes later. She greeted my mother with a polite smile and acted as if Dario were not there at all. "Would you care for some lunch, signora?" she asked with a sigh, unable to hide her disappointment at this unexpected ending of her holiday. As both Mother and Dario said that they would like some very much, she left the room singing in a false, high-pitched voice.

Dario and I waited in the living room while Mother went to get my birthday presents. He had settled in a low chair, and he sat there smiling at me while I beamed at him across the table from my sofa corner. "How's the new school?" he asked. "Do you like it better than the convent school?"

"Much," I said. "At first I thought the girls too fresh. Then I made friends with Oretta, who is the biggest rowdy in our class."

"So you became rowdy number two," Dario said, smiling.

"More or less," I admitted. "Oretta's so much fun."

"Are you learning anything, too?"

"Yes," I assured him, "though I still have to catch up with my Latin. But I'm getting some help with it now."

Zita was still singing in the kitchen, and I thought of the things she had told me. "What about your mother?" I asked abruptly.

"What about her?"

"Is she alive?"

"Oh, yes." He sighed.

"Don't you ever see her?"

"Very seldom."

"You never talk about her."

"That's because we have nothing in common," he said curtly.

"And Dario . . . ?" I asked, hesitating.

"Yes, *piccola*?" He leaned forward in his chair, waiting for me to say more. My eyes were fixed on his handsome black and chartreuse tie.

"I was wondering about your birthday," I said.

"June," he said. "June twenty-eight."

"What I mean is—how old are you?"

"Make a guess," he said.

"Twenty-two? Twenty-five?" I asked. He blinked at me across the table.

"It's a bit of both, you see. When I'm with you I feel twenty-two. Of course, that's awfully old for you, isn't it? And with older people . . ."

"You are twenty-five?" I said, as he stopped.

"Well, twenty-two is a bit young for them, wouldn't you say? Anything else you'd like to know?"

"Are you sometimes trying to make the perfect liar out of yourself?" I asked quickly. "You told me it's an art, remember, just like being completely honest."

Before he could think of an answer, Mother came in burdened with presents. She handed me a fine wool ruby-red dress and a necklace with a cultured pearl she had brought home from Paris, and a volume of poems by Verlaine. Then she gave me a small navy-blue leather bag my grandmother had sent me.

I was delighted with everything and went out to try on the dress and necklace. Dario and Mother both thought the dress a perfect fit and most becoming to my complexion, and I wore it for the rest of the day.

After lunch Mother took a nap, and then we were all to go to a show. While she slept Dario went through my homework with me, sitting on the sofa by my side. Time flew and mingled with the nearness of his breath, his serious gaze or his smile, the gentle touch of his palm on my shoulder.

When we had finished, he turned to me and said, "*Piccola*, I don't want to evade your question. About the perfect liar, I mean. It's true that at times I find lying most fascinating."

I was afraid to hear more and quickly changed the subject. "That's a lovely tie you're wearing," I said. "New?"

"Mammina brought it from Paris," he said. "You see, Nicole, you mustn't worry. To you I won't lie, I promise."

"You won't? Ever?"

"Unless . . ." he stopped.

"Unless?" I urged.

"Unless the truth should hurt. It can get very painful. And to hurt a child is the most cruel thing to do."

"In school I'm only a child. About twelve. With you I'm very old. Sixteen, at least."

"Oh?" He laughed. "I don't really care. You are my little Ventura citizen. Nothing else matters." He squeezed my hand.

"And why should you hurt me?" I asked, feeling a mixture of joy and dark misgivings.

Mother walked in at that moment, carrying a tray with three cups of *cappuccino*. Dario told her that he could not remember having enjoyed anything as much as studying with me.

"I shall engage you as Nicole's tutor number two," she said.

"Oh? And who is number one?" Dario asked.

"Sandra Manetti," I said. "She's actually a pianist and a music teacher, but she helps me with my Latin once a week."

"That's no competition," Dario said, "since I don't remember much of my Latin anyway."

50

Later we went to see Greta Garbo in *Regina Cristina.* In the dark of the theater Dario sat between us, holding my hand. Breathless with joy, I felt the warmth of his hand enveloping mine while enraptured by the sight of Garbo lowering a ripe cluster of grapes to her lips as she reclined on her lover's knees. As I glanced to the other side, I noticed that Dario was holding Mother's hand also. I kept telling myself that this was just as it should be to complete our harmony.

Dario remained with us a few more days. He slept in our narrow guest room, next to mine. Our beds were separated by a wall against which we would knock out messages or announce our daily awakening.

♣ ♣

A few days after Dario's departure, I was mounting the dim stairs to Sandra Manetti's floor, my Latin book pressed under my arm, when I heard an upstairs door open, then the tap, tap, tap of a cane, interrupted by slow, groping steps, descending.

I stopped and waited as the sounds came steadily nearer, and then my eyes fixed on a hand that grasped the bannister, the fingers sensitive and long, sliding toward the landing where I stood. When I looked up from the hand, I saw the white, heavy walking cane, then recognized a coat I had sometimes seen hanging next to Sandra's in the hall. I knew the particular salt-and-pepper pattern of the coat and the spot on the left sleeve where it was slightly worn.

I stepped back and held my breath so that the blind man would not know I was there. My heart thumped as he came closer and closer. If he should notice me and talk to me, what was I going to say? His face was like that of an apparition, with lids drawn over the vacant eyes that showed only a thin line of the white. It was a pale, elongated face, the skin drawn taut over marked cheekbones, clean shaven and almost ascetic. His light-brown hair was thick and long and wavy, with strands of copper tones. There was, as I have since frequently noticed in the faces of blind people, an intent expression of listening, as if to some barely audible music no one else could hear.

By now he had sensed a presence, and as I shrank back against the windowsill he came to a halt on the landing, his face turned in my direction.

"Who's there?" he murmured, stretching his free hand toward me. His fingers lightly brushed across my hair.

I recoiled, ducked, then noiselessly slipped past him and ran up the stairs, running a flight higher than where the Manettis lived so that he could not guess who I was. Then I waited, my pulse throbbing wildly, until I heard him go down the last flight, open the front door, and go out.

When I felt calmer, I went down to the Manettis' door and rang the bell. Sandra's mother, a small, unpretentious woman in black, opened it.

"Did you meet my son as you came up?" she asked. "He was just going out."

I said no almost inaudibly, since I could not explain my foolish behavior, and hung my coat next to the spot where his no longer was.

Sandra came out of the music room to greet me. "*Ciao,* Nicole," she said with her gentle voice and her lovely smile. She was dark blond and of medium height, and always wore skirts and blouses. As soon as we entered the music room, she too asked me if I had seen her brother.

"You never told me you had a brother," I said, not answering her question.

52

"Lorenzo used to be a painter before his accident. . . . He's blind, you know."

"When was that—the accident, I mean?" I asked. And for a moment the blind man's face hovered before me, a vague impression like a half-finished sketch. '

We lifted the piano bench, each on one end, and carried it to the desk. The cleanliness of the naked parquet floors added to the cold and somewhat austere atmosphere of the whole apartment. It always hit me like a draft, especially in the music room. This miniature room served as Sandra's father's study. Besides the desk it contained an upright piano, tall shelves with innumerable scores, and a narrow black leather-covered chaise longue.

Sandra and I sat down side by side on the bench. She looked at me with her warm amber eyes, and said in a subdued tone of voice, "It happened shortly after our father was taken to prison, about four years ago. You've probably heard about it?"

"Vaguely," I said.

Sandra's father was a well-known composer in town. Artists and intellectuals regarded him highly for his musicianship as well as for his personal integrity. We had heard rumors that he had suffered a great deal of persecution for political reasons and that Mussolini had sent him into exile at one time.

I had put Virgil's *Aeneid* on the desk, and now Sandra opened it. While she looked for the page where we had stopped reading last week, I admired her slim, well-shaped figure, her fair skin, and her finely penciled eyebrows. In contrast to most Italians I knew, she hardly ever gesticulated with her hands when she spoke. In spite of her straight posture there was nothing stiff about the way she sat or moved; on the contrary, her motions were fluid and graceful. She was only in her early twenties, but she seemed to me the epitome of maturity and wisdom. Still, beneath all this poise and unobtrusive discipline I could sense a feeling of despair and defeat she was struggling to subdue.

"I am sorry," I said, as she asked me to translate a passage from Book Two, "but I'm completely unprepared." I felt hot and dizzy, but preferred not to mention that I had felt ill all day in school, since it seemed such a poor excuse for my neglect.

"You don't look well, Nicole," Sandra said. She put her cool hand on my forehead. "You are quite hot, you know!" She closed the book and said, "Why don't we skip studying for today and have some tea instead?"

Before I could protest, she had left the room to put the kettle on the stove. She returned a moment later.

"Your brother," I asked shyly, as she had sat down again at my side, "how does he spend his days?"

"Oh, he does so many things," Sandra said. "He plays the piano much better than I, although he has never had a lesson in his life. But above all, he writes."

"How?" I asked, awed. "And what sort of writing?"

Sandra replied that he was able to write plays in a somewhat shaky though regular hand. "I type his work," she said, "and then read it back to him. You, too, are interested in writing, aren't you, Nicole?"

"Yes. How did you know?"

"Just a hunch," she said. "Is it poetry?"

I nodded. "And you," I asked before she could say more, "are you choosing music for a career?"

She shook her head. "When you grow up under the shadow of a father like ours," she explained, "you can't expect to measure up to him. And then to watch a man of genius suppressed and stifled in everything he tried to do! A musician's life is hard enough without political persecution."

54

"But why—and how did it happen?" I asked.

"One day, after a successful concert, they asked him to give a speech. Well, he spoke," Sandra said with pride. "He spoke openly, before a crowd of more than five hundred people, and he said that music, like any other art, could not thrive under a dictatorship. A bird with clipped wings cannot fly, he said, and the stifled spirit of a man can neither create works of beauty nor truth. He said a great deal more," Sandra went on. Her small hands, with the softly padded palms, and fingers pointed at the tips, were folded in her lap.

"Then other things happened. . . . It takes too long to explain. They came to arrest him. They put him in jail. You may have heard of the castor oil they force political prisoners to drink. Well, Papa wasn't spared that pain and humiliation! He was ill afterward, and they only waited for him to recover so they could send him into *esilio*." Sandra's voice rose to a higher pitch. "For two years he was forced to remain in Calabria. It was a barren, windy town near the sea, full of dark rocks, and the people shunned him. When he came back home, he hardly ever spoke to us about his suffering, his loneliness.

"He has been like a lion in a cage ever since," she went on, "a lion with a broken heart. He composes with a fury, and he's lonely and bitter, avoiding even the company of his family."

"And after all that, how can you be so gentle, so serene!" I cried out; and Sandra said, "Because we mustn't let ourselves be destroyed by either my father's bitterness nor our poor Mamma's meek resignation. Do you understand, Nicole? It's Lorenzo who gives me the strength to . . . Without him . . ."

She turned her head away for a moment, then went on softly, composing herself, "I don't know what carried me away to tell you these things. I should be more careful, since I don't even know your family's political attitudes. But somehow I feel that we have a lot in common."

"I abhor Fascism!" I cried. "We are democrats, all of us, and we hate tyranny and cruelty of any kind!"

Sandra seized my hands, then smiled at me with shining eyes, and said, "I am so glad to know you are on our side! But my tea—oh, I forgot all about it!" And she ran out into the kitchen.

Later, when we had finished drinking our tea, we carried the bench back to the piano, and Sandra played the slow movement of Beethoven's "Pathétique" for me. I sat on the black leather-covered chaise-longue, feeling the room growing hotter and hotter while my mind wandered back to the dramatic events she had confided to me.

I had met Sandra's father once, and now I kept seeing his gaunt, pale face with its dark-ringed eyes and bushy brows. My heart beat faster; I could feel small hammers pounding in my temples, and my hands grew wet with perspiration. The maestro's full, black moustache curled like two rich commas across his cheeks. It seemed to grow partially out of his nostrils. I could see him sitting in brooding melancholy on the narrow cot of a prison cell while I felt hot and cold chills running down my spine. Then I followed his tall lean figure, dressed in black, as he wandered across the barren rocks of a small Calabrian town. People turned their heads away at his approach, and the wind tousled his full mane of black hair. It seemed to me that from his dark and desperate heart rose the passionate music of wild and infinite longing, as it now rose in my own heart while I listened to Sandra's playing. I could feel the music burst through his bitterness and all the limitations of pettiness and oppression.

"Dio mio!" Sandra cried, looking at my feverish face when she had finished. "What's the matter, Nicole? Are you ill?"

                  ♣ ♣

Sandra summoned my mother who came immediately in a cab to take me home. I was put to bed at once. The fever rose high, and the people about me turned into shadows moving past the heavy, formless cloud that was life, without and within. The first two weeks passed like that. Afterward the fever fell from 104 degrees, and the shadows turned gradually from more distinct silhouettes into real people.

A great weakness followed. That was the time I devoured in semihallucination *The Brothers Karamazov.* Mother was summoned to my grandmother's deathbed. She left for Paris while I remained in the care of Zita. The news of my grandmother's death reached me at the time when my flu had changed into yellow jaundice. I recall the innumerable glasses of milk I was compelled to drink and the profound melancholy of those endless weeks of convalescence.

My body as well as my face had grown longer and thinner. I would lie or sit and dream for hours, languishing, with my hands in my lap. I began to see everything from a new perspective, steeped in sorrow and in the pleasure of poetic yearnings. The smallest provocation moved me to tears. I felt immersed in the heavy sweetness of my blood, the new consciousness of my growing breasts. Gone was the clear perception of childhood; contours blurred as I slowly emerged from my cocoon.

One afternoon Zita urged me to come to the telephone for a long-distance call. It was from Milan. The receiver shook in my hand.

"*Piccola*, how are you?"

"Dario!"

He was trying to say something, but I could hear only a noise. "Hello," I said, "hello, hello . . ." His voice came in angrily, distorted. I could hear him curse under his breath. "Dario!" I cried again.

"*Piccola*, can you hear me?"

"Yes. I can hear you now."

"Mammina wrote me about your illness. I was . . . Hello, hello!"

"Yes . . .

"Are you better?"

"Yes. Can you come to Torino?"

"What did you say?"

"Can you come?"

"No. I promised my relatives to join them for Christmas. I'll write you."

"How nice of you to call!"

His voice sounded anxious. "You are better, really better?"

"Yes," I said. Silence.

"This damned telephone," Dario said. "I can hardly hear you."

"Neither can I."

"*Addio, piccola.*"

His letter arrived two days later:

My dear little citizen of Ventura,

The thought of your illness is distressing to me, all the more because I can't come to see you and help you get better. I sent you a couple of books, Gogol's *Dead Souls* and a volume of short stories by Katherine Mansfield. I have just finished reading them myself and am sure that you will enjoy them both.

This is a bad year for me, since I have to sweat through my final exams. I have done well in German literature and Elizabethan drama so far, but now am worried about economics. You concentrate on getting well, and then study hard. We shall make up for lost time next summer in Rimini, I promise.

I think of you often. I miss you. You and *Mammina* are my real family now. Perhaps I can get away for a week end or two, later on. Write me as soon as you feel strong again, and have a good Christmas. A kiss on each of your cheeks, my little girl, in the hope to turn them rosy with good health.

Dario

Father came home shortly before Christmas. He came into my room at once, and scrutinized me disapprovingly. "You look awful, Nicole," he said worriedly. "I don't like the white of your eyes."

"That's the jaundice, Father. How was your trip?"

"Not so good. Restaurant food disagrees with me. And the dampness, everywhere. I hope your mother will come home soon."

"The day after tomorrow," I said.

"The funeral took place last week."

"You know there are many things she needs to attend to," I said, but even as I spoke I had a clear picture of Dario and Mother walking arm in arm through the streets of Milan. I tried to push the picture out of my mind, but it kept coming back, haunting me with pangs of resentment and envy.

Father shook his head and sighed. "I don't know whether anything else really matters with a sick child at home." He looked sad and resigned as he said it. I patted his shoulder in order to comfort him. "I'll be all right," I said. "I'm all right now."

♣ ♣

That spring, when I at last caught up with my Latin in school, Sandra dismissed me as a pupil and opened the doors of her house to me as a friend.

59

During my long convalescence she had come to see me three times, and when I first returned to her apartment—about twenty minutes' walking distance from our house, on Corso Galileo Ferraris—she said, "I can't get over how you have grown, in every way! You went to bed a child and have emerged a young lady!"

At the end of our last Latin session we heard the door outside, then the familiar tapping of the cane. "Lorenzo's home," Sandra said. I've told him about you, and he asked that you stay for some coffee. He'd like to meet you."

She went to open the heavy oak door in the wall connecting the music and dining rooms; beyond it I could now hear the clatter of dishes. "It's ready," Sandra said, turning to me. "They are waiting for us. You must forgive me if I have to leave you soon, though, since I'm expecting a piano pupil. I was unable to postpone the lesson."

As soon as we entered, Lorenzo, who was sitting at the other end of the massive table, turned his head in our direction. For an instant I could not believe that he was blind. Signora Manetti had an old woman's face which grew young as she smiled at me. Her hair was the pepper-and-salt pattern of Lorenzo's coat. She rose from her thick-legged oak chair, took my arm, and as if I were the blind one, led me to Lorenzo's side.

"Renzo, this is Sandra's lovely friend, Signorina Nicole," she said.

He got up from his chair for a moment, then stretched both hands toward me without hesitation. They felt soft and warm to the touch. In withdrawing them, he lifted one arm as if by accident, and his fingers touched my hair. Then smiling, he said, "Sandra has told me about you."

"S'accomodi, signorina," said Signora Manetti. I thanked her and sat down near Sandra, facing Lorenzo.

"If you could see how Nicole has been changing ever since her illness," Sandra told him. "Her face has a more mature expression each week." She poured the steaming black coffee into the white china cups and then lifted a black tray from the white table cloth and offered me some butter cookies.

"There's a deep truth in sickness furthering one's development," Lorenzo said.

At the other end of the room a door opened, and the gaunt, tall figure of Maestro Manetti appeared. Sandra had to introduce me again since he did not seem to remember me. He greeted me with an aura of absent-minded gloom, poured himself some coffee from the Neapolitan metal pot, took a golden cookie with a trembling hand, put it on his saucer, and then, without another word, balanced himself and the cup out of the room again.

Maestro Manetti and Lorenzo, I saw, resembled each other but slightly. The father's mouth was thin and pulled down at the corners; there was a fuller, more sensuous line in the generous curve of Lorenzo's lips. The older man was darker than his son, in coloring as well as in mood. But Lorenzo's hands, now folded around the cup, were exact replicas of his father's hands.

Sandra barely had time to drink her coffee when a ring at the door announced the arrival of her piano pupil. She patted my shoulder good-bye and withdrew into the music room. *"Con permesso,"* her mother excused herself a moment later, leaving me alone with Lorenzo.

I sipped my coffee in silent embarrassment. After a while, between the sounds of scales racing up and down beyond the wall, he remarked, "Sandra tells me you are interested in literature."

"Oh, well . . ." I said.

"She says you write poetry. Will you be a poet?"

61

"I'm too young to know what I really want—yet," I said.

"But once you grow older," Lorenzo replied, "you will feel that the time is too short. Now you can still be whole."

"Then I must do nothing at all," I said, smiling. "For as soon as I touch something, it's no good, it's gone." For an instant I remembered the mimosa bush in the park, near Lake Como.

"There is a poem by Leopardi," Lorenzo was saying, "in which the poet describes his feeling of the infinite as being strongest in front of a hedge. I don't know what makes me think of this just now."

"We both said one can be whole only as long as one hasn't done anything yet; or something of the sort."

"But that has nothing to do with the infinite," he said.

"Yes. Because everything is still one, untouched."

He stretched his arm over the table toward me. "You are right," he said. Then he pulled his chair closer to the table, propped his elbows on the white cloth, and cupped his face in his hands as he spoke. "In front of the hedge you can imagine how everything spreads and opens; you are still held together in some way. But beyond—let's say in an endless plain—you are lost and boundless; the infinite loses its sense of wholeness inside you. . . . What made you say it?"

"You said it. I wouldn't know how," I replied shyly.

"But can't you see?" he asked.

"I'm not sure," I said. "Perhaps you can teach me."

He laughed. "You are teaching me," he said softly as if to himself. "I can see you so well," he added, smiling. "But let's try anyway."

I put my cup down in silence, feeling something in my breast growing wider and the walls of the room widening as well.

His mother came in and asked if I wanted more coffee. I thanked her and said that it was time for me to leave. I stood up, and Lorenzo got to his feet and walked with me into the hall. There he put on his coat, took his cane, and said that he would go downstairs with me.

"Do you walk home?" he asked.

"I'll walk as far as you'll come with me," I said.

"Then prepare yourself for the worst."

The harsh beats of a Czerny exercise followed us as we went down the stairs. I saw Lorenzo groping for the bannisters, and I kept awkwardly at his side, wishing but not daring to help.

Stopping on the landing where I had met him for the first time, he turned to me and said, "It's strange, you know, in this darkness you never can tell what you dream or imagine and what actually happens or does not happen."

"It doesn't really matter," I answered, saying to myself that what one dreams or imagines is far more important than reality.

"Oh, but it matters a great deal!" Lorenzo exclaimed. Then, abruptly, "Maybe you're right. Do you think people run away sometimes from a blind man?" he asked. "Perhaps some people would like everyone else to be blind so that they could remain unseen."

"Maybe," I said timidly, "people run away from someone like you because they are afraid to be seen too well."

We stepped out into the brilliant sunlight in the street, which dazzled me all the more as I realized that to him it must be only an abrupt change of temperature. He took my arm on one side, his cane on the other, and walked briskly, almost dragging me along. His pale, ardent face with its strong, pointed chin was lifted upward as he spoke softly and breathlessly from the safeguard of his darkness into the protection of my child-

63

hood. There fell from us the artifice of convention which might be strong with him in the presence of adults and was so strong with me in the presence of the seeing.

Then, as we crossed Corso Vittorio Emanuele, we fell silent. After a while I asked Lorenzo if he would not rather turn back, but instead of answering, he said he was writing a play and had just finished the first act. "To walk home with you might help me find a beginning for the next scene," he said.

I felt too shy to ask him about his play. I looked at the magnolia trees in the gardens, the lilacs, and the red and yellow and blue flowers, wondering what impression they would make on Lorenzo if his sight were to be restored. A rebellion against the unalterable must then have taken hold of me. To feel pity for a man like Lorenzo was inconceivable, but I could not rejoice at what I saw without sharing it, and my spirits sank.

A gust of wind blew over the *corso*. I shivered, and felt cast out by him; or rather, he had cast himself out, and was now moving alone, and willingly so, having let go of my arm. It was as if we had crossed a bridge together, and then I had turned back to the other side and the bridge had been drawn up, and now we were separated. I was no longer the person he had seen so well, but merely a strange young girl, one of Sandra's friends. I did not dare glance at him, for I feared he might know what was passing through my mind.

"How strong the lilacs smell," he said, breaking a small branch and handing it to me as we passed a garden hedge.

"I've known this lilac bush," he explained, "as long as I can remember. Are they large, those magnolia blossoms?"

"Yes, very."

"Open?"

64

"Most of them are still closed."

In the silence that followed, I tried to imagine what he saw: something infinitely richer, no doubt, then the reality of scattered shrubs and flowers.

"I must go back now!" he exclaimed, turning to me and again taking my arm. There was a happy expression on his face. "Tell me is this Corso Re Umberto?"

And when I said yes, he turned around, tapping with his cane, then left me without saying good-bye.

FOUR

When I think back on those days, life in Turin, where we spent about nine months out of each year, appears as the shadowy counterpart of those blinding summers at the beach. Rimini rings stridently in my ears; Turin is hushed to a whisper. The most memorable moments of those winter seasons seem to rise as peaks from the flat lands of school weeks. Lilacs, magnolia trees, and the blooming candles of chestnuts bring Lorenzo to my mind. Dario needs no associations. Sandra still represents the elective sister.

My growth must have been as jerky as my movements. I spilled; I broke things; corners seemed to run into me. I hated waking in the morning or going to bed at night. Life was a brilliant landscape, full of joy and jubilation. Life was dull inert matter without sense or hope. I grew forward and backward.

At last the school year came to a close, and I could look forward to another summer in which to forget everything I had learned. A few days before the Manettis were to leave the city for their vacation in the Piedmont mountains, Lorenzo invited me to join him for coffee and pastry. Mother did not object to my going out for the first time with a young man alone.

I met him under the *portici* of Piazza Castello. It was a warm afternoon. I had put on a sleeveless knitted cotton dress with white and navy-blue stripes. I can't remember anything Lorenzo ever wore except for his old winter jacket, but I keep seeing his hands and the copper shade of his hair and the inward look of his heavy-lidded eyes and his touching smile. It must have been windy, for his hair was slightly disheveled, and mine probably was, too. We crossed the square, arm in arm, and I kept reassuring myself that this was only because he needed my help. His face was lifted to the warmth of the sun. Beyond the *portici*, the café we entered was dark as a grotto.

People crowded around the tall silver robot of the espresso machine; it hissed its vapors of roasted coffee beans in loud, sharp spurts through the smoke- and talk-filled room. I felt naked amid the elegant ladies in their summer hats sprouting with colorful assortments of artificial flowers and fruits. Sandwich-filled platters crowded the wide glass counters of the bar, side by side with a variety of miniature cream puffs, napoleons, babas au rhum, and pastries filled with almond or mocha cream.

We found a round marble-topped table in the farthest corner and ordered *cappuccini*. And when the waiter returned with our coffee, he set a tray of pastries on the table.

"So what are you going to do with yourself, Nicole, all summer long?" Lorenzo asked, biting into a napoleon.

"The usual," I said. "Swim and loaf. And read."

Lorenzo groped for a cream puff on the tray to his left and put it on my plate. "Soak up the sunshine and let the boys swarm around you, eh?" he said. He smiled vacantly across the table with a moustache of foam on his upper lip. "You know," he went on, "this is a day for celebrating. I've just finished my play."

"Congra—"

"After all," he interrupted me, "you inspired part of it, if only indirectly. Remember the day we met? I worked on it as soon as I got home."

"What is it about?" I asked.

"It's a drama about our own times," he said, "and it has political implications. This makes it impossible for me to show it to the publishers, and more impossible still to have it performed. You will think," Lorenzo went on, his fingers folding and unfolding the white linen napkin, "why then did he bother to write it at all? I wrote it for the people of Piemonte, our people, Nicole. For those who fight in their small and powerless way against the disease that threatens to devour Italy. And I wrote it because I hope and believe that it's not as critical as cancer, but that it is something from which Italy may recover soon. Blind as I am, my pen is the only weapon I can use for the battle."

He lowered his voice, and added, "I hope to distribute the drama among anti-Fascist groups in order to give them courage to go on fighting."

"I wish I were an Italian!" I cried out. "I wish I were older and free to join you and help you!"

"Goodness, am I making a revolutionary out of you?" Lorenzo asked, putting his napkin on the table.

"Not at all," I said boldly. "I would love to read your play!"

"It may be a bit raw and vulgar for you," Lorenzo said, hesitating. "All right. I'll ask Sandra to send you a copy to Rimini as soon as she finishes typing it."

I shall never forget the morning I received Lorenzo's drama weeks later in Rimini. Among other things it

68

caused the first painful quarrel between Dario and me.

That summer we had rented a different house in another part of town, and Dario joined us a few days after our arrival. He lived with his relatives on Viale Dardanelli as usual, but spent most of his time with us.

Lorenzo's manuscript arrived with the following note:

Dear Nicole,

The weeks are flying past, more for the blind and old than the young and seeing. I suppose this is because of the monotonous rhythm of darkness, which must have something in common with the sense of dwindling days like the repetitiveness of life's cycles to the very old. One lives in a timeless dream, perhaps closer to the heart of the earth, and there are no ups and downs, no highlights to await. Though perhaps this is my personal feeling. It may be quite the opposite with another individual. Patience, Nicole, is a quality life forces you to develop sooner or later, and to write, to write constantly, I mean, is the sturdy and dependable walking cane of an old man's (like myself) sedentary hours.

Sandra, to whom I am dictating these lines, asks me to send you her love. Although I am interested to hear what you think of the play, don't worry about it. If it bores you, if it should shock you, forget about it. You may return it to me the next time we meet in Turin, so don't bother to send it back.

Keep well. Absorb all the sunshine and minerals from the sea, and don't forget to bring some back to

Lorenzo

Dario was present when the manuscript arrived. It seemed to me that his dislike for Lorenzo began when I refused to show him the letter. "Let's read the play together," he suggested. "It will come to life when read aloud."

"I'd rather read it myself first," I said firmly, remembering what Lorenzo had told me about its political aspects. "I'm not supposed to show it to anyone."

"You are getting quite headstrong," Dario said, giving me a challenging look. "What's so secret about it?"

"I don't know. I haven't read it myself yet."

"Then why act so mysteriously about it?" Dario asked softly, walking up to me. Before I realized what he was doing, he had snatched the black folder from my hands, and settling in a sofa corner with his loot, he laughed triumphantly.

"Give it back, give it back!" I pled.

He paid no attention to me but turned to the last page of the typescript and began to read. His face darkened and two vertical lines appeared between his brows. "Listen to this!"

I stood motionless beside him, feeling the heavy *thump, thump, thump* of my heart, my indignation giving way to fear, as he read in a clear thunderous voice, a voice that reminded me of my father's:

PAOLO, *desperate, yet strengthened by his fury, writhes on the cot of his prison cell after the guards have administered castor oil to him:*
I shit on the Duce and all his henchmen, and I shit on your filthy black shirts and your filthy black souls!
The guards beat him brutally. Paolo lies still for a while, as if dead or unconscious, then weakly raises his head, and says in a clear voice:
May my excrement turn into manure to make the soil rich. So the seeds of truth will grow into strong, healthy plants for a better generation. May . . .

"Enough!" I interrupted in torment.

"And this is the man you have chosen for a friend!" Dario exclaimed beside himself with anger. "Why, the filthy, vulgar . . ."

I tore the manuscript from his hands and ran to my

70

room. After locking the door, I sat on my bed and anxiously started to read the play from the beginning. My hands felt clammy and I was filled with an unknown, helpless fear. As I read on, I became aware that I dreaded to become the cause of Lorenzo's undoing. Suppose, I told myself, Dario is a Fascist? Out of anger, jealousy, or envy even, he might denounce Lorenzo. . . . *Oh, God,* I thought, *what am I doing? How can I have such awful suspicions about Dario? I shall never be able to look into his eyes again!*

I tried to concentrate on the play, but as I read on, my fear turned to terror. For the first act, it turned out, dealt with problems of betrayal, and the tragedy that resulted from them made my limbs grow cold:

The shoemaker Giuseppe has a clandestine press hidden in his cellar on which he and his friends print anti-Fascist pamphlets at night. Giuseppe, a widower, has an only son, a journalist, Paolo. Paolo loves Dora, a factory worker. When Dora tires of him she turns to the Fascist Roberto, and later tells him about the activities that take place in Giuseppe's house. Roberto goes to the house and arrests Giuseppe. Giuseppe is accused of high treason and condemned to death. Paolo, in despair over Dora's betrayal, and feeling responsible for his father's tragedy, tries to commit suicide. He throws himself from the window of an apartment house, but instead of killing himself, he becomes crippled for life.

Oh God, I thought again, *what am I going to do?* I connected the drama not for a moment with Lorenzo's life, but with my own present dilemma. I could not go on reading; I must speak to Mother first. Perhaps she could persuade Dario to keep the whole matter to himself.

The house was empty; they had all gone to the beach. I decided that it was much too hot for Dario to do anything like writing to the police inspector in Turin, for example, about Lorenzo's play. He was probably talking to Mother under the tent awning now, and it would be impossible for me to talk to Mother alone.

I decided to stay home and finish reading the play. I wanted to find out what had made Paolo end up in prison and why he had said the lines Dario had read aloud. They were words that struck me as the speech of a heroic man who stands up in the face of torture and death for the ideals in which he believes. The words had a haunting power, even beauty, for me. I knew that Lorenzo would act just as bravely as Paolo.

The disturbing factor, during the second and third acts, was Paolo's bitterness and his incessant brooding about avenging his father's death. Then, in the fourth act, Paolo's actions seemed to me to be justified. At first confined to a wheel chair, and later with the help of crutches, Paolo remains politically active. He writes for another clandestine press that operates from the home of his best friend, a carpenter, Antonio Pucci. Paolo's vengeance turns into an act of self-sacrifice, for when the informer Roberto is about to arrest Antonio and their friends, Paolo shoots and kills Roberto. The desperate Dora, coming to her lover's aid, is spared when Paolo sees that she is with child. He convinces her that it was he who operated the press single-handed, and then gives himself up in order to save his friends.

It was a powerful, exciting play, and I still felt overwhelmed and dazed by it when Mother and Dario returned for lunch. At first Dario spoke only to Mother, ignoring me completely. He looked sullen, although he ate with appetite. Soon curiosity won over his anger, and he turned to me with a wry smile.

"Well, have you finished the masterpiece?" he asked.

72

"Yes," I said.

"Can you tell us what the play is about, darling?" Mother asked.

I thought for a moment, then decided it would be best to give them some information. It was one way of testing Dario.

"It's about Paolo," I began. "He loves a girl who leaves him for another man. And this man informs on Paolo's father because he prints leaflets against the regime." I looked at Dario, and our eyes met. "So Paolo tries to kill himself but is crippled instead. Later he kills the informer, which serves him right." I looked squarely at Dario.

"Bloodthirsty, aren't you?" Dario said.

"Anyway, in the end he gives himself up and saves his friends," I went on, ignoring his remark. "And then he says those words you read when they torture him in prison, and they finally murder him, too."

"Fine literature for a young girl!" Dario exclaimed. "I detest political writing. Only Communists and Fascists make up such propaganda trash. To me they both stink equally to heaven. As to informers and avengers," he went on, "it all sounds like a corny opera."

"It's not!" I protested, sighing with tremendous relief at Dario's reaction and being almost glad to feel guilty now for having suspected him. "It's good, strong writing, and it's not political propaganda. The largest part of the play has to do with human problems."

"Look how eloquent she gets when it comes to her hero!" Dario mocked. "Then, pray, tell me about these human problems, since you are determined not to let me read the play myself."

"Nicole is merely acting protectively when it comes to her friends," Mother said, coming to my rescue. "You

73

should appreciate her tact and not make fun of it. It proves that she's discreet about all personal matters," she added, looking at Dario significantly.

I paid little heed to her words and glance, concerned as I was for the moment with Lorenzo's work. Still those words left me with a sense of malaise. Dario kept on scowling, and was curt and brusque with me for the rest of the day.

Later that afternoon, as we were on the beach about to take a swim, he asked me again to tell him about the "human aspects" of the play.

"It's about Paolo's friend, Antonio, the carpenter," I said, hoping to close this painful subject once and for all by telling him what he wanted to know. I tried to extenuate the impression the last words of the play had made on him, although I knew that nothing I might say would change his antagonism. "Antonio is torn between his mother and sister on the one hand, and his wife and young son, on the other, while he slaves to make a living despite his involvement in all these family problems." I saw that Dario was listening attentively. "He envies Paolo his freedom from all ties, his freedom to work as a journalist."

"But that's ridiculous!" Dario exclaimed. "How can he envy a cripple and a man, as you said before, who went through such tragedies!"

"I was just about to explain," I said, forcing myself to remain calm, "that Antonio meets Paolo after these happenings and only learns about them in the last act."

"All right, go on," Dario said.

"Paolo envies Antonio for exactly the opposite reasons," I said, speaking quickly as I stared across the sea. "He wishes he had someone to love, someone to work for. The play shows the many good and bad sides of these two conditions. There's Antonio's sister, Mara, who would like to take care of Paolo, but Paolo thinks she wants to sacrifice her life for him and refuses her help. But the girl really loves him and is very unhappy."

"I get it," Dario said sarcastically. "Some Dostoevski mixed with Chekhov overspiced and brought up to date with Communist propaganda. It's been done over and over again."

"If you are so clever," I could not help saying, "why don't you write something better?" I pulled my white bathing cap over my head, ready to go into the water.

"Why don't you admit that it's hogwash!" Dario said, putting on his own black cap savagely.

I said no more but ran ahead of him into the sea. I was angry and upset, and all my guilty feelings were forgotten. After a moment I saw Dario at my side, looking horrid in his black cap, his eyes bloodshot from the salt water, and this new cold, angry look on his face. He was like a bitter, haggish woman, I thought. His nose seemed longer, and the scar below his eye had somehow reddened and deepened, drawing his eye out of shape. I hated him then, hated him with every fiber of my being.

"Hogwash, hogwash!" he kept saying.

"You aren't jealous of me and my friend, are you?" I finally asked. "You are jealous because you haven't written anything yourself. That's why!"

Dario's furious reaction convinced me that I was right.

"Go on, defend him, raise him on a pedestal," he said, "with your trashy little girl's mind! Cherish him in your lollipop heart !That doesn't make his so-called drama any better." He swallowed some water, coughed, then went on, "From the few lines I read I can tell that it literally and figuratively stinks to heaven! He's just trying to make an impression on you! I won't write unless I have something meaningful to say to a more intelligent audience than a silly schoolgirl!"

"How hateful you are," I said. "I wish I could give you a mirror, so you could hiss your poison at yourself."

I swam away, sobbing, swallowing water through my mouth and nose, which made me cough and almost suffocate. I swam and coughed and sobbed and swallowed, and wished I were dead.

"You make me sick!" I heard him call after me. *"Antipatica!"*

♣ ♣

"Darling, are you in love?"

My mother's casual and condescending tone is still in my ears. She had no suspicion of the quick light she had shed upon my confused emotions. Her oversimplification made me grow aware of my own complexities. I must have murmured some vague answer, or merely nodded my head.

We were crossing the Kursaal garden. It was dusk. My mother's arm lay warm and soft against mine, and there was the smell of bright red roses. Urchins came running out of the ice cream parlor, their tongues licking cones. From Zanarini's coffee house across the beach the Violetta song from *La Traviata* carried my longing beyond the rosy rim of the horizon. I repressed a desire to run away from them all—from my mother, my cousin Natalie, and her husband, Walter, who had come to spend the end of their vacation with us in Rimini, and were walking a few steps ahead of us between Father and Dario.

In my mind's eye I could see myself running, running over the deserted beach endlessly, until I fell into the cool sand, exhausted and breathless, and grew calm again under the night-blue sky full of stars. Instead I walked on as quietly as though my mother had never asked the fatal question. I wondered if she meant Dario. Or perhaps she thought I was infatuated with my handsome cousin

Walter. After all, young girls did get infatuated with all sorts of people; they fell, as the saying goes, in love with love. I was used to grown-ups and their lack of understanding, and took it for granted, as children always do. I was glad Mother pressed me no further. But now I asked myself the question, Is this love? It was so different from what I had read about in books or observed on the screen. Yet I would not want to miss it though it was like being sick at heart with a terrible hunger and thirst for something you could not understand.

That night after dinner Walter and Natalie went out again with my parents and Dario. I was not allowed to go along because I was too young. I was not too young to go to the Kursaal and see a picture in the open-air theater nor too young for the amusement park nor even too young to go out dancing once in a while, but I was too young to go to the pier with them and eat seafood and drink wine. My youth was merely a convenient excuse for them whenever I would be in the way. Now, I was only in my own way. For a while after they left, I tried to leap over my shadow by talking to Zita, but Zita was in a hurry to go out on a date, and I settled on the sofa with *La Chartreuse de Parme*.

I had a queer way of reading books in those days. Not, for example, that I would look at the last page first to see the final outcome of a story as Zita did. I would hunt avidly for the love scenes. They would quicken my pulse and fill me with unusual agitation. That night I was particularly impressed by the story of a young woman who had vowed to the Madonna that if her imprisoned lover were given back his freedom, she would never see him again. The Madonna granted her wish, and she kept her vow by never glancing at him, but received him in her chamber, after dark. I did not yet appreciate the writer's wit. My imagination was deeply stirred by the two lovers

77

holding each other in their arms, life and circumstances allowing them to be alone without restraint. I could hardly believe that something so wonderful was possible.

I slept restlessly that night. At six o'clock in the morning I was awakened by the familiar, strident voice of a market woman praising her fruits and vegetables as she passed in the street.

"Belle pesche! Bell'uva! Bella frutta!"

I put on a sleeveless white shirt and navy-blue shorts and then peeped into Walter's and Natalie's room to see if they were asleep. It would be nice if either of them wanted to come down to the beach with me, I thought, preferably Walter. I found Natalie's bed deserted and Walter soundly asleep.

Slightly disappointed, I walked through the empty streets toward the sea. There the door of our cabana was ajar. Natalie's clothes lay strewn on the floor as if she had torn them off in a hurry. Her black bathing suit and the pink dressing gown she always wore on top of it were missing.

The beach was deserted. I saw no swimmers in the sea. Barefooted, I walked along the water, my head bent. Then I noticed the imprints of two pairs of feet in the wet sand, regularly proceeding in the direction of the pier. I went on in a cloud of painful misgivings as if pushed by some invisible hand.

The variegated patched canvas of anchored sailboats swelled out in the breeze as I walked along the channel, on the mole. I passed a fisherman or two, and as we exchanged friendly greetings, I was soothed by their warm, living presence. There was no sign of Natalie.

I reached the last restaurant on the pier; peeping through an open window, I saw Natalie at a table, with breakfast before her, in intimate conversation with Dario. There was no one else in the restaurant. I turned slowly away, but they must have noticed me, for a moment later I heard someone opening the door and Dario calling my name. I went on, hesitating.

"Nicole!" His voice sounded angry.

I stopped, then turned around without daring to meet his eyes.

"Come and join us," he said.

I followed him inside, my eyes still lowered. Dario was moving a chair for me to sit down. "How did you know we were here?" asked Natalie.

"I didn't." I glanced at Dario and saw irritation and annoyance in his eyes, and the imprint of lipstick on his mouth.

"We wanted to swim in the open sea," said Natalie. "It's more fun out here."

"Do you have to explain to the brat," Dario said under his breath. "A nice way to come sneaking after us!"

I felt myself suffocating. "I wasn't sneaking," I murmured. I tried to stand up and go but felt so overwhelmed with pain that I could not move.

"Don't go away," Natalie said good-naturedly. "Have some breakfast."

I shook my head.

"Now, come on," Dario said. "You don't have to be upset. I'll forgive you."

"No, really," I said.

Dario rose from his seat, stepped behind my chair and put his hands on my shoulders. I knew he was giving Natalie a sign behind my back. "Well, let's go," he said. "Our morning's spoiled anyway."

Natalie pulled out a patent-leather purse from the pocket of her pink dressing gown which was flung across a chair, and handed it discreetly to Dario. "Sorry," he said. "I forgot to bring my wallet."

I hurried out first, blinded with tears, and they followed more slowly. Back at our cabana, I found Mother in a beach chair and Walter stretched at her side. Neither of them had changed into their bathing suits. They were talking excitedly, and obviously changed the conversation as soon as I was within hearing distance. Mother looked old and tired. Her face was swollen as if she had cried all night, but I was too absorbed in my own pain to pay attention to hers.

Walter frowned at Natalie. She sat down at his side. Her wet bathing suit clung to her firm darkly tanned body. The pink dressing gown hung limply from her arm. Dario remained standing in front of them, shivering in his maroon-colored trunks. His profile was turned to the sea. His face was drawn. Then Walter rose and walked a few steps away, summoning Natalie with an angry sign of his head. She shrugged, then followed him reluctantly, giving Dario a forced smile as she passed.

Dario seemed to hesitate. I saw Mother looking at him with a painfully distorted face. "You look tired this morning," she said. "You must have gotten up quite early."

He returned her glance with an ironical grin. All at once he bent over her, and I heard him whisper, "And you look like a fifty-year-old woman." Then he walked away with his leisurely gait.

I had sat down in the sand at Mother's side. She seized my hand, pressing my fingers convulsively as though they were nothing but the nearest hold for her despair. I began to shake. Mother looked at me without seeming to see me.

I felt the vague presence of a shadow cowering at my side. I turned and saw that Augusto had quietly settled at my feet, as he always used to do, letting the sand run through his fingers. I had not noticed his coming. He sat there resigned and immobile, like a living reproach.

"Please go away," I said. He sighed. "Can't you see," I went on rudely, as he did not budge, "that we have visitors? Leave me alone, just once!"

                         ♣ ♣

I can't remember how I lived through the hours and days that followed. Like a wounded animal fleeing into the thicket of a forest, I nursed my grief in loneliness. I hid between cabanas, locked myself in my room, and withdrew into my shell at mealtimes. No one paid any attention to me, and even the tears that dropped into my spaghetti went unnoticed. Walter and Natalie gave my father an unconvincing excuse for their hasty departure from Rimini, and soon after they left, the fights between my parents were resumed.

I was resigned. Since I knew that we might never see Dario again, nothing mattered any more. Life stretched dull and hopeless before me. The things that men and women did belonged to a forbidden, mysterious world. Mother's distress lasted too long to convince me, as she tried to make me believe, that it was over Dario and Natalie's betrayal of Walter. I was sure now that Mother loved Dario.

I can look back on this realization as the germ that grew slowly, almost imperceptibly, into the intricate web of self-deceit in which I began to envelop myself after that fateful morning. It was Lorenzo who told me at a later time that we choose our own illnesses. My "disease" developed out of the fear of losing Dario. I needed cowardice to find my courage, deception to discover truth, and disillusionment to start my life with hope. I decided never to confront my mother with their relationship. Once or twice I had been tempted to ask her, but something stronger than timidity or shame held me back. I had been afraid that Mother might be embarrassed and send Dario away.

Slowly my love for him grew stronger than pride, and I felt a dim hope of a reconciliation while an instinct warned me that a reunion could take place only if I went on as if nothing had happened. Perhaps during the night of their outing with Walter and Natalie Mother had made Dario angry, and he might not have been entirely to blame. It was best to hypnotize myself into forgetting what I had observed. In her anger and unhappiness Mother neglected me sorely. Sometimes I used Augusto in order to pass this time of misery. My parents bickered like children, and I realized that their bitterness was the result of the difficulty many of us find in living with ourselves.

As I understood more about grown-ups, they lost much of my esteem. My love for Dario, on the other hand, restricted my memories to the pleasant times we had spent together. I found excuses for his wickedness. Something must have hurt and troubled him. Whatever the wound in his heart, I was determined to help him heal it. I believed in my power to move mountains. Through the faith of my love, a love that must be all-forgiving, I would help him find his other, better self.

He avoided meeting us for several days. As I strolled along the beach I would sometimes spot him leaning against a cabana in his bathing trunks. He was always bent over a book as I passed. Perhaps he regretted his behavior but was too proud to return. I felt tempted to go to him as if nothing had happened, but pride forbade me. One morning he lifted his head from his book and saw me, walking along the shore, and called my name. I stopped and waited for him to get to his feet and move toward me with his graceful gait. I noticed he had parted his full black hair to one side.

"How are you, Nicole? It's good to see you," he said. "I missed you—dreadfully."

"You knew all along where to find me," I answered in spite of good intentions.

"I don't blame you for being angry with me." I wanted to say something, but could not speak. "*Piccola*," he said softly. "Please . . . It was awful, unforgivable to treat you like that! I thought you would never want to see me again."

I swallowed hard, then looked up at him and saw that his eyes were moist and shiny. "I didn't. But then . . ."

"Yes, go on. Tell me!" he said.

"I can't stay angry with you forever." I turned away from him and quickly wiped my eyes with the back of my hand.

"*Piccola*, you are the sweetest, the gentlest . . ." His hand stroked my hair hesitantly, then withdrew. "Please look at me." As I did not move, he walked around me, then put his finger under my chin, and slowly lifted my face: "You do forgive me then, don't you?" I nodded sadly. "But Mammina . . ." he said. "She may not ever want to make up."

"I don't know," I said.

He glanced at me sideways, then said as if to test me, "You see, she was terribly angry because of Natalie and Walter. She probably thinks I'm an awful heel. Oh, *piccola*, I'd so much like to make peace with her, so we can all be together again!"

"Why don't you go and talk to her now? She's in the cabana changing."

"I'd like to. . . . But what about your father?"

"He's in bed with an upset stomach," I said.

"Too many plums?"

"No, grapes."

We smiled at each other. I felt half relieved, half uneasy, at the facile turn of tone our conversation had taken, for my heart was still heavy. We began to walk back in the direction of our tent awning.

Mother looked up from her book only when we stopped beside her canvas chair. She frowned at Dario and hardly returned his greeting. I left them alone with the excuse that I had to get a book, hoping they would make peace.

Later I was rewarded by my mother's happy smile. At lunch she was friendly toward Father, inquired about his health, patiently listened to his complaints instead of interrupting him, as she would have done at other times, with, "It's no wonder after all those grapes you ate. I warned you!"

Mother and I walked back to the beach in the early afternoon, and although it threatened rain, the two of us went swimming with Dario. We were happy, and we talked and laughed and even sang together. After the swim we changed, then hung our wet bathing suits to dry on a line behind our cabin, and sat down to talk.

After a while I looked through the rows of cabanas toward the sea and saw a pair of familiar bare legs walking toward us. "Here comes Augusto," I said.

"Quick, let's hide in the cabana," Dario suggested, and the three of us rushed inside like children, locked the door, and remained standing tensely together as we heard Augusto outside.

We could glimpse him through the shutters of the door. He stood in the sand, shaking his head. Then he sat down against the wooden wall. We hardly dared breathe.

"Our bathing suits!" I whispered.

It started to rain, and thoughtful Augusto rose and took them off the line. A strap of my wet bathing suit appeared in the narrow space of a wooden shutter. We could see Augusto's fingertip pushing it through.

I was tempted to hook my finger into the strap and pull. The next moment Mother succumbed and put out her hand. Dario's hand clasped hers. My suit dropped, plop, to the floor. I stifled a giggle. Dario's other hand clamped over my face. My laughter turned into a groan.

Mother's face became contorted with stifled laughter. I put my hand tightly over her mouth, and she squeaked almost inaudibly as she threw back her head. The rain drummed on the roof. Dario shushed softly. I put my free finger on his lips as Mother's black bathing suit snaked in through the ribs of the shutter. We huddled together in the semidarkness, feeling each others' suppressed convulsions.

Next Dario's maroon trunks came through the slats and fell on top of the wet heap. Blinded with tears, Mother and I wiped our eyes on Dario's white T-shirt. At last we heard Augusto run away. When he was out of earshot, we gave vent to our hysterics.

It was stuffy in the cabana. We opened the door. It was raining hard. We remained sitting inside on the floor, Dario in the middle. He drew us to him and put his arms around our shoulders.

"*C'era una volta—un piccolo naviglio,*" Dario began to sing. There was once a little ship—"*che non sapeva, non sapeva navigar . . .*" which knew not, knew not how to sail. . . .

As he sang, I beat the rhythm with my toes on his toes. "*E dopo uno, due, tre . . . quattro, cinque, sei, sette settimane . . .*" And after one, two, three, four, five, six, seven weeks. . . . My big toe drummed on the five toes of his left foot, then on two of his right, as he went on at the top of his voice, "*il piccolo naviglio navigò. . . .*" The little ship did sail.

"We shouldn't go home too late," Mother said. "Poor Father has a bellyache."

"Oooh, ooh," Dario sang. "Poor Father has a bellyache . . . *E dopo uno, due, tre, quattro, cinque, sei—sette settimane* . . . the bellyache, the bellyache was gone. . . ."

Mother and I burst into another fit of laughter, and Dario's shirt absorbed a few more of our tears. He said he would never wash it again, for it was the merriest shirt ever.

It stopped raining. "Nicole, would you pick up the suits and hang them up to dry again," Mother said. "Dario and I would like to go for a walk. We'll be back soon." She kissed me. "You guard the cabana, will you dear?"

All the gladness of the day went out of me. I shrugged and said nothing. Dario gave me a friendly pat on the shoulder. When they left, I picked up the suits and hung them on the line. Then I resumed my position on the cabana floor, leaning my face on my updrawn knees. Because of Natalie, Dario had almost lost us, and still he was so sure of himself, so confident that he would win us back. I had brought them together again, I thought bitterly, while now I might just be in his and Mother's way as Augusto was in mine.

After a while I took my white leather-covered diary from the table, unlocked its golden filigree lock with a miniature key, and sat pondering over an empty page.

I never confided my secret feelings to the book, but wrote down thoughts I considered philosophical. At the top of the first page stood the following words in capital letters:

GOOD INTENTIONS ARE MY CURSE.
LOVE IS MY FAITH.

I began to write slowly:

If you want to hold on to something, it escapes at the slightest touch. Why is this so? You can think of the right words to say, but before you open your mouth they are gone. It's painful to be so blind and to have to grope for your way. Happiness is gone before you know you are happy. The friend's hand withdraws before you have shaken it. Why is life like that? Like a mimosa bush. Oh, the horrible, frightening emptiness of it, the leaves always escaping and closing under my hand! And it happens so gently, so quietly, that you only seldom really, really know about it. With each word you say to a friend, the leaves close, and you are more lonely than ever. . . . And it is as if you were waiting from day to day for the right touch. Your whole life you go on fighting and searching for it. . . .

♣ ♣

It was about a week after I wrote those lines that Dario looked at me guiltily and said that he had read my diary. We were standing at the counter, eating sweets at the café across the beach. Mother was at the espresso machine, drinking her coffee, and could not hear us.

"I couldn't resist the temptation," Dario said. "You left the key on the table. Will you forgive me, Nicole?" I nodded. "I know I shouldn't have done it. It's a warning that you mustn't leave anything about when I'm here. Don't ever trust me."

"But I do trust you," I reassured him, looking at a small blue notebook he was holding in his hand. "I always will, and I'll leave my diary open the next time so you won't even care to read it."

"I wouldn't be so sure," he said, smiling. "You are a good sport, *piccola*."

"Sometimes I succeed, and sometimes I don't. It's not easy to be so with you."

Our eyes met with a new sense of recognition, an almost painful awareness, beyond the masks of gesture and word. I felt I had known Dario since the world began. And from the way he looked at me I could tell that his feelings, at this moment, responded to mine.

Sometimes such emotions would make us stop in the midst of a sentence or a smile, our eyes melting with something that was more than love or hate or both, an affinity at once unique and frightening.

Mother paid the bill, and we strolled across the promenade and went down the steps to the beach. Mother immediately went to sit down under our awning by the water while Dario entered the cabana first, to put on his swimming trunks. I waited for my turn outside. He reappeared after a moment and said that he would go ahead and swim to the diving board.

I slipped into my navy-blue knitted bathing suit and looked for my cap. It was on the table on top of the blue notebook Dario had held in his hand. As I opened the door I remembered Dario's indiscretion. I turned back, opened the little book, and found the pages almost empty. Only the first page was covered with his neat writing.

"Yes, she is lovely," I read, "too fine and too good for someone so unworthy of her. She must remain the sanctuary of my life. I will treasure her jealously, will help her grow into that exquisite work of art she promises to become. Oh, why is she so unattainably young, so vulnerable and invulnerable at one time! What makes her constantly search for something lost in this world, something she carries within the core of her own completeness? Angel, child, woman, must you remain the unspoken yearning of my life, the dream of dreams?"

My heart thumped so violently that I pressed a hand against my breast. My head was on fire. I could not face Dario now. I took the notebook and pressed it to my face. Oh, Dario, Dario! I took the page and tore it into shreds, crying with happiness. Then I went out and dug a hole into the sand and buried the shreds of paper.

I wanted to be alone. I hid at the upper end of the

beach, in the shade between two cabanas. Then I remembered that Dario had said he would go ahead and swim
to the diving board. I tried to collect my thoughts. If it
was all part of an act—his reading my diary and telling
me about it, and writing in a notebook . . . and leaving it
there for me to read, then what was his true purpose?
He could not have meant to turn my head, since he knew
he had done that already. I must go to him and pretend
nothing had happened as if I had never read that page.
Oh, why had I torn it up in my first impulse? Out of fear
that it might get into the wrong hands?

"Nicole!"

I started at the sound of Dario's voice and looked up
as he stepped toward me into the narrow space between
the cabanas. His face was blurred in my unsteady glance.
He took my hand.

"You haven't gone into the water at all," I finally whispered.

"No. I told Mammina I had forgotten to give a message
to my aunt. I came back to wait for you."

I lowered my head and said nothing.

"Did you read . . . ?" I nodded. "*Piccola* . . . I wrote it
last night," he said. "I didn't even think of leaving it there
for you to read. But then I thought you should know."

"Know what, Dario?"

"How I feel. I'm no good, Nicole. If you think badly of
me, it's never bad enough. But I am like two different
people. I want you to keep in mind that the better one is
dedicated to you, no matter what I do or say. Will you
promise me to remember?"

I nodded. "We all are many people at the same time,
Dario. Sometimes I'm three or five or ten."

"Yes. But I can be so wicked. I don't know what
comes over me. I'm conscious of it, but I just can't
help it."

"Perhaps you have been hurt. We try to get rid of our wounds by pasing them on to someone else," I said.

"Oh, *piccola*, you are so wise and so childish, so silly and so clever, and so lovable and so hateful! Oh, why are you so old and knowing, and so pathetically, ridiculously young?" He was still holding my hand. "You know it too, Nicole. It's an ironical thing I should feel this for a girl of barely fifteen, but you understand my better self more then a living soul ever has. . . . Nicole, *amor mio*, you and I are one in the spirit, in our deeper selves."

"Yes, Dario," I said gravely.

He drew me to him slowly, then kissed my forehead, my temples, my cheeks. And as I let my head sink on his shoulder, trembling and weeping with a joy close to sorrow, he raised my head and kissed my tears away, saying tenderly, "I wish I would see you laugh more often, *tesoro*, I want you to be happy. You are such a poor, sad little thing. Go, now; I'll meet you on the diving board in a few minutes."

I went away, turning to smile at him several times. Then he called me, and I ran back to him, and he said he had forgotten something. And then he kissed my eyes again.

"What took you so long to change?" Mother asked as I passed her, running toward the water.

I mumbled that I had been busy with the diary. Before she could see my face I threw myself into the waves, then swam to the *trampolino*. This consisted of a diving raft with its wooden poles anchored to the bottom of the sea, its top forming a sun deck towering about ten feet above the water. I climbed up a ladder to the top, snorting like a seal.

Giobbe, a handsome swimmer I had met in the water that summer, was stretched on the sunny planks. He seemed to be sleeping, his blond head bedded in the fold of his arm. I stepped over him so that the water dripped on his suntanned back, and he leaped up angrily, shaking his great muscular body.

"Oh, it's you!" he said. "Wait, you devil, I'll throw you into the water one of these days! Are you going to dive?"

"Not yet," I said.

"You coward! I've watched you all summer long. You'll never dare."

"I shall before the summer's over."

"You have only a few days left. You don't have to go with your head first. Just jump, and hold your nose."

"But that hurts! You can die if you fall in a bad way."

"Not from three meters!" Giobbe laughed.

"I'm not in the mood today."

"So you aren't in the mood. I beg your pardon, signorina." He stepped behind me, put his arms around my waist and carried me wriggling like a fish to the edge.

"Let me go!" I screamed with nervous laughter, and then I saw Dario in the water below. "Dario, help, help!" I cried.

Giobbe set me down, roaring with husky laughter. Dario pulled himself out of the water, and as he came climbing up the ladder to join us, Giobbe said, "I bet you ten lire that she will never dive."

Dario smiled, and I said that I accepted the bet. "I almost did—yesterday."

"Almost!" Giobbe sneered.

"Yes, I was over there, in front. I imagined someone was dying and my jumping would save his life. But then I remembered nobody was dying anyway, so why should I?"

"Trouble with you is, you think too much," Giobbe said. "People who think never do things."

"How true," Dario mocked. "You are quite a philosopher, Giobbe. Maybe an empty head gets back to the surface faster. Maybe she's afraid with all her thinking she'll sink too deep. Why don't you show her how to do it?"

"I've shown her a thousand times," Giobbe said good-humoredly.

"Do, Giobbe, do!" I begged, wishing he would dive and leave.

"This is the last time," Giobbe said.

A moment later the board shook under the weight of his tall athlete's body as he leaped over it as if in flight. For an instant his taut bronze figure seemed suspended in midair, his blond hair in the wind, and, like an arrow flung from an invisible bow, he plunged into the deep blue water. He reappeared close to the shore, waving and shouting something we could not hear.

"I hope you haven't insulted him," I said.

"Oh, no. He wouldn't think of himself as an empty head," Dario replied. "Empty heads never do. Besides, we got rid of him. Isn't that what you wanted?"

"Yes. But I didn't want you to hurt him. Giobbe's such a nice fellow."

"Oh, stop talking with that chronic bad conscience of yours! How can you ever enjoy anything if you regret it at the same time?"

"Now don't start. Not today. Please."

"All right, *piccola*. I want you to get rid of that convent which seems still to be in your bones," he lectured me. " 'Be hypocritical and polite to everyone, never follow a healthy selfish impulse and be joyous! Amen.' Nicole?"

"Yes?"

"Would you jump if I wanted you to?"

"I don't know," I said, my pulse beating faster.

"I know you would. You will, right now. Listen. You are not saving anybody's life. It doesn't make any sense, but you will dive because I say so. Jump."

I laughed out loud, anxiously.

"I mean it in dead earnest," he said, frowning at me.

"I'm not going to," I said.

"Jump!" He was grinding his teeth. I remained motion-less. "All right," he said, heading for the ladder, "I'll re-member this."

"Why don't you jump yourself?" I asked weakly.

"Because I don't like diving. It gives me a headache." He stepped down the many rungs of the ladder, then swam away angrily.

I stretched myself out on the planks, my eyes pressed into the bend of my arm, feeling all drained inside. After a while I looked up and saw a puddle of water gathering about Dario's feet: Dario was smiling down on me, a dripping giant.

"We aren't quarreling today," he said. I shook my head. "I wanted to prove to Giobbe that you aren't a coward. The method didn't work. Do you think with love and kindness . . . ?"

"Yes. But not today," I said. "I'm tired. Tomorrow morning I'll try hard."

"Good." He lay down beside me, and for a long time we said no more, our hands touching, our eyes wandering over the sea.

♣ ♣

"Jump," Giobbe said. Giobbe was a huge brown bear running after me at the edge of a precipice. "Jump!"

I was unable to move as I felt the hot breath of the bear on my naked shoulders. "I can't!" I cried. "I forgot my cap. My hair will get wet!"

"Jump!" Giobbe breathed hotly upon me. Through a fog I saw many tall trees, and among them a figure moving toward me. I recognized Dario's face, but as it came closer it was an old, haggish woman's under his black bathing cap.

"Jump!" she hissed at me, and before I could recover from the sight of her, she held up a mirror in which I recognized my own frightened face.

"Sneaks must jump!" I heard another voice that sounded like Natalie's. "Jump!"

"Jump!"

"Jump!"

"Jump!"

I stretched my arms out for support, crying, "Mammina, help me, Mammina!" But my words were repeated from all sides by an echo, and then the terrible command to jump came back, this time more imperatively than before. I thought I had reached the outer edge of agony when a white-winged horse soared through the air. Mother was riding it, her red hair flying in the wind. Instead of coming to my rescue, she was crying for help as she dug sharp spurs into the bleeding flanks of her horse. "Mammina!" I cried once more, but the word froze on my lips as I caught sight of my father. He was running after her with a knife that he seemed ready to thrust into her back.

Then they all vanished, the figures and the voices, the fog and the trees. I heard the gentle tap, tap, tap of a cane and thought, *Thank God, I'm safe.*

"Nicole, are you ill? You were screaming." I opened my eyes and saw my mother's shadow bent over me in the dark.

"A dream . . ." I said groggily. "Mammina . . ." She pulled back my sheets and slipped into my bed, trying to soothe me with the soft warmth of her body. "Now go

94

back to sleep," she whispered, fondling me. "Sleep . . ." Her fingers moved gently over my eyes and temples. "Sleep, sleep . . ."

I lay awake for a long time although my eyes were closed, and when Mother left, thinking me asleep, I opened my eyes and stared into the darkness outside and into the darkness inside, and my heart beat with a strong, fearful beat. There was agony in my heart, and I was afraid that another nightmare might come, in sleep or in wakefulness, afraid with a terror that I knew my mother's presence no longer had the power to dispel.

FIVE

Ever since my mother's hands had lost their power to soothe me, life seemed to be a nightmare whichever way I turned. Leaving Rimini at the end of summer was particularly sad for me, for I did not know when I would see Dario again. He meant to enroll for another semester at the university in Milan, although he expected to be called for military duty any day.

Once back in Turin, we learned of the sudden death of Maestro Manetti, which was followed by a long period of silent mourning by his family. As the weeks went by, I tried to call, but the Manettis refused any visits of condolence or any manifestations of sympathy from outsiders. I waited in vain for Sandra to get in touch with me.

I felt shut out of their lives and saddened not to be allowed to share their sorrow, if only in a small way. Their sorrow merely helped to estrange me from them. Lorenzo seemed to have forgotten my existence. Since he had asked me to hold it, his manuscript was still in my possession. He had meant to call for it personally that fall. Gradually I began to feel a resentment against their beloved dead, who seemed to have appropriated all the space in their lives, just as Dario had in ours.

But now I added the Manettis' nightmare to my own. The mainspring of their lives was gone forever. And what, I asked myself in secret anguish, is holding our home together? Maxine had died, and we were living as if she had never existed. My father was more often abroad than not, and we were relieved when he was gone. To me it was Mother alone, and the thought that she, too, might die, and that I would then be deprived of her as the Manettis had been deprived of their father filled me with despair. The ground that had grown so shaky under my feet might one day give way and the crumbling earth would swallow us all as death had swallowed the Maestro.

That autumn I felt homesick for Dario. Every now and then I received a friendly letter enclosed in the more important one addressed to my mother. She never showed me his letters, but she always read mine. I did not particularly enjoy them since I knew they were written for her to see.

While Dario's presence alienated us—not openly, of course, but under the surface of our tender relationship —his absence drew us more closely together. Although we expressed our thoughts about him only obliquely, he was the object of our longing. How lovely a sunset there had been in Rimini the day we ate in that particular restaurant, we would say; or how much we had laughed at Dario's imitation of the gauche young man on the tennis court; and remember that charming scene in the theater, what was the name of the play again? Yes, *Una dozzina di rose rosse*. A dozen red roses. . . .

Like roses, petal by petal, memories dropped on the books upon our laps as we sat side by side on the sofa after dinner. Sometimes Mother would suggest we play a game of chess, and as we set the figures on the board, I knew she was thinking my thoughts: *I wish he were here now, I wish I could feel his hand touching mine under the table, his eyes seeking mine, or see his tender smile. . . .*

♣ ♣

One day after a movie, when I had left my school friend Oretta and was making my way toward the Piazza Castello I caught sight of Lorenzo's coat. Its shabbiness and familiar pattern stood out among the other clothes.

Crowds were moving under the arcades of the new Via Roma in the late rainy afternoon, and elegant ladies and gentlemen were coming out of the cafés and mingling with the window-shoppers and the workingmen heading for home. He was at the outer edge of a marble column, tapping his cane not in his usual assured and determined way but with awkward and unsteady motions, as if he were dizzy or ill, seeking an island of refuge away from the crowd.

At one point I saw him bump his head slightly against the column; then his hand wandered to the spot where it hurt. I edged myself toward him, desperately using my elbows, aching with pity for him.

"Good afternoon, Lorenzo," I said, touching his sleeve.

He turned to me a face that was flushed and angry. "Who are you! What do you want?"

"Nicole Steiner," I almost sobbed.

"Oh, it's you," he said more gently, his cane groping for the next step.

"Let's walk near the curb," I said. "One can hardly move in this crowd."

I shyly touched his sleeve to lead him away, but he seized my hand, pressing it roughly, and said, "Oh, come on. Don't be so fainthearted!" He gave a short, hard laugh that was close to a groan. Something was troubling him, and it was not the bump on his head. He had bumped his head because of that other pain which had made him heedless of where he was going. I felt too helpless to speak.

"Come, talk to me," he said harshly, almost dragging me as he walked. "Let me know you are there. To be in a crowd is like losing oneself in a desert, you are surrounded by ghosts. Make me feel you are real, as I felt you in your letters! I had Sandra read them to me many times. They were little-girl letters, but real, so real I could feel you breathing beside me."

"I haven't been able to thank you for your last one," I said. "Your manuscript . . ."

"Huh, the manuscript! Don't tell me you read it all. It's nonsense anyway. I have a real job now."

"Oh?"

"As the only male provider of the family, I am engaged to play in a *café dansant* three nights a week. High class. Hot stuff. A place where your girlish foot would never be allowed to tread. Fortunately I am blind to sin. But let's talk about you. How have you been? How's your lovely mother? Red hair, green-blue eyes, rather ample, very feminine, so easy-going, Sandra told me. You aren't as charming as your mother, Nicole, but you may be some day. More than charming, I'd say. Why can't you ever float? What's holding you down and burning you up inside? Those letters Sandra read me. I could feel all that restlessness between the lines, that constant wondering and pondering about the essential, with a capital *E*. We have two literary minds, you and I. Let's talk about the essential, ladies and gentlemen. Don't let it get out of sight for a moment! Cheerio!

He stopped every now and then as he talked, emphasizing his words with vivid gestures, Italian fashion. I could smell wine on his breath. His new and unaccustomed manner frightened me.

"The essential! Huh! It's the dreary, the dull, the ever-repeating limitations of life, the hopeless pattern. Remember it well! The real drama is never what you think it is. That's one of the tricks of Mother Nature. The tragedy lies in what is never said and never happens. Remember that, too, you foolish dreamer!"

"Lorenzo," I said, "you aren't feeling well. Let's go home."

"I feel perfectly well. You aren't afraid of me, are you? Sooner or later you'll know the crudity of men, so you may as well look at Lorenzo now. You think I am drunk. Yes, I am. Very drunk. And maybe some day I'll hate you for what I've said. But to whom could I say such things if not to you? No, it's just to you I shouldn't say them. . . ."

"Because I'm too young?"

"Nonsense. Because you understand too well. Because you and I can identify with Mitya Karamazov when he is willing to die from sheer enthusiasm. . . . To hell with literature!"

We had reached Piazza Castello and crossed the darkening street slippery with rain. Our tram was approaching.

"How are Sandra and your mother?" I asked as the tram came to a halt.

"Oh, we are a happy family these days!"

I helped him climb onto the platform, and then said, "I was terribly sorry . . ."

"I understand Sandra's going to call you next week," Lorenzo said brusquely.

We stood side by side in the overwhelming odor of garlic which always emanated from any crowd. Lorenzo spoke no more. I felt that neither words nor silence would bring us more closely together. It had grown dark outside.

I left the tram with him and saw that he got home safely, although he insisted that I must let him find his way alone. I stopped at the door of his house. Without thanking me or saying good-bye, he left and closed the door in my face.

I went back to wait for the next tram, thinking not so much of Lorenzo's words as of his helpless bitterness, the weight of which I now carried inside me without having relieved him of his pain.

A few days later Sandra called and asked us to come for coffee on the following Friday evening. She telephoned once more, confirming her invitation with Mother. When Friday came, Mother was at a loss as to what to wear, not knowing if there were going to be other guests. She finally decided on an elegant black velvet dress with a turquoise collar and sash. I put on my ruby-red dress, which the seamstress had lengthened for me. I took Lorenzo's manuscript along.

As soon as we entered the Manettis' living room we saw that we were the only visitors. Signora Manetti was wearing a plain black cotton dress, and Sandra had on a gray turtleneck sweater and a black skirt. Mother and I glanced at each other.

Lorenzo looked well and seemed to be in fine spirits. I gave him the manuscript, and he put it on the table. He drew me into a corner after both women had given me a warm embrace, and there he made me sit down beside him. The living room was sparsely furnished with heavy, rectangular, old-fashioned pieces. I felt nervous, and looking at Mother, I was overcome by a desire to laugh. This embarrassed me all the more since circumstances were quite sad in the Manettis' home. Mother looked beautiful and terribly overdressed. I could not repress a giggle.

"What's so funny?" Lorenzo asked.

"Have you ever come in shorts to a company of people in formal clothes?" I whispered. "You should see my mother's elegant dress while your mamma and Sandra . . ."

"You two over there," Sandra said from the other end of the room, "let us in on your fun!"

"Just a moment," Lorenzo said, laughing softly. "What is your mother wearing?" I described the dress to him. "But it's black, isn't it?" he asked. "Maybe she wanted to wear something dark for the occasion. Well, I guess it makes you feel good to laugh a little at her expense."

For a moment my mind wandered through Mother's wardrobe, and I realized that most of her clothes were either bright blue or green, or light red.

"Probably," I admitted, ashamed.

"And you, Nicole, what color is your dress?"

"Ruby-red," I said.

He laughed. "Oh, then it never occurred to you!" After a pause he added, smiling, "But I like to imagine what you both look like. Lovely, I'm sure."

Then we got up. He took my arm, and we joined the others near the brown sofa in the opposite corner of the room. "We were saying that clothes have only one purpose," Lorenzo told them, "and that is to make a beautiful woman look even more beautiful."

He settled down next to me on the sofa. His mother made room for us, brushing and smoothing the place where she had sat, then straightening her skirt across her knees.

Lorenzo sat between us, and taking his mother's hand in his, he drew her face to him and kissed her cheek.

102

"But there isn't a dress in the world that could make this most beautiful girl more beautiful!" he exclaimed.

"Ah, *figlio mio!*" Signora Manetti said, smiling tenderly, "don't make your old mamma blush in front of our visitors."

"I think Nicole was laughing at me, Signora Manetti," Mother said, winking at me, "because I am all dressed up. Wasn't that it, Nicole?" I nodded and grinned. "Frankly, I feel rather foolish."

"Let's dress up too, Mamma, shall we?" Sandra suggested gleefully.

But my mother held her back and said, "For heaven's sake, Signorina Sandra, don't! I feel much better now that it's out in the open. Your brother is right. Dress doesn't matter at all."

"Of course not," Lorenzo said. "Especially since I'm the only male present and exempt from the delusion of appearances."

"I saw that Nicole brought your manuscript back," Sandra said after a silence. "I would be interested to hear what you thought of the play."

"Please!" Lorenzo protested, raising both hands. Don't let's talk about it. It belongs to the past. To my revolutionary period."

"And now?" Mother asked. "What period is it now?"

"No particular period," Lorenzo said. "I do have various projects, Signora, but nothing specific. Certainly no plays at the moment."

"But your drama," I protested, "was so good! You can't just discard it! It wouldn't be fair!"

Lorenzo let go of his mother's hand, then turned to me and took both my hands into his. "Well, well, Nicole!" he said with a look of pleasure and surprise, smiling broadly and showing his fine, slightly uneven teeth. "I'll

103

engage you as my agent. Signora Steiner, I'm afraid I've made a revolutionary out of your daughter!"

"You couldn't influence her if you tried," Mother said, laughing. The turquoise collar gave her eyes a green-blue sheen. "She has always been rather high-spirited," she went on. I did not like the turn of this conversation, but could not prevent Mother from adding, "When she was quite small, I remember, my husband and I sometimes had to send her to stand in the corner because of her contrariness." Mother spoke quickly. The odd French-American mixture of her clipped Italian accent did not seem to trouble her in the least. "Then, when she felt she was being stubborn," Mother went on good-naturedly, "she would climb off her chair of her own accord and stand there with her face to the wall."

"You must have been quite a girl," Sandra said in her melodious voice, enunciating the words clearly and softly and giving me a sympathetic smile. "I completely agree with you, Nicole," she added. "Of course, Lorenzo gets tired of a work that cannot be performed. But that time will come some day, I'm sure."

I looked at her gratefully. She had let her dark blond hair grow long and was wearing it in a neat French bun.

She left us for a while, and then asked us to come into the dining room, where she had set a simple though festive table. There was nothing but coffee and cake, but the white linen napkins were folded into small fans on each plate, held together at the base by the prongs of a fork, and the bouquet of forget-me-nots and wild red roses we had brought was in the center in a silver vase.

For the rest of the evening Sandra as usual preferred listening to the talk of others, but her gentle, graceful touch could be felt in everything she did. In a wordless way it complemented the warmth Lorenzo expressed so eloquently.

"You mentioned various new projects, Signor Manetti," Mother said presently. "What are they?"

"Oh, about two months ago," Lorenzo replied, "Sandra brought me a book of myths in braille. I became so interested that now I am combing the whole town for material pertaining to all kinds of myths, legends, folktales, fairy tales." He paused. "You see," he went on slowly, "I became really fascinated with the origins of man. How he saw himself and nature; how he began to visualize his gods through his fears. I have found incredible similarities in these original myths. They occurred at a time when no communication existed and during different periods in apparently unrelated cultures. . . ."

♣ ♣

On our way home from the Manettis' that night, Lorenzo was in my mind all the way. Mother and I got off the tram and walked home in silence, and there in the brightness of our hall Dario was sitting as if he were a just-unwrapped package, a living surprise.

Mother looked overjoyed at his unexpected presence, but he seemed like a stranger to me. I had not seen him since we left Rimini. He must be about to be called to Romagna for his military service at any time now.

"Where have you been all evening?" he asked us reproachfully. "Here I come all the way from Milano to see you and you are out!"

"We were visiting with the Manettis," Mother told him, as he helped her take off her coat.

Dario frowned. "So you go out to visit your beaux when I can't see you, eh?" he said, annoyed. I felt more remote from him than when he was in Milano.

"Come now," Mother said, and she explained about the Maestro's death. "We were just paying a visit of condolence."

For several weeks my mind had been at peace. Mother had been calmer and for once seemed to belong completely to me. I had improved my work in school, although I had yearned for Dario in a constant, quiet dream. But now his unexpected nearness struck me as unpleasantly strange, particularly after my visit with Lorenzo.

In the living room, as Mother spoke to him, he secretly glanced at me from time to time. At last, Mother said, "It's way beyond your bedtime, Nicole."

"But Dario's just come! Let me stay up for a while!"

"You didn't seem to care much anyway," he said.

"I have to get used to you first."

"We'll have a good-night session when you are in bed," Mother promised.

I hurried to my room and called them five minutes later. They came in and sat down on the edge of my bed, Mother right next to me. She turned her back to Dario, who sat behind her with one hand propped on my mattress. While he talked, gazing at me from behind Mother's shoulder, I felt the contact of his arm against my leg through the blankets, warm and familiar. My body was a stream under the bridge of his arm, and I began to pay less and less attention to what was being said, thinking, *He's here; he has come back; he's here, so close, so wonderfully close. . . .* I could not understand why, only a moment before, I had felt estranged from him and oppressed.

"I'm dying of thirst," Dario said. "May I please have a glass of water?"

"I'll get it." Mother rose, and Dario took her place, closer to me, as she left the room.

"So you have to get used to me first," he whispered, bending over my face until his breath mingled with mine, and I could no longer see him, so large had he grown with closeness. As I heard Mother turn off the light in the kitchen, I felt his lips closing on mine, soft and warm.

Mother came back. Dario moved away, and I could see him once more. I watched the shadows on the wall, and Dario's Adam's apple moving as the water went down his throat. Mother kissed my cheek; Dario brushed my temple with his lips. The lights went out; the door closed. Silence.

I felt myself sink into bottomless space. Flames shot through the black particles of night; my heart remained suspended outside my body; I counted the strokes of the three-quarter hour on Corso Orbassano. The two of us were blissfully floating upon a cloud. A moment later I had a vision of the first kiss under a hedge of roses, the kiss of two angels touching.

But such images vanished as I relived the instant of that real kiss, tasting and retasting the sweetness of Dario's lips. I was kept awake for hours by a burning desire for more and more and more.

After a long time I heard whisperings in the hall. The click of lights turned off. Silence and darkness. I wondered about the two of them together in that mysterious world of adults, where everything seemed to be permitted yet everything was so vague. I sought refuge in the cloud of my kiss, in the world of my pleasant delusions.

Toward morning I heard Dario in the guest room. Soon Zita roused me out of a light slumber and said it was time to get up. She had to come back twice, shake me roughly, and shout that I was late for school.

It was cold and dismal. I went through the anguish of being tardy. Later I was unable to concentrate on my lessons. When I came home for lunch, Dario and Mother had not yet returned from their walk. There was barely

107

enough time for me to eat and rush back to school. After dinner the two of them went to a show, and I was sent to bed.

I had hardly dared look at Dario and felt that he, too, was avoiding my eyes. The second and last day of his visit turned out to be very much like the first. In the evening Mother and Dario went to the opera. I read in bed until I heard them come home, then turned off the light and remained in sleepless agony.

When I went to school in the morning Dario was still asleep, and when I returned home for lunch, he was gone. Mother noticed my disappointment and said that Dario had sent his love to me and promised to come back on his first army furlough. I remained silent and oppressed for the next three days. At last Mother asked me if anything was wrong.

"Mammina . . ." I hesitated.

"What is it, darling?"

We were in the midst of dinner. I put down my knife and fork and began to fidget with my napkin ring.

"There's something I must tell you," I forced myself to say. I could not be dishonest with Mother. I wiped my mouth and took a sip of water, then pressed the ring in my hands and was silent.

"Is it that hard?" Mother looked at me and smiled.

I sighed. "I . . . Dario kissed me," I whispered, lowering my eyes.

Mother put down her knife and fork. Her hands trembled. I glanced at her. The color had left her face.

"When?" she asked.

"The night we came home from the Manettis'."

"On your mouth?" she asked sharply.

"Yes," I whispered, lowering my head again.

"Was that the first time he ever kissed you?"

"On my mouth. Yes."

108

"Nicole, you must never let this happen again!" she said severely. I nodded. "You must promise me. Never."

I burst into tears. Zita came in with the fruit, and I lowered my head so she could not see my face.

"Hey, what's the matter?" she said. "Trouble in school? Cheer up, *ragazzina!*"

"*E lasciami!*" I said, jerking her hand off my shoulder.

"All right, all right. Don't bite me," she singsonged, carrying out the tray.

We left our oranges untouched. I had never seen such a strange, cold look on my mother's face.

"Why must everything be wrong for me when it's all right for others?" I said defiantly.

"What do you mean?" She looked at me sharply.

I checked myself and said, "Well—he kissed Natalie." I saw my mother stiffen.

"How do you know?" she asked.

"I saw lipstick on his face when they were having breakfast on the pier." It was Mother's turn to look down at her plate. "After all," I went on, "she's married to Walter. I . . . I am not married."

The tone of my voice sounded shrill and unfamiliar. Mother kept staring at her plate. I knew it was on her mind to ask, And what else do you know? But she controlled herself and said, "Dario's behavior is inexcusable. You are much too young."

"That's all I ever hear! I hate to be young! I hate you all!" I cried, stamping my foot under the table.

"Nicole!"

"You don't understand me! You never have, and you never will!" I screamed. I had begun to sob helplessly, and then I ran out of the room.

I fell on my bed, shocked at my outburst. I thought I had forced myself to tell Mother in order to keep our relationship honest and intact, yet Mother's reaction had brought forth other feelings: resentment, jealousy, anger. I had hit out at her cruelly and so marred the image I had of myself. Besides, I was afraid Mother would come and confront me. I would be unable to deny the depth of my love for Dario—I had never lied to her before—and then I would lose him forever.

She came in a few minutes later and sat down on the edge of my bed, hesitating. I kept my head turned toward the wall. As Father does, I thought bitterly.

"Nicole . . . Did you really mean what you said—that you hate us all?"

I shrugged my shoulders.

"Do you know something? Maybe I don't understand you the way I should, but you are a moody and complicated child, and it's not easy. Sometimes it may seem to you that I don't love you enough, but I do, I do . . ." Her voice was breaking. "If you should ever hate me for any reason, I mean not just be angry, but really hate me . . . I, I . . ."

I felt my bed vibrate with her weeping. Oh, the power of her tears! I turned around quickly and flung myself into her arms, whispering, "Stop it, stop it, will you please stop it!" And we shook with tenderness and sorrow, holding each other in a strong embrace.

"Oh, my darling, then you don't hate me!" she sighed with relief, pressing me against her heart, and for an answer I gave her a silent, intense response.

The incident was closed. Neither Mother nor I mentioned it again. For the next few weeks peace was restored, and life, outwardly at least, went on as before Dario's visit. My mind, however, kept wandering back to his forbidden lips—in school over my books, at home while I talked with Mother, in a thousand instances. Since Dario was far away and I was quite safe, I dreamed of being kissed again, not by surprise, but gently, knowingly. At night I often lay sleepless, pressing my pillow against my breast and imagining that it was Dario into whose ear I whispered all my tenderness.

Two days before my father's return for the Christmas holidays Dario came unexpectedly for a brief military furlough. One Sunday morning while taking my bath I heard his voice in the hall. I hurried out of the tub, wrapped myself in a huge towel, and opened the door.

"Dario!" I called in a whisper.

"Piccola!"

We were facing each other in front of the wardrobe, he in his soldier's uniform. He stepped toward me with his hands upraised as if he meant to take me in his arms; then his hands sank slowly down.

"Piccola," he whispered again, staring at me with an expression of awe and astonishment.

"Dario, what is it?" I asked, almost crying with joy.

"It's . . . I'm seeing you for the first time." He shook his head and let a finger glide gently over my face without coming closer, always looking at me in wonder.

"Go and get dressed," he said, stroking my hair. I remembered then that I was merely wrapped in a towel; I blushed and ran to my room.

Afterward Mother and Dario kept me company while I ate breakfast, since they had finished theirs a while before.

"How long have you been here?" I asked.

"Oh, for about two hours."

"Why didn't you wake me up?" I asked reproachfully.

"We thought you needed your sleep on Sunday," Mother said.

"I see."

"I'm going to stay for at least twenty-four hours," he reassured me.

"Oh."

"That's the length of my furlough."

"Then you won't be able to come anymore?" I asked anxiously.

"For a little while," he said. "But I'm hoping to get transferred to Turin, after next summer. Then I'll have more freedom as an officer and shall be able to stay with you almost all the time."

That afternoon Mother lay down for her nap and Dario stretched out on the couch in the guest room. I was going into my room on tiptoe to get the books for my homework when Dario opened his door and beckoned me to his side.

I sat timidly on the edge of the couch. He took my hands. "Nicole, stay for a minute, will you? You are so adorable. . . . I shall never forget the way you looked this morning, like a little white angel."

He drew me down toward his face.

"So you told Mammina about my kiss. She was very upset and reproached me for it. We must be strong in the future. Let's see how strong we are. . . . He drew my head down closer and closer to his face, until our lips were only an inch apart, and held me there for what seemed an eternity.

"The loveliest mouth I've ever seen," he whispered, "like silk and velvet. . . . Don't you dare to ruin it with paint! It's mine, and no one else may ever kiss it. . . ." He let go of my head. "Aren't we strong, you and I, like two lions! Go now, I can't stand this much longer!"

I reeled into my room, where I was unable to concentrate on studying, took my books and went into the living room. The words swam in front of my eyes. I leaned against the back of the sofa inertly and closed my book. Again I was overcome by a power that left me powerless. After some time the door opened noiselessly. Dario came in and sat down at my side.

"You aren't studying," he whispered.

"And you aren't sleeping."

"What are you supposed to do?"

"A canto from the *Inferno*," I said. He took the book and opened it.

"Did you get as far as Francesca da Rimini?" he asked.

"Beyond that."

"Let's read it again."

He opened the last page of the fifth canto and began to read to himself at first, and then softly whispering, as I listened, my heart stopping its beat.

> Noi leggevamo un giorno per diletto
> Di Lancialotto, come amor lo strinse;
> Soli eravamo e sanza alcun sospetto.
> Per più fiate gli occhi ci sospinse
> Quella lettura, e scolorocci il viso;
> Ma solo un punto fu quello che ci vinse.
> Quando leggemmo il disiato riso
> Esser baciato da cotanto amante
> Questi, che mai da me non fia diviso
> La bocca mi baciò tutto tremante.
> Galeotto fu il libro e chi lo scrisse!
> Quel giorno più non vi leggemmo avante.

> (One day for dalliance we read the rhyme
> of Lancelot, how love had mastered him.
> We were alone with innocence and dim time.
> (Pause after pause that high old story drew
> our eyes together while we blushed and paled;
> but it was one soft passage overthrew
> (Our caution and our hearts. For when we read
> how her fond smile was kissed by such a lover,
> he who is one with me alive and dead
> (breathed on my lips the tremor of his kiss.
> That book, and he who wrote it, was a pander.
> That day we read no further.)

He put his arm about my shoulder. My head sank against his chest. I wanted to rest there forever. We did not move for a long time; we were like one, whole and complete and at peace through one another. He supported my head as he kissed me. Later he looked at me and said, "Why do you think Mammina doesn't want me to kiss you?"

I felt his keen eyes on me as I lowered mine. "She says I'm too young."

"Yes, you are. Exquisitely young." Then, after a pause: "And you, what do you think?"

"Think about what?"

"About her real motive."

"I don't know," I said, avoiding his searching eyes. I was bewildered by his probing. At the same time I felt tempted to confront him about himself and Mother, for this seemed to be an ideal moment. But I was afraid of his answer, afraid he might lie, and still more afraid of the truth.

He put a finger under my chin and forced me to look at him. "Nicole," he said, "you needn't be afraid of me, ever. I shan't hurt you. There are a few thing sacred even to a scoundrel like me, and you are one of them."

He looked at me tenderly. I always knew at such moments that he was completetly sincere. Strange Dario, rejoicing in his small games, and yet so vulnerable and sentimental in other respects! The fine embroidery of what he tried to make of me and our affinity was to compensate for the thwarting of passionate desire. He was breaking the stems of flowers elsewhere while cultivating his orchid. . . . How long it took me to understand! He would kiss his Galatea to see her white cheeks turn rosy, but he would never destroy his careful creation. Little did he know of the spirits he had called forth, of the newly created life growing in its own unexpected way, groping out of the darkness of hothouse confusion into the clear air of wide open spaces. . . .

Like two guilty conspirators, we drew apart before Mother awoke. Again I was alone. Mother peeked into the room and then went to see if Dario was still sleeping. We had coffee, and then the two of them went for a walk while I did my homework. I could concentrate on nothing but the joy of loving and being loved, the yearning to be near him, alone with him all the time. . . .

We gave each other signs of tenderness in every free minute we could steal: in the hall as I said good-bye leaving for school after lunch, in the living room whenever Mother went out for an instant. Her strict order that Dario must never kiss me again worried me no longer. I felt that my love was good and deep, and quite arrogantly thought that others were too limited to understand its greatness.

♣ ♣

"And where's my pudding?" Father asked, frowning.

Each of his homecomings was connected with a black monster of a train entering a windy platform. Mother and I would wait for his return at the railway station, holding hands. I wondered whether my anguish was passed on to her at our touch or whether her own increasing nervousness was the cause of mine. The fact that neither of us expressed the feelings aroused in us by his return made conspirators of us. An hour or two before he was to arrive even Zita stopped singing her strident couplets.

He came back from France about two days after Dario's departure. I felt relieved whenever he forgot to bring me a present from his trips, for his thoughtlessness gave me cause for resentment, and my resentment lessened a constant sense of guilt. This time he not only failed to bring us a souvenir but he seemed to use us merely as objects on which to vent his feelings of discomfort. He was tired, ill humored, and had caught a cold on his trip. Home was just his bed, I thought, and the hot-water bottle at his feet that Zita had to refill at regular intervals. He remained with us over Christmas and New Year's changing the joyful season into one of discontent and dreariness. He was so wrapped up in himself that he did not show the slightest interest in what either Mother or I had done or what preoccupied our minds.

At dinner a few days after Christmas, for dessert Zita brought in a bowl of chocolate pudding for us and a dish of applesauce for Father. Mother had especially asked her to prepare this dish for him since he had complained that starches did not agree with his stomach. As he asked, "And where is my pudding?" it sounded as if he felt robbed of something precious that he strongly desired.

Mother passed a plate with the smooth brown heap to me, telling him, "I had Zita cook some apples for you, Richard. You told me you don't want rich desserts."

"I said nothing of the kind! Give me my pudding!"

"There is only this bit left for Zita," Mother said.

My father beat his fist on the table so heavily that the glasses and plates shook under the blow. We both sat paralyzed and dumbfounded.

"Can't I eat what I please in my own house!" he thundered. "To hell with you!"

He poured insults on my mother; she sat speechless and then burst into tears and left the room. He went on with his shouting, and I did not know if he was aware that she had gone or if he was talking to me or to himself. With trembling knees, I rose from my chair. Somehow I reached the door and went out to look after Mother while his voice continued to rage in the dining room.

I rushed into the guest room where Mother lay sobbing on the couch. "He's so mean! How I hate him!" I

116

cried out, clenching my fists, for an instant wondering if he was now devouring the pudding we had both left untouched.

Mother turned to me and seized my hand. "Nicole, you mustn't talk like that!" she said. "You know you don't mean it. After all, your father is good and honest. He loves you . . ."

"I don't think he loves me!" I flared up. "He loves only himself. He frightens me, and I hate him!"

"He thinks of nothing but the family, our well-being. Perhaps sometimes he's not a kind man," she went on, as if talking to herself, "but he's good and honest and straight. . . ."

Her repetitiousness destroyed her point.

"I don't care! He's like a stranger to us. To think that Sandra and Lorenzo had to lose such a father, while I. . . ."

"Nicole!"

I hid my head on my mother's breast, appalled at what I had said.

For three or four days my parents did not speak to each other. I shunned my father's eyes. I could not look at him, and at such moments became almost physically aware of how my eyes were veiled with insincerity.

On New Year's Day, when things were back to normal, Father took me to the cinema. We had time enough to stop at a café for hot chocolate.

"Would you like another piece of cake?" he asked.

"No, thank you."

"Give me a cup of tea," he addressed the waiter. "You know, Nicole," he said gently, looking at his plate, "we are going to have a nice afternoon together, you and I. I know you think your father is a monster, but really, I feel hurt the way you and your mother treat me." He did not look at me as he spoke. The waiter came with his tea, and he waited until he had left. "Yes, yes," Father went on. "Don't try to protest, Nicole, I know how you feel. I see more than you realize. But everything I do, child, is for your benefit. Do you think I would travel around Europe most of the year if it wasn't to give you both a secure and comfortable life? I know you hate me; I know how your mother is trying to influence you against me."

"That's not true!" I protested again. "I've got eyes to see for myself. I'm not a baby!"

"No, but you are influenced. You have grown up fast, Nicole, I can hardly believe it. You are a young girl now, and must take good care of yourself. After all, we live in a southern country. Hot climates make people act strangely . . . and Italians are reckless men. You have to watch out. . . ."

I looked out the window at an old woman in black passing by. Father went on with difficulty. "For example, Dario Ventura . . . Has he been here lately?"

"Just once, for a day or two," I lied.

"I don't like his being around you so much. I observed him last summer. It's all right to be a friend of the family, but in a couple of years you'll be of marriageable age. . . ."

"Goodness, Father," I said, laughing nervously, "I'm not going to get married for years!"

"In any case I wouldn't like you to marry an Italian. There is a great gap between our outlook and theirs."

"I don't want to get married at all!"

Father finished drinking his tea, beckoned to the waiter, paid the bill, took his umbrella, and buttoned his coat. We went out in silence through the cold and almost empty streets. We saw *Lost Horizon* with Ronald

118

Colman; during the show we forgot our conversation, but later, going home, we were silent and embarrassed.

Mother had asked the Manettis to come for an early dinner. Signora Manetti had declined the invitation because she was not well. Father was animated, and as usual took care of the conversation for the entire evening. At times Mother would try to say a word or two in vain. I felt awkward and ill at ease with Lorenzo in Father's presence. Every word I said seemed forced and unnatural. I knew that Father was keeping an eye on me, with such a reckless Italian at my side. . . .

He addressed Sandra with great respect and sympathy. I could tell that he had taken a liking to her. She looked radiant that night and responded with interest to everything he said.

Later Mother and Lorenzo played the piano, and Sandra promised that they would come more often to make music together. I was allowed to stay up until the Manettis left. At last, on saying good-bye, I had a moment alone with my friends.

"What a fine man your father is, Nicole!" Sandra said. "You must be proud of your parents. He is so well read, so imposing!"

I said nothing.

"Well, let's go," Lorenzo remarked. "Nicole must be tired."

"No. The evening just flew away."

"Did it?" Lorenzo asked. His face looked tired and drawn. He had been unusually quiet.

"I can sleep late tomorrow," I said.

"Right. You are having your Christmas holidays. Let's take a walk tomorrow afternoon," he suggested.

"All right."

"Three o'clock on Piazza Castello?"

"All right," I said again.

♣ ♣

It was cold the next day. Lorenzo and I walked briskly from Piazza Castello to the Po River, and from there up to Monte Cappuccino. When we reached the top of the hill, we went over to the stone wall.

A young couple stood leaning against the low parapet, arms entwined around each other's waists, their backs turned to us. I looked down across the sluggish river, the symmetrical streets, and the gray buildings dim in the winter fog.

"I suppose there isn't much to see," Lorenzo said, standing close to me. He looked taller, more imposing than usual.

"No, it's dismal. I can't even see my old *collegio* over there in the hills," I said.

Lorenzo pulled off his gray knitted gloves and held them out to me. "You forgot your mittens," he said. "Take these. My hands are warm."

"Just for a little while. Thank you," I said. His gloves felt like roomy warm nests.

Lorenzo leaned his white cane on the other side of the wall, put his left hand into his pocket and his right around my shoulder. His hand felt weightless; his touch was a soft spot on my shoulder. He stood so close to me that I dared not look at his face. Dario's hand would have been heavy and his touch would have lighted a spark and run like a current through my blood.

To my right I saw the young man bend over the girl and kiss her. Her black hair, in a page boy, bobbed on her shoulders as she tilted back her head.

"Any more people around?" Lorenzo asked, and I said casually, "Yes, just a couple."

The girl was resting her head on the young man's

shoulder. I could glimpse her profile now. Her eyes, half-open, seemed to be empty, colorless. Though not meaning to be inquisitive, I felt compelled to look at her again. Yes, she was blind. Her lover opened the buttons of her coat; his hands disappeared in the darkness inside. She abandoned herself to his fondling and kissing.

As I turned my head the other way, I wondered if perhaps the blind had a deeper need for love and tenderness than the seeing. Lorenzo might sense the lovers' excitement and be either embarrassed or stirred up by it. I was afraid that the hand on my shoulder might draw me close, that he would begin to kiss me before I could disentangle myself from his embrace. As I imagined the feel of his lips on mine, Dario's face seemed to hover between us. My heart thumped heavily at the thought of my deception. How easily betrayals could occur—by the mere sliding of a hand from a shoulder into a coat, or a careless word escaping from one's lips! It could happen in a split second and be remembered as something dreamlike, unreal.

"You must have been lonely in that school," Lorenzo now said. To my relief, he withdrew his hand and put it in his pocket.

I knew I would have been unable to resist him, but now, free of my desire to yield to his needs, I felt slightly disappointed. Dario's image no longer interfered. Exempted from actual betrayal, I grew bolder in mental deception. As I felt drawn to Lorenzo for one intense moment, I began to understand some of Dario's ambiguous sentiments, and how torn and confused he must be. My feeling for Lorenzo had the nature of an immense blue expanse, forever widening and serene.

"Have you been able to learn more about your myths?" I finally asked, disregarding his last remark.

"Not as much as I'd like. Since Father's death there hasn't been much time for anything outside of making a living."

"It must have been an awful blow," I said.

"Not really." His blunt statement gave me a shock.

"I thought you . . ."

"Idolized him?"

"Yes." I was confused. "From the way Sandra used to speak about him. . . ."

"That's because Sandra sees only the good in people." His breath came like smoke from his lips. "It's cold up here," he said, taking my arm.

I pulled his gloves off and gave them back to him. "Oh, no, that's not what I meant!" But I forced one glove on his right hand. "All right," he said, "but you must keep the other. Let's go back to the piazza and have some hot chocolate."

I put on the glove, he picked up his cane, and we walked downhill for a while, and then he stopped and said, "Of course, we all admired our father in many ways. I felt sick with guilt when he died because I had been a bad son to him." He pulled me closer as we resumed the descent. "I detested him for what he did to my mother."

He was leaning heavily on my arm, letting his cane trail along the ground on the other side, and then he went on speaking with the passionate intensity that had moved me so much in his play. "I want to be honest with you, Nicole. I want you to think and never take appearances at their face value. At home my father was exactly what he fought against officially—a small dictator. And because I tend to be like him—I mean I have a tyrannical streak and am irascible and quick-tempered too—he and I could never get along. So before I can fight for his cause on the outside, I have to fight my father inside me, step by step."

We had reached the foot of the hill, and now stopped to wait for the tram to take us back to the piazza. "You sound just like me and my own father," I said.

"I know. I waited for you to say that."

"Is that why you told me?"

He pressed my hand. "It wasn't to speak ill of my father. The poor man certainly suffered enough. No, I feel you are entitled to know the truth because . . ."

The bells of the tram interrupted his sentence. When it came to a halt, we climbed in and sat down in the empty rear of the car.

"Because?" I reminded him anxiously.

"Oh, yes—Because I wouldn't want you to sit in judgment on either yourself, your father, or anyone else. The young are so intolerant."

We said no more. At each stop more people got on the tram, mostly workingmen returning from their jobs. I took Lorenzo's hand, and shortly before we arrived at the piazza I made a path for him through the crowd. It was dark by the time we settled down at a table inside a café.

"What was it your father did to your mother?" I asked softly. Before he could answer, the waiter arrived, and I made him aware of this. Lorenzo ordered two cups of hot chocolate.

"He destroyed her joy for living," he told me when the waiter had left. "He made her give up everything she most loved to do. She was a pianist and a singer in her own right, and I believe this was part of what made my father love her in the first place. He demanded complete subordination from her—to his career, to his whims—Oh, it would take too long to explain."

123

"Yes, I can imagine," I said. "My mother wouldn't like that."

Lorenzo smiled. "*Ecco*," the waiter said, returning with our order. He put the steaming white cups in front of us, then hurried to another table. A small cloud of whipped cream floated on top of the brown bubbling foam.

"What would your mother have done?" Lorenzo asked.

"Fight back, I suppose."

"I don't believe that would have worked with my father either," he said. "Is that what you would do, too, under those circumstances? Fight back like your mother?"

"I don't know. I probably wouldn't fight in *her* way."

"Your mother is more like a sister to you, isn't she?" —I did not answer—"Or maybe something like a rival . . . ?"

"Perhaps," I admitted.

"You probably think a husband should be an understanding friend," Lorenzo went on, "and not a tyrant."

"Yes, that's it. That's it! Then there wouldn't be the need to fight in the first place."

"No. But how is one to predict anything? People grow and change. Love happens unexpectedly, even without friendship. It's unfortunate that friendship rarely turns into the magic of love."

"No, it's good!" I protested. "You and Sandra, for example, are the best thing that ever happened to me."

He found my hand and held it for a moment. "But wouldn't you think that if really good friends fell in love, we would have many happier marriages in the world?" I pondered this in silence as he stroked my hand softly, my heart beating faster.

"Would you care for more chocolate?" he asked.

"No, thank you."

124

He withdrew his hand and, after a silence said, "You shouldn't let anyone clip your wings, Nicole. Don't let the little things choke you. I know how they can close in on you."

"How can one help it?" I asked.

"Leap over your shadow!" His hand made a wave in the air. He smiled warmly. I was inside the wave of his hand, the warmth of his smile.

"I wish I could. If I were like you . . . you, in spite of your . . ."

"Be careful of projections!" His cheeks were flushed. He straightened his shoulders against the back of his chair and turned his face toward me. A strand of hair had fallen over his brow and made him look younger, more carefree.

"I guess we all project more or less," I said, wondering if his eyes had once looked like Sandra's. "What do you mean—projections?"

He laughed. "It's when you put your own feelings into other people, and can no longer see them as they are." His spent eyes of a blurred gray-blue under thick lashes seemed to look straight at me. "For example, remember Paolo's love for Dora in my play? The girl who betrayed him and his father?"

"Yes, quite well."

"If Paolo had realized what she was like, his whole tragedy could have been avoided."

"I felt all along that Paolo should have loved his friend Antonio's sister, Mara," I said. "She wanted to be useful to him, to be needed. I think she would have been so right for him."

"Yes, wouldn't she," Lorenzo said softly, smiling. "It's probably time for us to go home," he said, groping for his cane.

Later as I rode back with him, he asked me if I had

read *Electra.* "Well, it's probably too soon," he said. "You might get more out of it in a few years."

Lorenzo wanted to take me home, but I insisted on getting off near his house and taking the next tram. We alighted, he took my arm, and we walked in silence until we stopped at his door. He opened it, ready to disappear as usual without taking leave.

"Lorenzo!" I said. He turned around. "Why don't you ever say good-bye to me when I go away?"

"Because you never leave me." He stepped through the door, holding it, then turned to me once more and added, "Or probably because I forget."

SIX

For some reason she did not trouble to explain, the following summer my mother made arrangements for us to go to another beach. Two weeks before my summer vacation began, she made a trip to Tuscany alone in order to rent a house in Forte dei Marmi. I knew that she had told me the truth as to her reason for making the trip but that she had carefully concealed her plan to include a detour to the province of Romagna. I could tell this from the radiance of her face and from the meticulous care she expended on herself the day before her departure. She packed a new white summer dress and had her masseuse come to the house a week sooner than usual to knead her body and face, after setting up all kinds of pots and cloths and ointments in her bedroom. Mother's face emerged from a beautymask as smooth as a baby's bottom. Her full short hair had been cut in the latest style, and its color touched up with golden highlights. All this had fascinated me at other times, but now filled me with sadness and jealousy.

I had not seen Dario for several months with the exception of one brief furlough in April, which had been interrupted by his hasty departure. Mother had caught us kissing in the hall as I was leaving for school. When I returned home three hours later, Mother did not reproach me, but Dario was gone.

After this incident we hardly ever spoke of him, and we made an effort to go on living as if nothing had happened. I existed in the sole hope of seeing Dario the next summer in Rimini. Now I wondered if we would ever meet again.

"It's a fine beach," Mother told me, upon her return from Forte dei Marmi several days later. "It's time for a change, Nicole. There are so many lovely places in Italy." And she added with forced cheerfulness that she had rented a nice summer house close to the beach.

I was unable to appreciate her heroic renunciation. I think Mother was intending to save me from Dario's clutches.

Zita packed trunks with summer clothes and household silver and sheets and tennis rackets, and even an ice machine. I stood watching the men who came to fetch our trunks and boxes, which looked like coffins to me, especially when I remembered the happy anticipation I had felt last year . . . how I had laughed as I said it looked as if we were a huge family leaving on an expedition, and Mother had answered I should have seen *her* father and mother preparing to go to Brittany for four weeks with five children and two maids and dogs and eiderdown quilts.

Zita left the day before we did. The three of us— Mother and Father and I—followed gloomily; we sat in the train as though we were heading for a funeral instead of a holiday sojourn at the beach. Since Father had to accept this decision of Mother's when it was already a *fait accompli*, he acted like a martyr. I expected nothing of the future but the slow unrolling of gray and tepid days. I knew what my life would be like as I watched my father bite too eagerly into a tomato, splattering the juice over his collar and tie, while Mother gave him an angry look as if inwardly stamping her foot. I knew it all by heart as I saw her holding her tongue out of regard for our fellow passengers. But she was expressive enough when she pushed a paper napkin toward him like a dagger.

Zita awaited us in the freshly cleaned summer house, which smelled nauseatingly of chlorine. We ate a late dinner in weary silence, and later went to sleep in the barely furnished, inhospitable rooms.

Zita and I were to share a bedroom. I watched her pin up her hair in large metal curlers and cream her face, and I smelled the pungent odor of her perspiration mingled with that of the chlorine still clinging to her hands, as I listened to her gushing account of her new romance with a corporal whom she always called by his last name.

"Merletti's going to give me an engagement ring when we come home in September," she said. "I'll introduce you. All right?"

"To the ring or Merletti?" I said without interest.

"No kidding! This time it's serious, Nicole. Merletti's the first man I've ever really loved. Some day you, too, will find out how wonderful love can be, *nè?*"

The first morning we ate breakfast complaining of mosquito bites. Then we went out to the beach, which was as large as Mother had described and as dull as I had expected to find any beach without Dario. Moreover it was almost deserted since the season had not yet begun. Of Forte dei Marmi, I still remember the short pine trees, but I have forgotten how the cabanas looked or what the sand and the sea were like. As we lazed through the morning I could feel that my mother and father were pervaded by the same sense of ennui that made me oblivious to all the beauty around us.

A week went by in which we became more and more of a feast for the mosquitoes. Zita closed windows and shutters at night and sprinkled our rooms with some penetrating insect powder. We covered our heads with the bed sheets and tried to sleep like birds, but the anti-insect powder did greater harm to us than to the mosquitoes who continued to relish sucking our blood.

"Ah, *le zanzare!*" Zita sighed.

"Let's go to Rimini," Father said.

"There are fleas in Rimini," Mother warned. "I'll try to get some mosquito nets in town."

"But we are used to the fleas," I said. Mother glanced at me quickly.

"This time we are going to do as I say," my father said firmly.

Mother might have easily convinced him to go to the mountains, but fate, Father, and I wanted it otherwise. Against so many forces she was powerless. Perhaps my exuberant joy at the prospect of returning to the beloved beach of Rimini was contagious.

Mother and I stood in the corridor of the train, watching in the distance the Republic of San Marino on a high mountain that rose from Romagna's countryside. We were like two happy children, and at each familiar sight we pressed each other's hands. Here we belonged; here we had memories and hopes; here we would suffer or be joyous; but in any case be alive, oh, alive! said the pressure of our hands.

The house Mother had rented by letter was not far from the beach. A narrow staircase led to a three-bedroom apartment. There was a small dining room and a parlor with old-fashioned green plush-upholstered furniture. The bedrooms were connected by a long ivy-covered balcony that faced the front.

As of old, I would run down to the beach in the morning to watch the sea under its whitish sheet of mist, which gradually dissolved like a layer of ice under the warmth of the sun. I cherished each familiar sight and face: a waiter from the café across the promenade as he took his early morning swim; the tattooed old guard who would stop every day and talk to me as to an old friend; the still deserted rows of the white *capanne* over whose flat, tar-papered roofs my glance would fly toward Riccione on one side and the mole on the other.

It was good to be home again, home with the matrons in the Kursaal pharmacy, home in the ice-cream parlor, home in this ancient town, with the arch of the Malatesta reminding me of Francesca da Rimini, her life, her love, her cruel untimely death—and of Dario's hands and voice and kisses.

I was afraid I would come upon him unexpectedly. Then after two weeks I began to feel restless and disappointed. I no longer wondered what would happen at our first encounter; I knew we would halt and speechlessly contemplate each other—no more. Life would stand still, and darkness would no longer alternate with light. We render great moments static in our daydreams, I thought, and static is our concept of paradise.

One sunny midafternoon in July, as we sat drinking coffee with my father across from the beach, Mother and I caught sight of Dario. He was sitting at one of the white metal tables in the open-air café a short distance away from us. His back was turned to us, and he was bent over a paper spread open before him. From time to time, and without moving his head, he reached for his cup, still reading, and slowly sipped his coffee. He was wearing the same blue linen jacket and the immaculate white summer trousers in which I had met him at Lake Como.

On top of a platform right in front of us a string trio was playing a tune from *The Gypsy Baron* when Dario rose. He moved in our direction with his deliberate, rhythmic gait without noticing us. I stared at the three musicians in their dark suits, aware of Dario's legs coming closer; when they abruptly halted I knew he had finally seen us.

"Dario Ventura!" I heard my father exclaim. "I've been wondering what you were doing this summer. In fact, I've asked my wife if you were hiding from us!"

Dario shook hands with my parents, asked Mother a polite question, and then, before I had really felt it, the pressure of his fingers was being removed from mine. I felt Father's eyes on me as mine remained fixed on Dario's sharply cut chin. Father's stare made the blood rise to my face, and I looked away with feigned indifference.

Father pulled up a chair for Dario, and they exchanged bits of conversation while I stared steadily at the tall, white-haired violinist. I wanted to flee to the beach, but remained nailed to the chair, from which I rose with difficulty after the others had got to their feet and Mother motioned to me to come. She had not taken part in the conversation, and she now walked at my side, a step behind the men.

"And how have you been, Nicole?" Dario asked, turning to me as if nothing had ever happened, as if I were merely the daughter of a Mr. and Mrs. Steiner whom he had not seen in some time.

"All right." I tried to say the words cheerfully, but

132

they were scarcely audible, so I cleared my throat emphatically to show that I was hoarse.

"Passed your exams?"

"Yes, all except history of art. I must try again before the term starts in October."

"History of art, of all things!" he exclaimed. "I thought it was your favorite subject?"

"Yes, but not in school." I turned my head toward the beach, away from the blinding sun.

"So the mosquitoes drove you out of Forte," Dario said, laughing, to my father. I wondered if Mother had quarreled with him again that last time she had seen him in Romagna.

"You can say that again!" Father replied.

Then Dario turned back to me. "I can imagine how boring it must be to study beauty from textbooks."

"Are you coming down to the beach with us?" Father asked.

"Thank you, Signor Steiner, I'll join you some other time." He stopped to take his leave. I was aching with disappointment.

"Queer fellow," Father remarked later as we descended the steps to the beach. "He used to be so friendly. Could I have said anything to annoy him? Never saw him so stiff before."

"He may have had some other engagement," Mother said.

In the cabana I undressed slowly, feeling how strange life was, and how there was so much wasted time and conventional beating about the bush until one touched its essential points. It was as if most people spent their lives playing hide-and-seek with each other. "The real drama," Lorenzo had said, "lies in what never happens and is never mentioned."

I walked to the shore past Mother in her beach chair

133

and sat down near the blue, placid sea, a book about Leonardo da Vinci open in my hand. But the book was merely part of the game, a screen to hide my thoughts. I took a fistful of sand and let it run through my fingers.

"You haven't been reading much since yesterday, Signorina Steiner," I heard a voice say, while Carlo Sarditta, a young lawyer whose acquaintance we had made at the beach, sat down beside me.

He was in the habit of talking wittily to me for a while every day near our tent awning. Although he was attractive and I felt flattered by his attention, I was not interested in him or in any stranger. It was odd, I continued to ponder—as Sarditta said, "I have just finished an excellent biography about Michelangelo"—how many people one knew and how few one chose for inner communication.

"Do you know the one by Romain Rolland?" he asked.

I shook my head. I remembered all the men and women who had come to our house in Turin. With the exception of one or two, they touched one's life no more than passersby in the street whom one sat observing from behind the window of a café.

"Pardon me?" I asked, and Sarditta inclined his head toward me, looking in the direction of the awning next to ours. There a young blonde Polish singer sat in the shade, surrounded by a swarm of admirers.

"What was I saying?" he asked, frowning, as the young woman threw her head back in melodious laughter, beaming through half-closed eyes at one of her young men.

It came to me in a flash as I caught Sarditta watching her from behind his rimless glasses, that it was not my company he had chosen all this time, but the nearness of that much sought-after woman.

I checked an impulse to tell Sarditta to stop pretending and go and sit at her feet like the rest of them, but I was not angry, since I had come to observe and learn about people. There always seemed to be a thick glass between oneself and others. I felt that people were like the colorful fish one watched in the aquarium. The ones surrounding me seemed to live in an element into which I had neither interest nor desire to penetrate. It reminded me of my cousin Natalie's world—jolly, reckless, and adventurous. These were the kinds of people from whose gaiety I would flee years later in nameless sadness, after hearing my own laughter ringing out with theirs.

Murmuring some timid words to Sarditta, who paid as little attention to me as I to him, I rose, and still holding open the page of my book, my fingernail digging into the line where I had stopped reading, I walked away in the direction of the mole. Yes, there were on the one hand men and women enjoying themselves without giving much thought to anything, and on the other, men like my father who were honest and moral and virtuous in the conventional sense, and made themselves and those about them uncomfortable and unhappy. Was it not easy to be virtuous if one did not love and felt no temptation?

"Nicole, where are you going?" my mother called after me, but I pretended not to hear her. I did not want to have the flow of my thoughts interrupted. There was something I must find out.

I began to think of Mother, whom I had never before considered as a person detached from myself, with a life and a personality of her own. Who was she? And where did she go? Dario had once called her feminine, motherly. Love, music, and well-being were the only things she seemed to care for—she, too, liked to enjoy the moment, yet in a warmer, more generous way than those other pleasure-loving people. Did not her greatest joy consist in giving, in spreading harmony and happiness about her, at least for those she loved? But what was her aim in life? She seemed to be untroubled by this constant search for meanings that I had found in Lorenzo, myself, and perhaps, Dario.

And who was I? Would I ever find myself and know, and then find It, the great message for which I had been put on earth? I asked myself, If I weren't living for that magnificent day—although I had no idea in what form it would present itself—then what purpose would there be to life? And if It revealed itself, what would I have to do in order to show I was worthy?

"*Piccola!*"

The sand seemed to give way like a marsh under my feet. The book I held still open in my hand closed instantly. I turned toward the sound of his voice, and he stood there smiling at me in his uniquely charming way. He had changed into swimming trunks, and he raised his tanned arms and let his hands slowly sink on my shoulders.

"At last," he said. "Tell me, *piccola*, how have you been all this long, terrible time?"

I looked around worriedly, aware only at this instant that I had almost reached the mole. Then I glanced at his hands on my shoulders. He withdrew them at once.

"Mammina doesn't want us to see each other alone," he said. You see . . . ever since our argument, last time, in Torino. Now fate has brought us together again. At least we can talk and be friends and see each other once in a while."

"I don't know," I said, asking myself, *Fate . . .* ?

"How I missed you saying these words!" He smiled tenderly. "Once I heard you say them in a dream. Nicole is always wanting something she doesn't dare express, I told myself. In the fear that it might not please me, she heroically tries to overcome whatever it is, but can't quite go all the way, and so remains suspended, poor darling, in the middle with her 'I don't knows.' Am I right?"

"I don't know," I said, smiling.

"And something else." He pointed at the book in my hand. "A minor characteristic showing me the difference between you and your mother. I followed you just now. You were holding a line in your book with your finger. When I called you, you let go of the line and the page altogether. Your mother's finger would still cling to that spot."

"It's only a mechanical gesture," I said.

"No. It tells me a great deal. What were you thinking about when I called you? I have been following you for some time."

"Nothing much."

"Tell me the truth, Nicole. You were beginning to forget me, weren't you?"

"A little," I lied. "But I had better go back. Mammina . . ." I said nervously.

"Yes, do. I'll visit with you all tomorrow morning at the beach. I don't think she'll object. Run along now, you devilish little angel you."

♣ ♣

I was drying myself in the beach hut after my swim. Dario was waiting for me under the tent awning to join him for a game of chess. Mother had not objected to his seeing us at the beach. For the last two weeks he had stayed a little longer each day.

Mother and Father sat talking in the shade behind

the cabana. They had not heard me come in, and I made no noise lest they should call me.

"I think we had better move to France as soon as possible," my father was saying. "It's getting too tiresome with all this traveling. I have been thinking of selling my share of the business. We disagree on too many things."

"Would you rather travel for Moirots?" Mother asked.

"I know it has its drawbacks. The income will be about the same, though I know it's better to be on my own. But with Moirots I practically will be, without the present headaches and worries."

I stood still, listening intently.

"But it's not for you, Richard. You have always been your own master."

"Right. I've thought about it. There are other considerations. Italy is getting unbearably Fascist. I don't think we'll be safer in France in case of war, but at least we'll be where we belong. You always said you wanted to live in Paris near your brother."

I slipped into a dry bathing suit, then stood motionless, listening to Father's words and to the thumping of my heart.

"But Mother's gone! And we can't uproot Nicole all the time. I hate the idea of having her change schools again. It's been enough of a strain getting through these last years."

"Nicole won't have any language difficulties this time, so the change will only make her lose a few months. What plans does she have for the future?"

"She would like to study belles lettres."

"She should learn something more practical. But if she is really keen about it, I shan't object if I can afford it."

Everything my father said was kind and sensible, and

he would expect me to jump for joy at such a proposal. At other times the thought of becoming a student in Paris would have been most attractive, but now it filled me with fear and anguish.

"There is something else I meant to tell you," Father said. "I don't like Dario to be around Nicole all the time. She has grown so womanly of late. I abhor the idea of having her marry an Italian."

"Oh, but Richard, how ridiculous!" I heard Mother give a short, forced laugh. "She's only a child!"

"You can trust my judgment, Clarisse. I am a widely traveled man, and I know this sort of Italian better than you do. He considers us well-to-do people. Nicole is beautiful, intelligent . . . ."

"I beg you not to make such a fuss about a casual friendship!" Mother exclaimed irritably.

"I know better. No one can fool me! That artist she sees in Turin, the blind man, I mean. . . . I don't know what's going on, but I don't object to him. His sister is a fine young woman."

"You would mind Manetti as much as Ventura if he were not blind," Mother said.

"Be that as it may. What I mean is, Italians can't be divorced. And if my daughter should . . ."

"You are ridiculous to worry about it now while Nicole is just a schoolgirl!"

I opened the door noiselessly and ran out.

"What took you so long?" Dario asked, hiding the pawns in his fists.

"I overheard a conversation between my parents."

"Eavesdropping, were you?"

"I couldn't help it."

"Why didn't you clear your throat or something?"

"Well, I was eavesdropping."

"Drop it to me."

"Father wants us to move to France."

"So? Don't worry about it. I won't let you go."

"I hope we'll stay here, for a while at least," I said.

"As long as I'll be in Torino for the remainder of my military service, you mean?"

"But that's not even sure."

"As good as sure. I'll go to Torino next month to make them decide. Come on, it's your first move."

I pushed the pawn in front of a rook into the next square and said, "Dario, do you think us well-to-do?" I asked, after we had made several moves in silence.

"Why on earth do you ask?" He laughed. "Fairly, yes."

"Do you think I'm beautiful and intelligent?"

"Let me think . . ." He inclined his head sideways as if scrutinizing me for the first time. "Your forehead is strikingly high and pure, like alabaster. As far as intelligence is concerned, such a forehead can be deceiving, especially in a woman. Your lips are perfect, your teeth like freshly peeled almonds. How she drinks in every word I'm saying!" He pointed a finger at me scornfully. "Here she sits, woman, vain, avid to hear herself praised! Come on, I just moved my queen."

We sat on beach chairs facing each other, the chessboard on our knees. My legs were imprisoned between Dario's, who pressed them hard as he spoke. I paid no more attention to the game. I felt faint; I saw Dario through a haze while he slowly sank his eyes into mine. My blood was a single wave undulating through my body, and the wave of his blood through the touch of his knees floated together with mine. I heard a gentle murmur from the sea as I covered my blazing cheeks with both hands and tore my eyes from him, lowering them to the chessmen on the board, which I did not see, thinking, *It's your move. Come on, vain woman! Oh God, what's happening to me?*

140

"Your nose is a fine little bud, which may still grow into a bulb within the next few years. In its straightforwardness it adds a slightly tart note to your face, which otherwise would be almost too regular," Dario went on, obviously finding pleasure in my embarrassment as he continued his survey. "Your eyes . . ."

But I hardly listened, yielding to the heavy sweetness in my blood, closing my eyes, leaning back in my chair, absorbed by his touch, which filled my body and soul with ecstasy.

I yearned for this contact to last forever, and that I might sink into oblivion under its almost mystical fulfillment.

"Nicole, don't you want to play?" I heard Dario whisper. His legs withdrew from mine.

As I opened my eyes, I saw him put back some chessmen that had been upset, while I noticed my parents approaching. I bent over the chessboard and thoughtlessly moved my queen against Dario's. I had been suddenly cast out into cold, empty space.

Dario saw me shiver and smiled, saying that I was lost. Yes, lost to you forever, I thought, watching him move his rook against my king who was now surrounded by a threatening regiment of figures.

"Check!" he said. "I think that does it. You had better surrender."

"I do," I said, putting the figures back into the box.

Mother and Father had stretched out in their canvas chairs a few steps beyond us, Father reading the newspaper, Mother gazing idly at the sea. Beyond their heads I caught sight of the Polish singer, who was looking in my direction with a smile.

Dario turned his head to see at whom I was nodding, then said, "Come on, let's have another swim!"

In the water he inquired, "Why did you ask if I

thought you well-to-do?" I splashed him, laughing, and swam away. "Tell me!" He came after me, out of breath.

"You look so awful in that old black cap." I giggled. "I'll give you a couple of lire to buy yourself a new one!"

"Tell me!" he said again. He had caught my foot and was holding it tightly. I shook with laughter, struggling to get free.

"What's so funny?" he shouted.

"That you should want to marry me because we are well-to-do people and I'm beautiful and intelligent!" I was choking with laughter.

"Is that what your father said?"

I nodded, fighting for breath.

"Well," he said. "It's not such a bad idea. I must think it over."

      ♣ ♣

The prospect of visiting the ancient town of Ravenna had not displeased me until Mother said she would not come. Father was going to leave us at the beginning of August. A few days before his departure he suggested we should go there on an excursion, but Mother said she had already seen Ravenna time and again.

"Mammina, please come along!" I begged her the afternoon before we were to leave as we rested in her room after lunch.

"Oh, darling, you'll enjoy it just as much without me!"

"I don't want to go without you. I'm sure if Father had asked Dario you would come!"

"That's a silly thing to say."

"No, it isn't. You are happy to get rid of Father and me for a day, so you can be alone with him. I know, I know it!" I stood in front of her bed in my slip, feeling very hot and angry.

142

"We'll just have a chat on the beach, Dario and I, like two good friends," Mother said. I looked at her with actual hatred. "So you don't care that I don't come along?" she said. "You are only begrudging my being with Dario, eh?"

"So if I do! I don't want to go to Ravenna without you!" I shouted.

"Hush! Do you want the whole neighborhood to hear you?"

"I don't care!" I cried, stamping my foot.

"If you want to be treated like an adult," Mother said quietly, "you have to behave like one."

I could hear my own dry, suffocating sobs. I wanted to beat my fists, my head against a wall and scream, but I remained on the spot, gasping for breath.

"Nicole, control your temper! You are worse than your father!"

Oh, the blind, murderous fury that boiled up in my blood at those words! I glared accusingly at my mother through a haze of tears, wishing to kill her, to strangle her, so that she would no longer be able to speak. The truth about my boundless irascibility struck home, leaving a gaping wound.

"Go to your room and rest. We can talk when you are normal," she said coldly.

With my fists clenched in front of me, I took a step toward her: "I hate you!"

"Nicole, go to your room!" she cried, pushing me away.

I ran out of the room and out the front door and down the steps toward the street.

"Nicole! Where are you going!" Mother came panting after me.

I hesitated; I felt her hand clutching my arm. She

pulled me back harshly. "You are out of your mind, crazy, crazy! To run into the street in your slip!"

I collapsed on the stairs, sobbing helplessly.

"Now, come on, try to calm down, you little fool. I'll go with you tomorrow, all right? I didn't expect you to make such a fuss about it," Mother said, sitting down by me and patting my head.

"What's going on there?" Father's voice came sleepily down the steps. "Can't you be a little more considerate while I rest? You know I didn't sleep a wink last night!" He went back to his room, banging the door in anger.

I began to shake with hysterical laughter. Here was Father, thinking only of his sleep and not even wondering why we sat on the steps in our slips! Still trembling with tears and laughter, I put my arms about Mother and whispered, the pain once more overwhelming me, "You will, you really will?"

"Yes. Let's go upstairs."

We returned to her room. I sat down on the edge of her bed, my head lowered with shame, saying that I was sorry. I let my head sink on her breast feeling nothing but love for her now, and guilt for what I had said only a moment before.

"But you mustn't sacrifice yourself for me," I murmured.

"I like to go with you," she assured me.

"No. Stay here. I don't want to force you to come along."

"But you don't, silly darling."

"Yes, I did. You stay. All right?"

"You don't mean it."

"Yes, I do. I love you. I'll have a pleasant time, I promise."

"You are sweet. You really mean it?"

"Yes. I swear it."

144

She kissed me and I smiled at her fondly, feeling proud of this victory over myself. How I wanted her to be happy.

Early the next morning Father and I set out. On awakening, I fluctuated in my decision. My spirits sank, but I wished to test my magnanimity.

"We can travel third class," Father said, as he bought the tickets. "It will only take an hour."

"I like it better anyway," I said.

"Why? It's more uncomfortable."

"Because it's Italy," I said.

The train was waiting at the platform, the wooden benches of the third-class compartments crowded with laborers and peasants.

"Second is Italy enough for me," Father was saying. "Garlic, a black pomaded curly head, a curious stare, toothpick in mouth . . ."

His description hurt and irritated me. "Second and first are filled with people you can find anywhere," I said, "but the real Italy is here." I pointed through a window to where a bearded old man sat next to a middle-aged peasant woman whose ample figure spread over two seats. She had a triple chin and large black eyes full of kindliness.

As soon as Father pulled the compartment doors apart, the old man lifted a large basket from the woman's side into the net above while she willingly withdrew half of her bulk and squeezed into the corner to make room for us. Thanking her, we sat down.

On the opposite bench a pale young woman sat nursing her child. I could hear the gurgling sounds as the milk went down the baby's throat. No one paid attention to the mother, who seemed to dwell in a world apart in rapturous absorption. I kept staring at her in wonder until Father nudged me roughly as if she or I

145

were doing something shameful. I turned my eyes toward the fleeting countryside. A connection between my love for Dario and this nursing woman flashed through my mind. Was not our rapture as complete, as pure and as apart from the rest of the world as hers?

Like two good friends . . .

Mother's words haunted me in the rhythm of the moving wheels. *Like two good friends, two good friends, two good friends . . . He's my friend, my friend . . .* What were they doing now? Here I was sitting beside my father, who nudged me angrily. For an instant I wished I could destroy his blissful ignorance and pass on to him some of the torture I was enduring.

Father was speaking to me in French, lest our fellow passengers should understand, not because he had no feeling for "the people," but out of embarrassment about his own gentlemanly air.

"I wanted to show you Ravenna," he said, "since this will probably be our last summer in Italy." He had spoken about his plans once more in my presence. I said nothing. "What's the matter, Nicole, you have goose-pimples on your arms. Are you cold?"

"No, I'm all right."

My eyes fell on the inscription on a brass plate: *Non sputare nella carrozza;*" "Don't spit in the carriage." It had been the first Italian I had learned when we arrived from Zurich, many lifetimes before, with Maxine. I had said those words proudly to a friend of my parents', while getting off the train in Turin.

The peasant woman smiled at me, and amid tears I smiled back into her broad, motherly face. Our last summer in Italy. Italy . . . now that I had become a part of it and could no longer see it as an alien country . . . I had taken it for granted like my own mother until for some

146

powerful reason I had begun to see her as a person apart from myself.

"La Signorina è francese?" I heard the woman ask.

"No, sono italiana." I felt I was speaking the truth in saying that I was an Italian. Father gave me a disapproving look.

Non sputare nella carrozza. "Look, girls, we are now in Italy," Mother had said. "Can you tell the difference?"

We had pressed our noses against the window of the train, which had just left the Swiss border. The mountains were strewn with huts and farms that seemed stonier than the ones we had seen in Ticino.

"It's all the same," Maxine had remarked, disappointed. "Only the houses look shabbier."

"And dirtier," I added reproachfully. I had expected Italy to begin right at the border, but had consoled myself thinking that maybe it would start a little later. And in that long distant past I had waited for a palm or orange tree to appear.

Now the little black inscription on the brass was telling me that this was the beginning of the end of that immense journey. Again, I wondered: Where had my Italy begun? With Father Giacomo's tears at Maxine's death?

"Going to Ravenna?" the woman asked.

"Yes. For a sightseeing trip."

"It's a beautiful town," she said, her eyes flashing with pride.

She rose, reached for her basket in the net above, put it on her knees and opened it. *"Gradisce?"* And she urged upon us apricots and luscious peaches and berries, and finally a piece of fried chicken. It was impossible to refuse. I bit into the meat, repressing a sob. Both Father and I thanked her repeatedly.

"Do you live in Ravenna?" I asked.

"No. We live near Forlì. We are going to visit the family," she explained. "My daughter has had her second baby. Imagine, it's a boy! Papa and I are so happy," she added with tears in her eyes. The old man nodded at us, beaming.

I had an impulse to throw my arms about her and kiss her dear warm face as if it were the face of my beloved, chosen land.

"Take more," she said. "You see, we have so much!"

Take more, take more! My Italy was here, was in these faces, was Sandra and Lorenzo, was Dante, was Mazzini, was Garibaldi, was this man and woman, that nursing mother. And Dario, Dario . . .

♣ ♣

After Father left us in August, Mother and I often lay stretched side by side at night in long chairs on the beach with Dario between us. A faint murmur came to us from the sea, or perhaps it was the murmur within our hearts. We spoke little, but lay and watched the sky, feeling as a living presence the whispering black concentrated mass of the sea. It should, I thought, reflect the stars, but it never did. The sea was too deep, and those glimmering needle heads were too high, too far away. I wondered how it would be if the sky were to fall on us and we would be caught in its infinite, sparkling net. Sometimes a shooting star flashed through the firmament. Then Dario would press my hand for me to make a wish, but it was gone before I could think of one. I waited for the next falling star, wishing for Dario to be at my side and to love me forever; but no star would fall for a long time. Then one would flash through the sky so unexpectedly that I missed wishing my wish again.

One night in our apartment we stood on the ivy-covered balcony and I told Dario that my personal star was a small one close by Venus. I asked him where his was, and he pointed at me and said, "There." I was wearing a red silk dress with tiny white dots, and we were waiting for Mother to get dressed to go dancing.

As soon as she was ready, the three of us went down to the *corso*, where we found a carriage to drive us out to the open-air *café-dansant* at the other end of town. The trees glided past us like tall, whispering silhouettes, and the air was drenched with the perfume of roses and jasmine.

At the *café-dansant* tall spreading trees enclosed the white metal tables that encircled the dance floor, and garlands of colored bulbs hung from the branches over our heads. Through twigs and subdued lights, which had turned the leaves red and violet and blue and gold, came the soft insinuating sounds of music. A breeze caused the leaves and the bulbs to tremble. I remember the touch of the soft red silk against my body and the beat of Dario's heart against mine as we slowly rocked to the tune of a fox trot, among the dark figures of elegant dancing couples. One of Dario's hands felt like a flame upon my back, more scarlet than my dress; his other hand was clasping mine. Our fingers could no longer be told apart, and the rhythm of our steps was the same. I dreamed I would dissolve in the wind, and be reborn tomorrow upon the waves of the sea. "Non scordarti dell mie parole, Bimba, tu non sai cos'è l'amor . . . ," a man in white tails crooned from the platform where the band was playing, and the words poured over the pivoting couples from loudspeakers in the trees.

"Let's sit down," Dario said. "I'm fed up with his greasy voice. The cheapness of this place makes me sick."

We joined Mother at the table and sipped our wine. Dario danced the next waltz with her. When they returned, he pointed at me and said, "Look at her eyes! I wonder what she's seeing. Isn't it good to be young!"

I looked at him happily. While we watched the people chatting and moving about us during a pause between dances, I felt Dario's eyes upon me and found in his glance the same expression of love and wonder as on that morning in Turin when I had run to greet him, wrapped in a bath towel.

The lights flickered into a darker tone; the air grew sultry as the first sounds of a tango swept over the dance floor. A stranger was heading toward our table. As soon as he bowed before me, Dario rose and drew me away.

"Why did you do that?" I whispered, as he guided me through bending, courtseying, and twisting couples to a spot where Mother could not see us.

"I must have you alone for a moment," he said, leading me along a path to the wall of a house where we could remain unseen and unheard.

He made me stand against the wall, and then bent my head backward with his hands: "Nicole, is it really true, is it you, or are you a dream?" he whispered. "If you could forever stay like this, if we could only hold this night, this instant! Do you know that what seem like miracles to you are nothing but dull, worthless things, and that it is you who enchant! I can't stand the thought of having you dancing in the arms of another man! You are mine, do you hear, mine forever!"

He took my hands, and tying them with his behind my back, pushed me more closely against the wall, leaning his body against mine. Thus imprisoned, I saw his eyes and lips over me as he whispered once more: "You will be mine, you will wait for me. We will belong to each other forever!" Then I seemed to lose consciousness under his kisses until the music stopped and he led me back to the dance floor. Again he pressed my hand and said, "Will you wait for me?"

"Yes," I murmured drunkenly.

Mother looked at us suspiciously, asking where we had been. "There was no room left to move," Dario said. "This crowd makes me sick. I walked with Nicole up and down the path out there."

♣ ♣

A few times each summer Zita cooked our midday meal, put the pots and plates into a basket, and brought everything down to the beach for us. This was part of our particular freedom, of doing things we liked on the spur of the moment. We sat on the beach like Turks, and later dug our dishes into the sand. Dario said there was nothing better for cleaning plates. He said he would enjoy living in a country where the women had to wait for the men to eat and be contented with what was left over.

He was with us most of the time. Every morning for our swim we would row out on a *moscone*, a boat consisting of a narrow raftlike base holding two wooden benches and a pair of oars. We used to take turns rowing, reading, and swimming. Dario meant to improve his German by reading to us from Goethe's *Wilhelm Meister*.

We would row for long stretches of time out to the placid, open sea from where the beaches of Rimini and Riccione looked like spots of colorful ink. Mother would open her sun umbrella and I would seek protection under its shade, huddling against her, and listen to Dario's droll accent, his voice groping warily as if over ice, and feel the water gurgle and splash through the wood against my feet. Sunlight rippled on the sea; at times its surface shivered under slight gusts of wind. Whenever we paused simultaneously in our reading and rowing, silence seemed translucent in the limpid air.

One morning as we rowed by the diving board, Dario and Mother caught sight of Giobbe, and Dario asked if I did not want to join the lad and dive for a while. Dario had been unkind to me all morning. It was obvious, I thought, that he wished to get rid of me.

"I don't care," I said.

"Yes, why don't you?" Mother insisted. I looked toward the diving board in torment. "If you want to be alone, you may as well say it openly," I murmured.

"Don't be silly, Nicole."

"All right. So we want to be alone!" Dario exclaimed, irritated.

I pulled my cap over my head and plunged. I swam to the board, and while climbing its ladder saw Dario and Mother row out to sea, the small parasol turning over her head.

"*Ciao*, Nicole," Giobbe said. "Going to dive?"

"Later." I stretched myself on the dry sunny planks and hid my face in the fold of my arm.

"You are in a bad mood today, *signorina mia*."

"No. Just tired."

"Tired from sleeping too long?"

"No. Tired in my mouth to talk."

Giobbe shrugged his shoulders, took a run over the board, and leapt. A moment later he reappeared, snorting, on top of the ladder, took another run, and dived again. The *moscone* moved farther and farther away. The parasol had changed to a tiny white spot.

I rose, walked to the edge of the board, and plunged in, head first. I let myself sink deeply and swam on underwater toward the horizon, where the dots of three or four *mosconi* seemed to have come to a standstill. The sea, at least, accepted me fully in its cool, impersonal nothingness. I swam on and on, and then floated on my back, motionless, looking at the sky. Then, moving my legs, I sailed along under the vaulted sky, merging, evaporating, until I was one with the blue particles of ether and the blue particles of water, thoughtlessly, blankly, listlessly.

I do not know how long and how far I had swum when I heard my mother's anxious voice calling my name. Let her call, let her worry, I thought bitterly, let them feel sorry, afterward. And, accelerating my strokes, gasping for breath, feeling my heart like a heavy inert stone in my chest, suffocating amid effort and faintness, I tried to get ahead of those recklessly swinging oars.

"Nicole! Are you out of your mind?"

Yes, I am. Leave me alone! What do you care? I felt their hands reaching out for me, dragging me, heard their reproachful words, the anguished tone of their voices, and struggled to get free.

"Come, come, you little fool," I heard Dario's gentle voice. Then, unable to fight any longer, I let myself be pulled up on the planks of the boat, where my head sank weakly over my updrawn knees as I sobbed breathlessly, dripping with water.

For the next few days Mother and Dario went out of their way to be kind to me. Dario left our house when it was time for me to go to sleep, and Mother sat on my bed with me for long, tender good-night sessions. Once or twice I heard an outside door close softly an hour after I was supposed to be asleep, and I knew then that Dario had come back.

Sometimes I sat up in bed, tempted to go out and face them. But then I sank back on my pillow, asking myself what good it would do. There would be a scene. Mother

153

would have to send Dario away, and we would all be unhappy. It was a terrifying prospect. Besides, I loved them so much, and would never wish to give them cause for misery. I decided to play along with their game, concealing my own torment.

Before the end of the month Dario would have to be in Turin for the rest of his military service. Mother decided we would travel home with him, so Zita went ahead with most of our luggage. My mother had an excellent excuse for this early departure since Father was to come back from Paris in order to prepare for another business tour for the fall and winter seasons. Dario said that staying as an officer in Turin would be like being close to home, near us, his real family.

Nothing had materialized with the Moirot brothers yet, and we were not to move to France for six months at least. The day before our departure from Rimini, Mother was busy with preparations at home, and I went down to the beach for a last time. It was almost deserted. Every now and then a solitary voice could be heard across the sand like a gust of wind over the quiet sea.

I was alone, but Dario had promised he would join me later for a last meeting at the beach. From a distance I saw Augusto walking briskly in the direction of the mole. He had stopped being my wordless shadow and no longer reproached me with his mute, cumbersome presence. In a pensive mood I watched him come closer, for the first time realizing how cruelly I had treated him and how I had gradually destroyed his constant devotion to me. I called him once, but he did not hear me. I waited until he was nearer and then called again. He started, saw me, and came to my side.

"*Buon giorno*, Augusto," I said.

154

"Good day," he answered stiffly.

"I want to say good-bye to you. We are leaving tomorrow."

"Oh." He began to whistle through his teeth.

"I don't think we'll be here next summer."

"Oh?" he said again, and went on whistling, looking at me in a supercilious way.

"Well—if you were going somewhere, I don't want to keep you. I just meant to say good-bye."

"Really? It's convenient I happened to come your way."

"Don't be silly, Augusto. I meant to look you up before we left."

"You can't expect me to believe that."

"If you want to act like an offended old maid, I'll buy you a green sofa to sulk on," I said irritably. Why must he act so self-righteously! Still—had I really meant to look him up?

"I wish you a pleasant trip," he said. "And good luck for the future, if I don't see you again."

He took my hand and shook it, his hand like a log in mine, then walked away with dignity without turning his head. I stood looking after him with the strange sensation that I was Dario and that Augusto was myself. Yes, my very image—tender, irritable, withdrawn into his shell, a poor lost shadow unable to express his strong, bewildering emotions.

"What are you so thoughtful about?" Dario said. I had not seen him come up. He stretched himself on a beach chair a few steps from where I stood and opened a thin paperback novel on his bare, brown knees.

I told him that I had said good-bye to Augusto and that we had parted almost enemies.

"Here you go again," Dario said. "You don't really

care about the boy. You only meant to clear your conscience by being nice to him at the last minute, when it's too late to make it up."

"That's true," I admitted, sitting down on the sand at his feet.

"You can't be lovable to everyone who will fall in love with you," he went on. "It's enough if you are with me. If you give your little finger, they will take your whole hand. Either you'll break a great many hearts or you'll be unable to say no, like me; and then you'll lose shape and spread out like a huge ink spot on blotting paper."

"You know I only meant to be kind," I said.

"Kindness is fine with women, children, and old people. But with the opposite sex, you can become just a little too kind before you know it."

"Have you been too kind with me?"

"You know better, silly one." He leaned forward and put his hand on my shoulder.

I looked at the book in his lap and read the title, *Le Diable au corps* by Raymond Radiguet. "What kind of a book is it?" I asked.

"It's the love story of a boy almost as young as you are," Dario said. "It's called *The Devil in the Flesh*. He wrote it at the age of seventeen, and died three years later. Will you wait a few minutes, darling? I'm almost finished."

"It sounds so sad," I said, staring across the water and wishing to prolong this day forever. Once or twice I must have sighed audibly, since Dario groped for my face, pressed my cheek against his leg, and asked, his eyes still on the page he was reading, "What's the matter? What's bothering you?"

"Oh, Dario," I said, "this may be our last day here together! I wish I could roll up Rimini like a carpet and take it with me wherever I go, sea and all."

156

"Rimini isn't so special," he said.

"It's our place, Dario. Can there be anything more special?"

"Now, now," he said. "You will come back."

"No. Never. Next summer we may be in France."

"We'll have other places."

"But other places won't mean the same thing. To come back somewhere after a long time can never be the same, either. You grow away from a place, or a place grows away from you. Somehow you both change."

I thought of places and of how their importance grew large or small to people according to their memories. Never would the sea shine as bright to me as in Rimini, or the sky be more azure, or the sun set more majestically from any pier.

"Finished," Dario said, closing the book.

"Yes," I said. "If we could do that. Just close the book, put it away and say, 'Finished.' How was it?"

"Oh, quite excellent," he said, stroking my hair, "especially if you consider the youth of the author. And almost as romantic as you," he added. "It has the saddest ending."

He looked for a page as he skimmed through the slim volume, and then, when he had found it, he read slowly and softly to me in his poor French, caressing my shoulder as he read:

> When she slept thus, with her head upon my arm, I leaned over to gaze upon her flame-lit face. This was a perilous game. One day I came too near, although my face did not touch hers, and I felt I was like the needle which trespasses by one millimeter upon forbidden territory and thus becomes the magnet's prey. Is the magnet or the needle to blame? Thus it was that I felt my lips on hers.

While reading, Dario had pulled my head against his

chest. I looked across the empty beach and the motion-less sea. The landscape seemed hushed and darkened, as if I had cast a veil of sadness across it. Dario read on.

> Her eyes were still closed, but like those of someone not asleep. I kissed her, aghast at my own audacity, while in reality it had been Marthe who had drawn my head down against her mouth.

Dario's husky voice, with its guttural rolling r's enveloped me slowly, slowly:

> Her two hands clung about my neck; had she been shipwrecked, she would not have clung more desperately. And I did not know if she wished me to save her, or if she wished us to drown together.

Now he stopped and bent over me. I saw the world go dark in the bright sunlight. Turning my face toward his own and with his lips almost on mine, he whispered, "Doesn't it remind you of something, *piccola*?" Without waiting for an answer, he closed my lips with a kiss. His hand glided slowly, searchingly from my shoulder into the opening of my bathing suit.

Half intoxicated, half frantic with sorrow, I tore myself from his embrace, seized his hand, and kissed it, sobbing: "Oh, Dario, it's the end of something, I don't know what! The end is always sad. Is there never a happy ending to anything?"

"What seems to be an end to you may be a new beginning," he said, holding me close. "Besides," he added tenderly, "even though you can't roll up Rimini, you can roll me up like a carpet and take me with you to Turin this time. Remember?"

SEVEN

O nce settled in Turin, Dario rented a room in our neighborhood. He took his meals at an officers' club in town, but often dined with us, listening as of old to my father talk. Father would always find fault with him, as with everyone else, but you could see he enjoyed Dario's company. I thought that Dario looked extremely handsome and elegant in his new officer's uniform.

He had apparently been taken back into Zita's good graces, since she had an incurable weakness for the military; she proved this by often serving Dario a dish that he particularly relished—hearts of artichokes wrapped in boiled ham and thin slices of veal, baked in a casserole with a savory tomato sauce. She would bring it to the table with a large bowl of rice, begging us to eat it all up since she had prepared herself an egg, some fried potatoes, and a little salad, her favorite supper. This she would tell us time and time again, with her hand on her heart and eyes turned ecstatically upward as though reciting a poem. I never knew what was coming when she looked like this, whether it would be about her Corporal Merletti or her egg and fried potatoes.

I had not seen the Manettis for a while. Sandra had casually informed me of her engagement to a young professor of literature who had just accepted a position at the University of Turin. She said he had always been a friend of the family, but because he taught at the University of Milan they had not seen each other for several years. She spoke no further about him or her plans, and I dared not ask questions, but I found her announcement rather sober and matter-of-fact. I had always thought of Sandra as having a romantic and passionate nature, and therefore attributed her subdued tone and manner to her usual modesty and restraint.

Late in October, a few days before Father's departure, Mother invited her to drop by for an aperitif with her fiancé and Lorenzo. I remember the glasses filled with red drinks that Zita brought us on a silver tray. All the lamps were lit, and there was a white tablecloth embroidered with golden leaves on the living-room table and stuffed olives and deviled eggs on trays.

Professor Leonini reminded me more of a spider than a lion. He was short, slight, and sinewy; his complexion was strikingly white. His fingers were like long tentacles, their backs covered with black hair, and his brown eyes were piercingly intelligent. It seemed to me—as I furtively watched him talk to my parents and Sandra on one side of the table, while I gravitated toward Lorenzo on the other—that fine threads of humor were leaving his lips as he spoke and smiled. I liked him—he was definitely *simpatico*, although his presence awed me a little—but I could not picture him as the prospective husband of Sandra.

While I was pondering the possible nature of their relationship, the doorbell rang, and a moment later Zita announced the arrival of Dario. My pulses beat faster at his unexpected arrival, for I realized that he had never met Lorenzo. He did not enter with his usual ease, but remained standing close to the door, hesitating. He looked at Sandra and Lorenzo, and when he caught sight of Professor Leonini, who was staring at him in obvious surprise, he paled. All this happened in a split second, perhaps unnoticed by anyone but the professor and me. Dario ran a finger under the collar of his shirt and then stepped forward to shake hands with everyone, while my mother made the introductions. He greeted Sandra first and told her how glad he was to meet her after all the nice things I had told him about her. The truth was that I had consistently avoided talking about the Manettis to him. Although his approach to the professor was deliberately casual, I could tell he was hiding embarrassment under his usual bravura. Sandra exclaimed, "What a coincidence, so you know each other!" and the professor answered, "Yes," quietly, and explained that until last year Lieutenant Ventura had been one of his students. He then turned back to Father, and, after a strained moment of silence, resumed the interrupted conversation.

"And this," Mother said, guiding Dario to Lorenzo's side, "is our friend Lorenzo Manetti. Signor Manetti, meet *Tenente* Ventura."

"Ah, the famous Lorenzo!" Dario exclaimed. His hand, stretched out to shake Lorenzo's, stopped in midair. It always took Lorenzo some time to register a new presence. To a stranger it probably appeared as a reluctance, a hesitation to be admitted into the realm of an imagination that must be crowded by ghosts. Lorenzo smiled to show friendliness, but his smile remained as vacant as his delicate, groping hand until it was enveloped by Dario's ruddy fingers. The shocked look on Dario's face made me realize that I had never told him Lorenzo was blind. He narrowed his eyes and glanced at me. Then he

161

let go of Lorenzo's hand, pulled a chair to his side, and sat down beside us. Zita came in with an additional glass of Campari. This gave Dario a moment to recover from the double shock. He took his drink, leaned back in his chair, and took a few sips with an air of intense preoccupation. Lorenzo asked Dario if he was a regular army officer, and I wondered what kind of unpleasantness might have passed between him and the professor. For the first time I grew aware of another side of Dario's life, of a man's world, impenetrable to women— Mother and I only knew him in relationship to ourselves. And although I was having a glimpse at another dimension, one that might forever remain a mystery to me, I would have given anything to save Dario from this afternoon's embarrassment. I should have warned him of Lorenzo's blindness.

"No," Dario was saying, "I am putting in my time of military service." He was silent then, obviously pondering the situation.

Mother began to make small talk with Sandra, her fiancé, and Father on one side, and Lorenzo and Dario on the other. She offered the food from the trays, saw to it that silences did not grow tense, and, with her usual *savoir faire*, looking as elegant as ever in a navy polka-dot dress, she managed to steer the boat around the rocks. From time to time Dario looked at me, shaking his head slightly. "So *that* is Lorenzo!" his eyes seemed to say.

"When is Sandra going to be married?" Mother asked Lorenzo, who had grown quiet and was leaning back in his chair motionlessly, as if oblivious to his surroundings.

"Not before Lorenzo has his eye operation," Sandra answered from the opposite side of the room.

"It's the other way around, signora," Lorenzo protested, coming out of his shell. "I shall wait till Sandra is happily settled, and then . . ."

"Why, is there a chance," I asked excitedly as he stopped, "a chance for you to . . . ?"

"If the operation should be even mildly successful," Lorenzo said, "I shall go to a small Greek island off Rhodes, where I have always wanted to live."

"To escape?" Dario asked unexpectedly in a low voice. He put his empty glass on the table.

"No, *tenente*," Lorenzo answered emphatically enough for all to hear, "to pursue my own life."

"You must forgive me, Signor Manetti," Dario said, "but I had no idea . . . Nicole has told me so much about you, but she never mentioned that you were . . ."

"Blind?" Lorenzo finished the sentence for him.

"Yes. Were you born that way?" Dario asked.

"No." Lorenzo sat immobile, his long, slim fingers folded on his knees. There was something stoic in his posture. He looked as if he had cast his own figure in marble by a sheer act of will.

"Please, don't take my directness for indiscretion or curiosity," Dario said, "but I am genuinely interested . . . Again he ran his finger under the collar of his shirt while Lorenzo listened with the air of a deer, scenting something about Dario beyond his words. "I have always wondered whether it isn't harder to come to terms with blindness after one has been able to see for a time?"

"I can't really tell," Lorenzo said, now coming to life and turning his head in Dario's direction, "although I don't think so. To remember colors and shapes, to be filled with visual concepts, seems much less of a strain on the imagination."

163

I saw Dario watch Lorenzo reach for his glass right in front of him on the table with a sure, dextrous movement. He took a sip and added: "How else is one to have some kind of inner panorama, *tenente*?"

Now everyone was listening. The room seemed to take on livelier shapes and colors as Lorenzo grew more animated. Sandra was glancing from me to Dario and then at Mother, as if wondering in turn what Dario meant to us, and the professor looked at Dario, or rather through him into the past where he might once have seen him in a different light. Dario pretended not to notice, and the professor said something to Sandra I could not hear; then he turned back to Father and they resumed their discussion.

"You may be right," Dario was saying to Lorenzo. "Have you found that the loss of sight really creates a greater sharpness of the other senses, a finer intuition?"

"That's an old wives' tale," Lorenzo said. "People imagine all sorts of things." He took another sip of Campari, set the glass on the table, and put both hands into his trouser pockets.

Dario's hair was combed back straight and finely cut at the temples, as if chiseled by a sculptor's tool. Lorenzo's light brown hair fell over his brow as he moved his head. Next to the tanned, sanguine Dario Lorenzo's sensitive features seemed more delicate than usual, almost fragile; yet of the two of them it was Lorenzo who seemed to be the stronger, the more resilient. I could feel almost as a physical presence his quiet assurance that did not need to assert itself, while Dario's bravura could break at any time.

Lorenzo went on, saying, "From the medical point of view it's a fallacy—although I believe that one does try to compensate." My heart went out to them both: with tenderness for Dario and his frailties; with devotion and deep respect for Lorenzo.

At that moment Dario asked, "How long has it been since you lost your vision, Signor Manetti?" I could tell he was driving at something specific.

"My sight, not my vision, I hope," Lorenzo said. Dario caught my sympathetic smile and frowned. "I had an accident about six years ago," Lorenzo added.

"Then your play is somewhat autobiographical?" Dario said.

I saw Sandra turn her head and look at me across the table with a shocked expression. I stared at the ruby and diamond ring I had inherited from my grandmother and was wearing for the occasion, and began to turn and twist it so hard with my thumb that my finger felt sore. Lorenzo waited a moment before answering. I felt choked as I heard him ask softly, "Oh, have you read it, *tenente*?"

Mother quickly offered Dario another canapé, perhaps hoping to prevent him from saying anything further by filling his mouth with food. But Dario shook his head, thanked her, and asked, "It's no secret, is it?"

I was burning to tell Lorenzo that I had never let Dario see the manuscript, but I felt too shy to speak up in front of all these people, especially in the presence of Sandra's fiancé and my father. I knew Dario was taking advantage of my helplessness.

"Of course not," Lorenzo said. "I didn't know you were in Rimini." I sat paralyzed.

"Ever since the Steiners came to Italy," Dario said almost in a whisper, after making sure that Father was not listening, "we have spent our summers together."

"I see," Lorenzo said. He had never seemed so blind to me as at that moment. The stones of the ring, inside my palm, a drop of ice and a drop of blood, shone in the glare of the electric bulb. Again I saw Sandra glancing at us, a worried look on her face.

"Well, I'm off to London again day after tomorrow," Father was saying as Sandra rose to leave.

"To change the subject," Dario said, "Nicole, have you ever shown your friend the books I gave you?"

"No," I said coldly. Father, Mother, Sandra, and her fiancé were standing about the room exchanging good wishes.

"I recently gave her *Sons and Lovers* by D. H. Lawrence," Dario said. "Do you know it?"

"I read it a long time ago," Lorenzo said.

"One doesn't quite know what to give Nicole at her age. I mean," said Dario, "how much she'll understand."

"That depends on one's memory," Lorenzo remarked. "I mean, how much one is able to connect."

Sandra came over to him and touched his arm. "We are leaving," she said.

"How much did you understand when you were that young, *tenente*?" Lorenzo asked, getting up.

"I don't recall," Dario said.

"Nicole will remember," Lorenzo said.

The professor shook Dario's hand and said good-bye to him briefly in passing. I was grateful to Lorenzo and furious at Dario. Sandra went out to get Lorenzo's cane. I wished to set things right, to explain that I had never betrayed Lorenzo's trust, but I could not do it now.

Dario remained with us for a few minutes after the others were gone, in order to talk to my father and to wish him a pleasant trip. Then he excused himself and left, and I was unable to confront him alone for a single moment.

♣ ♣

Two days later, as soon as Father had left for England, Dario began to take most of his meals with us. He often spent the night in the guest room. I asked him at the first opportunity why he had wanted to give Lorenzo the impression of having read his manuscript, but he brushed my question aside and said he had no intention of fighting about that boring play with me all over again. I felt it would be wise not to insist and said no more about it.

"What happened between you and Professor Leonini?" I asked casually, the next time we had a moment alone with each other.

"What do you mean?"

"He obviously avoided talking to you," I said.

"Oh, we had some sort of argument the last time, in class. I thought he was rather petty to act the way he did at your house."

"And that's all?" I asked.

"Yes, what else should there be?"

Military life gave Dario much leisure, and I hated the long dreary hours in school, knowing he was at home or out taking walks with Mother. He was angry with me for not being a good student—as if he were not the cause of my failure! It was agony to sit on a school bench, unprepared for my lesson. I would fix my eyes on the teacher's face before a question and concentrate all my will power against her asking me to recite from memory long excerpts from Dante's *Purgatorio*, which I had read but once or twice.

I would come home from school at noon, usually before Dario and Mother returned for lunch. He would enter the living room, walk over to the sofa where I sat reading, stretch out his hand toward me, and say, "Good morning, *piccola*. How are you?" and I would shake his hand and reply, "Fine, thanks. And you?"

It was an answer I could not help giving, and it never

failed to irritate him. One day it made him so furious that he shouted at me like a madman, " 'Fine, thanks. And you?' Can't you give me a more intelligent answer, idiot?"

I rose, stunned and trembling, and fled to my room. There I leaned limply against my cupboard consumed by a terrible, murderous impulse. If I wanted to die, I no longer wished to do it passively. I wanted to strike back first. I was burning with a deadly white hatred.

Mother was aghast when she found me in this condition. For the first time, I think, she understood the depths of my torment. "Nicole, please calm down!" she said. "I'll send him away, I promise! I won't let him hurt you any more!"

"Yes, send him away!" I cried, "I don't want to see him ever again!" I beat my fist on the cupboard door while Mother tried to stop me.

I continued knocking my fists against it until they were sore. Mother did her best to comfort me, but I paid no attention to her. She offered to bring some food to my room and told me to take a rest before going back to school. I sat down and said that I would never eat or go back to school. She kept urging me in a gentle, worried voice to accept the endless, mechanical efforts of daily living, but her words of common sense were as strange to me as Chinese. I began to hear undertones of impatience, although she tried to conceal her annoyance. Then I became unaware even of sounds, but simply looked at her, watching her lips move as one watches the breathing mouth of a fish under water, opening and closing, opening and closing, with no sound.

At last, in exasperation she left me. Once I was alone, I could not bear it. I hated no longer, but was as tired of myself as Dario seemed to be. Oh, to make an end of this burden! I must be like a stone around the necks of those I loved, incapable for a single instant of my mother's gaiety or Dario's charm.

The next day I went back to school, and Mother allowed Dario to return. He came and apologized to me. It took a great deal of time and effort for him to reassure me that his outburst had been incomprehensible even to himself, and was probably caused by a physical pain he had been feeling for the past few days. He made me withdraw my wish not to see him again and to beg my mother to forget what I had said in a moment of frenzy. Thus, again, a few happy days followed. I was constantly being given respites of bliss or harmony. In those moments when my appetite returned, and after a good night's sleep, I was able, ironically enough, to gather strength for new afflictions. And new afflictions seemed to wait around each corner.

A new crisis occurred one evening when Dario arrived at our house unexpectedly, writhing with pain. Zita had opened the door for him, and I found him curled in an armchair in the library, his officer's cap pushed back on his head. Zita went in to call Mother.

"What is it, Dario?"

"That ghastly pain again!" He was holding his side, moaning.

I bent over him, helpless and frightened. Mother came out of the living room.

"Come," she said, trying to help him up. "You had better lie down on the couch."

"I can't!" he cried.

"I'll call the doctor." She hurried back into the living room.

Dario continued to moan and once, between the more violent attacks of pain, he looked up at me and said,

169

"That's what I meant the other day, *piccola*. It's no excuse for my awful behavior, but these pains . . . You didn't seem to believe me."

"I'm sorry. I had no idea . . ." I said. "I hope it's nothing serious. The doctor . . ."

"*Ai-ai-ai-ai*, here it comes again!" His eyes were full of tears.

Mother returned and said that an army doctor would arrive in a few minutes. She had Dario stand up slowly, carefully, and put his arm over her shoulders, and then walked with him to the guest room.

I followed them helplessly, step after halting step. I would gladly have freed Dario from his pain by taking it on myself. If only the doctor would get here soon!

Mother bent down, easing Dario gradually onto the guest-room couch. She took off his shoes, gently lifted his legs, made him stretch out, and covered him with the Scotch plaid. She always knew what to do under stress, while I felt utterly superfluous.

To make my misery complete, she sent me to my room. In the dark, I walked over to the window and leaned my forehead against the cold pane. A moment later the doorbell rang, and I rushed through the hall to let the doctor in.

A gray-haired man swept past me through the door toward Mother who was motioning him to follow her from the rear of the brightly lit hall. I saw him disappear around the corner with his black doctor's bag as if Mother had pulled him in like a magnet.

Peeping through the open door of the guest room, I prayed that Dario would not die. The doctor was bending over him, his back to me. Mother saw me at that moment and gently closed the door in my face. I was too worried to go to my room. The shadows of the doctor's and my mother's heads kept moving beyond the milky texture of the glass door, but I could not hear what they said.

A moment later I was trying to catch the doctor's words as he spoke on the telephone. Must I forever stand behind closed doors, I wondered, trying to decipher whisperings?

When someone seemed about to come out, I slipped into the darkness of my room. Mother came in a moment later and said, "Darling?"

"Yes!"

"It's appendicitis. The doctor called an ambulance to take Dario to the hospital. They have to operate on him right away."

"Oh, Mammina!" I threw my arms around her, trembling with terror.

"Don't worry, dear. He'll be all right."

"Will he? Will it hurt very much?"

"Only tomorrow, when it's over. He'll be fine in a few days."

"Are you sure?"

"The doctor said so."

"Are you going to the hospital with him?"

"No. I'll stay here with you."

"But he may need you."

"What good can I do? He's in pain, and he'll be put to sleep right away. Besides, they wouldn't let me."

"At least you could comfort him!"

"We'll visit him at the hospital, as soon as they'll let us. All right?" Mother patted my cheek reassuringly.

I followed her into the hall, repressing my sobs. Zita looked out of her room, like a sleepy porcupine with her pincurled head. "What did the doctor say? What's wrong with the *tenente*?" she asked.

"He has to go to the hospital," Mother said. "Appendicitis."

Zita yawned, reasurred that it wasn't a matter of importance, shrugged her shoulders, withdrew her head, and closed the door. We waited in the library.

After a few minutes the bell rang, and Mother opened the door. I noticed how pale she looked. Two men in white entered, carrying a stretcher. Again I was terrified.

"Where's the patient?"

Mother showed them through the hall. A moment later they came back with Dario on the stretcher, followed by the doctor. Dario glanced at me as they carried him past me, and I tried hard not to show him my despair. Mother pressed his hand and whispered a few encouraging words. I wished I could say something, too, but I felt choked.

The doctor followed the men into the elevator, and we stood on the threshold watching. The elevator doors were shut, and I listened to the humming with the awful feeling that Dario was being borne into the underworld.

Mother drew me inside and closed the door. "Come to bed," she said. She looked worried. "You haven't had any supper."

"I don't want any."

I kissed her good night in the hall. In bed I heard every quarter hour strike from the church spire through the night. I was sure that Mother was counting the quarter hours too.

The next day Mother spent most of her time at the military hospital. Since Dario was in great pain, I was not allowed to see him for two days. On the third day Mother took me to the clinic where Dario shared a room with a young cavalry officer who had broken his collarbone. Dario introduced him to us as *Tenente* Corvelli. He looked quite healthy in his white nightgown, a handsome youth who probably spent most of his time outdoors.

Dario looked at me, his eyes dark and grave in his thin, pale face. I put my hand gently on his, feeling as faint as if I myself had gone through an operation. He seemed so angelic in his white nightgown that I moved on tiptoe and spoke in a whisper. I noticed that he gave himself entirely into my mother's hands now, sighing with relief and gratitude as she adjusted his pillows or dabbed some eau de cologne on his temples, or showed him the magazines and books she had brought.

His eyes clung to her with the helpless, tender affection of a boy who depends entirely on his mother's care. At the same time he seemed unusually serious and introspective, as if he had done a great deal of thinking. Once I saw that he was trying to hide his tears. He made a painful grimace to indicate that his wound was hurting, but I knew that this was merely an excuse.

There was only one chair, and Mother sat on it at his side while I stood at the foot of the bed. Dario looked at me as a brother might look at his younger sister, and I smiled at him. What had been between us seemed gone forever, with the old Dario.

I had a painful feeling that a curtain had fallen and my part was finished. The only thing I could not understand was that my life had not had enough good sense to end there also. I had a vision of myself, or rather of an astral body of myself, standing naked in the wind, disintegrating like the substance of pain itself, until I had returned to infinity and everlasting peace.

"*Piccola*, aren't you uncomfortable standing there like that?" Dario was saying.

From the slippery white of the walls to the metal white of the bed my eyes found their way over the softer white of his sheets to the angelic white of his gown. It was winter; the snow must be falling silently outside. The mourners were wearing black boots and they wandered with heads bent against the wind, holding small bouquets of white gardenias in their hands. At last they reached the cemetery. Here was my grave. It had no stone, no name, and was recognizable only by the gentle mound of snow. They bent down and set the gardenias like petals of snow upon the wave of snow that was my grave. Each one of them cried a silent tear, and each tear fell on the flowers and gleamed there like a dewdrop before it froze, reminding them for an instant of spring.

"*Piccola*, why don't you get that chair from *Tenente* Corvelli's side and sit down! Do you hear me?"

I nodded. I saw my mother smiling as my legs wandered obediently to the lieutenant's bedside. My hands took hold of the chair.

"This chair cannot be removed," the lieutenant said. "You have to sit down right here."

"Yes?" I asked seriously.

"Yes," the lieutenant said. "Ventura is still too weak to entertain two lovely ladies."

"He expects them to entertain him," Dario said.

"I don't think it's fair," Corvelli said. "You must take pity on me, signorina. Look, the nurse brought me oranges, and I can't even peel them while he gets every attention—his pillows fixed, his forehead refreshed . . ."

"Why don't you call a nurse?" Dario said.

"Are you joking? Do you see the rich man's avarice, signorina? Those shriveled nuns are worse than this, believe me." He held up a dry-skinned orange. "And he wants to talk me into a nurse! Yes, if we had lovely ones like you!"

"I'm afraid I'm not qualified," I said, looking at the frank, handsome face of the young officer, "but I'll peel an orange for you."

I sat down near his bed, thankful for something to do,

174

feeling as the oily aromatic moisture from the orange peel sprayed my face, his insistent, almost amorous stare. "Finished," I said, spreading the sections like a star on his plate.

"Thank you, signorina. This is the best orange I've tasted yet. And you said you were not qualified! Why, what nurse would ever think of transforming an orange into a star?"

That night I dreamed Dario was my mother's son. He was not my brother, but he was Mother's child, and when she put him to sleep, she sat down at the edge of his bed in the guest room and stroked his temples with eau de cologne. He smiled at her sweetly and put his head in her lap and was suddenly a little boy. He called her "Mammina," just as he used to when the three of us were alone, and when I awoke I thought, *Maybe he needs her the way I need her, and his love for her is the love of a son for his mother.*

❧ ❧

Ten days later Dario was restored to us. *Tenente* Corvelli sent me a postcard from Aosta, where he was to finish the last few days of his military service before returning to his native Rome. He wrote that he thought of me each time he peeled an orange, and also when he peeled none. He would return for one more day in Turin on his way home and would take the liberty of calling on us.

"Here we go," Dario said, looking at the card. "I think Nicole has made a conquest."

The lieutenant telephoned early one afternoon and asked if I would like to meet him on Piazza San Carlo. If my mother allowed it, he said, we could spend the afternoon together and go to a show. Mother allowed it, and I said I would be down within half an hour.

As soon as I hung up, Dario said, "Why didn't you ask him to come here?"

"It didn't occur to me," I said, smiling at him. "Maybe he'd rather talk to me about oranges alone."

"Your daughter is getting too independent," Dario said to Mother. "Why isn't he asking us to come along? After all, we knew him first."

"Maybe he wants to propose to her," Mother said, smiling.

"Would you marry him?"

"Well . . . let me think about it," I said.

"You would have to ask my permission first."

"To think that Nicole's just as old as I was when the first man proposed to me," Mother said.

"What did you do?" I asked.

"I cried and ran to tell my mother."

We laughed, and went on chatting as I put on my coat.

"I don't think anyone will propose to me. Men don't do that any more," I said. "I wonder what Corvelli really looks like."

"That's right," Mother said. "We saw him only in bed."

In the tram I tried hard to remember Corvelli's face but could not. I saw his nose and mouth and eyes, and meant to piece them together, but the pieces would not fit. It had pleased me to see that, in spite of our casual conversation, Dario was not indifferent to my meeting another man.

As I alighted on Piazza San Carlo, Corvelli was waiting for me on the sidewalk. I had only a moment to recover from my shock at the sight of his stocky figure and reddish face, which was pleasant but far less handsome than I remembered.

He took my hand and shook it joyously. "I'm so glad

to see you again, Signorina Steiner," he said. "How are your mother and the *tenente*?"

"Fine, thank you. They reproached me for not asking you to come to our house. I didn't think of it."

"I would have called on you, but I don't have too much time."

"Time enough for a movie," I said, as we walked under the arcades, side by side.

"Well . . ." He cleared his throat. "I thought it would be nicer to see you alone. And to talk about something other than oranges . . ." he added shyly.

"We could talk of apples and bananas," I suggested.

"Now, don't be naughty, signorina! May I call you Nicole? And will you call me Roberto, please?"

"Yes, *tenente*. Roberto, I mean."

"Where would you like to go?"

"There is a picture of Katharine Hepburn at the Rex," I said.

"All right, if you'd like to see a picture. Unless . . . you'd rather talk."

"As you wish," I said politely, but I involuntarily directed our steps toward the theater.

"Nicole, I've been thinking of you so often. I have interrupted my journey only because of you . . ." He stopped, and I waited at his side, too embarrassed to look at him.

"You know very little of me," he said, breathing hard through his nose. "But I'm a man who makes his mind up fast when he finds what he wants. Nicole, tell me, is there hope?"

"Hope for what?" I asked, wishing very much to cry but not daring to—or to run away to tell my mother.

"Hope for learning more about each other, hope for me to join my life to yours?" His voice shook with emotion.

177

"*Tenente*," I whispered, "I'm only sixteen . . . a mere schoolgirl!"

"That's all right, Nicole. It need not hinder us from planning for the future. I'm a Roman. I come from a good and wealthy family. I . . ."

As I stared at his stolid face and listened to his solemn declaration about himself and thought of our conversation at home, I was overcome by an overwhelming desire to laugh. I put my closed fingers in front of my mouth and bit into my glove in order to repress my laughter, but this only made it worse, and I burst out helplessly as I averted my face.

"Is this so funny to you, signorina?" Corvelli asked, stopping short.

"I am sorry," I managed to say, composing myself, "but it came as such a surprise. Don't be angry, please, Roberto," I begged.

"Then tell me, Is there hope?" he asked again, and I answered gravely that there was none.

"Give me a reason!" We were standing in front of the Rex. "Unless your heart belongs to someone else . . ." he added in a whisper.

"It does."

"Good-bye, then, signorina." He bowed before me coolly, touching his officer's cap, and walked away with dignity, leaving me standing in front of the theater like a jilted bride.

I paid for my ticket and went in.

♣ ♣

Later that evening Dario and Mother sat on my bed as of old, saying good night. On leaving my room, Mother turned off the lights and closed the door. After a moment or two my door opened again, noiselessly, and

I saw Dario's head for an instant as he whispered, "*Piccola*, I'll come back for a little visit later."

I lay in the dark, my heart throbbing wildly. As soon as Dario had returned to the living room, I slipped out of bed and crossed my room to find that Dario had left the door slightly ajar. I went back to bed and waited. I waited for an hour and heard nothing but the church bell from the Corso. If Dario would only come! I wanted and dreaded his "little visit." Was there anything he meant to tell me? This was a possibility since Mother never left us alone even for a moment lest Dario should kiss me. Or was he curious to know what had happened with Corvelli? I had told them that he had indeed proposed to me, without mentioning my reaction, nor his to mine, nor that he had left me to see the picture alone.

It was after midnight when I heard the guest room door open and close gently, and Dario tiptoed into my room. He sat down on the edge of my bed and took my hands in his.

"*Piccola*," he whispered, "I was afraid you might have fallen asleep."

"What is it, Dario?"

"Nothing, darling, I just want to be near you," he murmured, stretching himself at my side on top of my blankets. "Sometimes I'm afraid you are going to slip through my fingers before I know it. You have grown up so fast. Men are beginning to swarm around you. It's frightening, you know."

"You only care when you are afraid of losing me."

"You know better, *tesoro*. But the thought of it drives me out of my mind." He began to stroke my hair, my face, my shoulders.

"It's not as bad as you think," I said.

179

"Don't you care about the *tenente?*" he asked anxiously.

"Oh, Dario . . ." I had never said the words to him. I had kept them inside me for years. It was as if no one had ever said them to anyone else before. "I love you," I whispered, and the words spread and grew larger than the night, filling the whole universe.

He covered my face with kisses, then kissed my lips passionately. "You are mine then, all mine!" he whispered, covering my face, my throat with small burning kisses, his hands pulling at my blanket as I tried to hold it firmly over my chest.

"No, Dario, please don't," I protested, frantic with fear and desire.

"Let me feel your warmth just once!" he begged, pulling down my blanket and seeking my breasts as he unfastened the top of my nightgown. "I won't harm you, darling; you mustn't fear," he whispered, his hands stroking my hips and stomach, his lips on my breast. "It's easy to lose one's head over you, but I won't hurt you, I promise!"

I closed my eyes and abandoned myself to his caresses and my ecstasy, yet holding his exploring hand away from me in nameless fear.

"You are so sweet, so indescribably lovely and warm," he said after a while, tucking the blankets about me and stretching himself once more at my side. For a long time he let his hand glide over my eyes, waiting for me to sleep. The bell from the church had struck three o'clock when he left my room. Until dawn I lay with my eyes open, wishing for him to come back and hold me in his arms in the darkness of a night that was never going to end.

And so for the days and weeks that followed I obeyed my mother's order to go to bed more willingly than I had ever done before. Later in the darkness of my room I would anxiously wait for Dario to open my door, which was the sign that I could count on his visit. He would come to me every other night or so, saying that I needed time for sleep and recovery from such late hours. But if my door stayed closed, I would be unable to sleep and be kept awake by my feverish yearning. We spoke in whispers lest Mother should hear the slightest noise and grow suspicious. Often we listened to her snoring gently beyond the wall.

Shivering with cold and weariness, I would wait for the tram in the mornings, always late for school, hating and dreading the discomfort of the school bench, the lessons awaiting me. Sometimes I would fall asleep at my desk, my head on my arm.

Yet it gave me a secret joy to spend long days in the old routine as if I were still a schoolgirl, to laugh over the same jokes and childish schemes with Oretta and other classmates while within me I was burning with this passionate love. My rapture was attributed to my notorious absent-mindedness. Oh, if my companions knew! I was now a grown woman, burning through lonely nights in torment and desire for some unknown and sublime fulfillment. For such were my emotions that each touch of his hand made me glow with an almost religious joy, each moment in his arms had become purest enchantment.

By contrast, my anxiety grew as I waited for hours and hours in the dark. I was no longer capable of deceiving myself about the hushed motions outside. Yet an instinct of self-preservation made me cling to the last remnants of my child self, made me refuse to grasp what I knew. In lucid moments I would abruptly sit up in bed and listen, holding my breath. I had visions of Dario and Mother in her bedroom beyond the wall. Was

181

he doing with her the very things he did with me, and more, much more? I would ask myself, burning in despair. All those vague forbidden things, so dreaded and desired?

I would find myself standing at the door in my bare feet, my heart pounding, my fist pressed against my mouth in order not to scream. I would stand petrified, until I was numb and stiff with cold, tempted to step out of my room and open my mother's bedroom door without knocking. Something always compelled me to return to my bed and bear my torment in silence. No description in Dante's *Inferno*, no matter how deep and low the circle, could express the torture of those hours.

I never tried to solve the mystery of whether Dario came to me fresh from my mother's arms or whether he chose my company for the nights he abstained from her embrace. Perhaps it was a little of both, for some nights he would wearily stroke my hair and face, and at other times he would kiss me with ferocious passion. I would then remember every precious tender moment of our past: the day he met me between the cabanas in Rimini and told me that his wider, better self was dedicated to me alone; our first kiss; our reading about the love of Francesca da Rimini; each moment that he sought my touch, my eyes, or told me how much he loved the sound of my voice.

All these and many other memories again fed my hope and pride and rekindled the fire of my delusions. What other reason but love could make him seek me out whenever my mother left the room? And yet, I asked myself, why did he treat me as a child in her presence, as well as in the presence of strangers, and then act so passionately toward me as soon as we were alone? Was he ashamed to let anyone know he loved me because these were the truest, the enduring feelings of his life, and he cherished them as deeply as I by keeping them sacred and untouched in silence?

"Nicole, *tesoro*, I am waiting for you to grow up. . . . Remember, whatever happens, you are the dream of my life," I could hear Dario saying. If this was so, time was on my side: Mother would grow older, and if I had the strength to endure, Dario would some day turn to me alone. The maze of my doubts, hopes, and contradictions was enough to drive me out of my mind. Thinking did not help at all if I wished to keep my sanity. Instead, I told myself in anguish, I must abide by my faith in Dario and my love for them both.

This was how I reasoned with myself in order to excuse my reluctance to act in an intolerable situation. The truth was that I had lost myself in the thicket of my passionate desire for Dario. Addicted to his touch, I could not find the strength to will that dreaded separation from which nothing but self-deceit could momentarily save me. I still believed in the impossible, still felt that the power of my love could miraculously transform the beloved.

Conflicts and dangers were temporarily put off by my father's return shortly before Christmas, and Dario appeared only for sporadic visits. I was haunted by the presentiment of a final disaster drawing closer, closer, every instant.

♣ ♣

Christmas vacation had almost ended. I was sitting on Sandra's bed in the tiny cubicle of her room. Outside, the city was buried under snow. The sky hung full and threatening, and my throat felt parched and my limbs tired as if from the weight of snow in the air. I shivered with cold.

183

"Wrap the cover around you," Sandra said. "Would you like me to call your mother and ask her about tonight?"

"Perhaps I'd better ask her myself. I have to go home in a few minutes anyway."

Sandra had invited me to go to a dance that evening with the professor and Lorenzo. She had said that if I went, Lorenzo was sure to go. I had not seen the Manettis since that embarrassing afternoon, and Sandra's invitation made me feel happy and reassured. At any other time her flattering remark about Lorenzo would have made me proud and heightened my self-esteem, but now I was only concerned about the continuity of our friendship. I was anxious to tell Sandra that I had not let Dario read the manuscript.

I had a glimpse at her slim body in her pink slip as she took off her dress and quickly covered herself again with an old flannel robe. There was something vulnerable about her figure, modest even when exposed. I responded to it as to the tremolo of a small but singularly fine voice and felt a tenderness combined with a desire to protect her, wondering if the professor would caress her smooth white skin and fondle her as Dario used to fondle me. Or was theirs one of those regular long Piedmontese middle-class engagements, where everything was proper and the couple did not trespass beyond the holding of hands in the parlor under the eyes of a chaperone?

"Keep me company while I fix my nails," she said, sitting down in front of her wardrobe mirror. "Help yourself, if you like." She opened a narrow drawer and pulled out a pair of scissors, a file, and a bottle of pink nail polish.

I watched her spread vaseline on her cuticle; in spite of the shortness of her nails, her supple fingers looked

184

graceful, elegant. I took the file from the top of her dresser and began to work on my thumbnail. I was dying to find out if the professor had told her anything about Dario.

"Are you going to wear lipstick tonight?" Sandra asked.

"I've never used any."

"You are a young woman now. It might make you feel more like one."

I thought of Dario's voice, saying, "Don't you ever dare ruin your mouth with paint! It's mine, and no one else may ever kiss it!"

As though she read my mind, Sandra, rubbing the towel over her nails, asked, "Have you ever been kissed?"

I was so surprised at her question that I had no time to think about it and said Yes, then casually bent over my nails before she could see my face.

"The *tenente*, I suppose," she said, untwisting the top of the nail-polish bottle. When I did not answer, realizing that she was as interested in my relationship with Dario as I in hers with the professor, she stopped for a moment and looked at me. Her amber eyes were full of fine starlike specks; her full, well-shaped lips expressed a vague dissatisfaction and sadness.

"Yes," I admitted.

"You are starting young," she mocked good-naturedly.

I continued working savagely on my nails.

"Did the professor tell you anything about Dario?" I finally ventured to ask.

Sandra hesitated. She brushed the light pink polish deftly across her thumbnail, leaving the half-moon free.

"Not much. He said he was one of his favorite students. Bright, thoughtful—" She was holding her right hand up and looked at it, waiting for the polish to dry.

185

"He did helpful research for Alfredo until one day . . ."

"Yes?" I asked fearfully as she stopped.

"He mentioned something about plagiarism. Alfredo didn't want to talk about it, and I didn't press him."

I felt the color rising to my face and realized that I was blushing for Dario. "And Lorenzo," I asked, putting the file back on the wardrobe, "do you think he liked Dario?"

"I'm afraid he was a little disturbed about his reading the manuscript. After all," she said softly, "Lorenzo sent it to you. He didn't say you should show it to others."

"But I didn't!" I was wounded by her reproach.

"Oh, I'm so glad!" She pressed my hand, and looked into my eyes and said, "Nicole, don't ever betray Lorenzo's trust. He's had enough of that."

I felt stunned. "You know what I really think?" she went on. "If Lorenzo disliked your friend, it was probably for personal reasons. Men!" she exclaimed. "Even the most unselfish ones are possessive."

"Lorenzo possessive?"

"It may be my imagination," Sandra said. "Maybe it's wishful thinking on my part. I was hoping that you and Lorenzo . . . His sight might be restored . . . No, no, I realize how foolish it was to imagine . . ." Sandra stopped, withdrew her hand from mine, and started to work again on her nails.

"But Lorenzo and I are only friends!" I was deeply disturbed. "Real friends, I mean."

"Maybe you feel that way, Nicole. But what makes you so sure about Lorenzo? I've never seen two more kindred spirits. . . ."

Sandra must be wrong. I was desperately clinging to the old friendly relationship. It was the only comfort I had left.

"Why would Lorenzo care for me?"

186

Sandra looked at me with surprise; her face grew radiant. She came to me, put her arms around me, and held me in a tight embrace.

"Oh, how late it is!" I cried. "I must run home now. I'll call you later about tonight."

Zita was ladling out the soup when I entered the dining room. Father looked sullen and reprimanded me for being late. I decided to wait and ask him after dinner. He might be more benign on a full stomach.

Mother and Father were conversing, but I hardly listened. I was thinking that if Lorenzo and I sat and talked together tonight while Sandra was dancing with her fiancé, I would hear every word, see every gesture in a new and confusing light. All at once I lost my desire to go to the dance. Anyway I had nothing to wear for the occasion.

"Ask her," Mother was saying impatiently. "Ask Nicole."

"My child," Father turned to me, "I hope that you, at least, will listen to reason." I said nothing, waiting for him to go on.

"I was telling your mother that I am going to begin working in Paris next May, a few weeks before the end of your school term. Now you are a bright girl. I see no reason why you shouldn't be able to finish your semester there."

"It will be awfully hard," I said. "Couldn't we just wait until I finish?"

"I can see it's useless to talk to either of you," he said angrily. "My wishes don't count at all in this house! I'm just to provide for you so that you can do anything you please!"

"It's not that, Father. I am grateful for the things you have given me."

"This is lip service, Nicole. I am asking you for one small favor once, and you are unable to say 'Yes, Father' with a smile."

"I am sorry. I wish you wouldn't work so hard. Don't do it for me, please."

"And for whom else, pray, but for you and your mother?"

"We could have lived on less, for many years . . . and been happier."

I don't know what gave me the courage to say it. Mother looked at me in wonder, and I was sure my father's fist would pound the table or that his voice would thunder with outrage at my daring. But nothing happened. Father sat silent, staring across the carpet, as if he had forgotten our presence. He looked sad and old.

His silence aroused guilt and sorrow in me as neither fist nor voice had ever done before. I looked across the rug, the same rug which I had sat on as a child watching him behind his paper, and in its Oriental pattern I saw a gap opening wide before my eyes, the gap of his lost years into which he was now staring, wasted in the drudgery of hard lonely work, the cobblestones wearing down his heels in hostile towns and strange streets, the burden of samples in suitcases dangling heavy from his tired hands, the gray mornings in hotel rooms, trains, taxis, business offices, the glib smiles and handshakes of strangers, the books filled with numbers and orders and cancellations, the quarrels with partners, the winter cold, the summer heat, and the loneliness—above all, the loneliness. And all this so we could have a beautiful apartment and a maid, and summer vacations at the beach, and concerts and good schools, and Dario!

For the first time in my life, my heart cried out to him in agony and compassion. *Oh, Father*, I thought, *why have you never been my father? Why have you never paused to love?* And I desperately wished I could say Yes with a smile; but it was impossible because if Mother and I had never existed, he would still have carried his suitcases and done all the things he said he did for us because it was his life and he could not change it. I could not say Yes to him because I could not break free of my love for Dario.

We said nothing more during dinner. Then Father and Mother went to sit and read in the living room in silence. I called up Sandra and told her that I could not go to the dance. She seemed disappointed and said that now Lorenzo would certainly not go either.

Father had many business matters to settle in town, and remained with us longer than usual. There was some satisfaction mingled now with my disappointment at being able to see Dario only occasionally, for Mother, too, saw him less often. At least I was spared the nightly torture of waiting for him in mad jealousy. But soon I began to realize that Mother was going secretly to Dario's quarters. For one thing, she stopped taking a nap after lunch. Instead, she had all sorts of errands to do, and left with me when I went back to school. Even without those outings I would have noticed, since I had learned to read the signs: the careful choice of dress, the happy expression on her face, the gentle, peaceful way in which she would respond to my father's ill humor.

To spare myself suffering, and also because I had no proof, I tried not to think of these secret rendezvous. But my suffering could not be held at arm's length, and I would cry in the silence of the night, or find my pillow wet with tears when I awoke. I felt hopelessly trapped by the many tentacles of my predicament. It was not enough to bear the threat of separation from Dario, for besides this there was the burden of my complicity, my jealousy and anger, and my grievous love for my mother. It was not easy to face the world as though all these things did not exist and to keep up my scholastic standards as though tests and papers and exams were all the problems I had in life. Now I was further charged with the responsibility of convincing my mother that moving to France, and moving as soon as possible, was the only right thing for us to do.

Father would take me aside and urge me to use my influence, hoping she might listen at least to my persuadings. I was too afraid to say No to these demands, yet unable to say Yes, just as in that convent school I could neither kneel nor stand erect during prayers. There was nothing I could do but go on with my tightrope dance. Would I ever reach the other side?

I told Mother what Father had asked me to tell her, listened to her counterarguments, and reported to him what she had told me. By the sheer law of motion, it kept us in even balance until Father left once more at the beginning of March, exasperated and determined, and Dario was restored to us. Although we avoided talk of separation, it constantly hung in the air. We tried to be cheerful, to forget, to make the best of the moments left us.

One Sunday we went on a picnic in the country as Mother and I had done in previous years. But now the grass was greener. The songs of youngsters we met on the roads sounded more sonorous. The white walls of houses shone brighter; the wells were deeper; the water was more refreshing to me. For Dario was there now, but perhaps soon would vanish from my life. His presence and the fear of his absence colored everything I saw, veiling it at the same time with an almost unbearable grief.

On that day I was able to delight in the moment without thinking of the future. It was a radiant morning. There was a humming in the air, in the valleys, in the hills. Mother, Dario, and I left the train, which had crept through the countryside as though paralyzed by spring fever, and wandered through open fields, heading for the hills. Every now and then we passed through a hamlet where we would stop to drink from a fountain.

As we climbed up the stony, winding path there was a cool silence in the woods, but the sun filtered through the young foliage of the trees, dappling gold on blue-green grass and shady trunks, on moss, brook, earth, and wanderers. We climbed in silence, sometimes stopping to take a deep breath.

It was past noon when we reached the top of the hill where a clearing opened to the most breath-taking scene. Surrounded by trees on all sides, a large meadow full of daffodils in bloom lay before us—a carpet of green and gold and white. In its midst, as graceful as a deer, rose a tiny white chapel, its pointed red roof piercing the sky. There was an intoxicating perfume of narcissi as a gentle breeze passed over the meadow, rocking the star-faced flowers like tiny sails in a sea of grass.

As we put down our knapsacks and stretched out on the ground, the surrounding scenery no longer seemed something apart from myself. I felt the earth under my back and looked at the sky through the tall grass, at the petals quivering above my white dress, then closed my eyes and felt drawn to the heart of the earth as though I were about to be initiated into some kind of mystic ritual, some pagan rite.

I heard Dario murmur, "You are like a child of light dropped from heaven," and then I knew that I belonged, belonged to sky and earth and flowers and brooks. The flowers knew; the veins of the earth had known long

191

ago. I pressed my wrists to the ground and felt the pulse of the world beating together with mine, heard the brook at the edge of the grass flowing with the blood in my veins. I had always belonged obscurely, unknowingly. Once I had been a part of it all in darkness. How lovely it was, this fresh knowing, this awakening, this streaming and flowing!

"*Piccola*, what's the matter?" I turned my head and saw Dario's eyes upon me. I could see every hair in the fine arch of his brows, and the small wrinkles engraved by smiles and laughter around the corners of his eyes. The sun was in his eyes, and the sky and the meadow's green and white and gold, small particles of quivering green and brown and gold—my love was in them, the echo, the call answered was in them. *Narcissus*, I thought, *No, it's you, the You, You, You. . . .*

"You are so sweet today, I've never seen you so happy," Dario said, and Mother looked up from her book and reached over to press my arm affectionately, still marking her line with one finger of her other hand, as I said, "Yes, I am, let's make a garland of narcissi."

"I'll make one for you," Dario said.

As his arm stretched out before me, I felt an irrepressible desire to kiss his hand. I stopped him as he was ready to pluck the first flower, made sure that Mother wasn't looking, took his hand, brushed his fingers with my lips, and said, "No, let's not."

He looked at me tenderly. I thought, *Give me the life of all the flowers unplucked, and not the death of a few!* Then he whispered, "If you were a wood and my thoughts chirping birds, you would hear their singing in your tree tops, day and night."

Mother looked up from her page and, shaking her head, somewhat annoyed, said that we both seemed ready for the booby hatch—a bite of lunch might restore us to normal. So we unpacked bread and chicken, cheese and fruit, and a bottle of wine. Dario and I ate and talked nonsense and laughed and then, like Henry VIII, tossed the chicken bones over our shoulders. I felt reckless and gay and did not trouble myself about the look on Mother's face.

As we marched back through the woods, Dario and I sang. The sun began to filter in oblique rays through the trees. Once Dario took a shortcut down a slope, and I ran after him before Mother realized that I had left her side.

"Come down here!" Dario called. "Look, how lovely!" I ran from tree to tree, following his voice, and then sat in the grass and let myself glide down the mossy slope until I stopped at his feet. He threw himself at my side. I lay under the arch of his arm, the arcades of trees, the expanse of the sky. To our left a brook murmured, leaves rustled over our heads, flowers rocked everywhere. We looked at each other, motionless, our eyes echoing each other's love; yet it was not like an echo, for there was no call and no answer, but waves, rhythm, unity.

"Where are you?" We heard Mother's voice.

"Here!" Dario answered dutifully, too softly for her to hear. "Who are you?" he whispered. "And who am I?"

"Nicole! Dario!"

"Here!" Dario called.

"Where?"

"Here! Here!"

I was lost under his kiss. Then he helped me up, and we walked back to the road, holding each other close until we caught sight of my mother.

She looked at us suspiciously and urged us to hurry. We marched on briskly. Dario held my hand as we stepped onto the train, held it while we stood in the

193

overcrowded compartments where Mother was offered a seat, held it while we stood facing each other in the crowd at a distance where she could not watch us. Many of the travelers had garlands of withered narcissi around their necks, and dead bouquets were in the nets above our heads and on people's laps, intoxicating the air like a sweet narcotic. Youngsters began to sing rustic songs about love and youth and the mountains. Everyone joined in. There was joy on the people's faces in the glow of the setting sun. Soon the train began to wind through the countryside like a winged, singing serpent, moving into darkness, into the roaring station of Porta Nuova.

We walked out of the station into the city, but the dream was still ours. We carried it home where Zita greeted us with the promise of an exquisite meal.

"I'm too full," Dario said, looking at me. "I can't eat."

Mother had gone to refresh herself. Dario and I stood facing each other in the doorway of the dining room. When Zita came in with the soup tureen, we held our hands above her head, and she stooped under the arch of our arms as she stepped over the threshold.

"I can't eat," Dario whispered again.

"You don't say," Zita chirped, "Are you sick or something?"

"It's worse, Zita," he said, "I've been wounded by a mortal arrow."

"Oh, stop kidding now!" Zita said. "You go on, eat. I don't see you hurt!"

EIGHT

Father returned the middle of April with the news that he was definitely going to work for the Moirot brothers, and in a month would make his first trip for that firm.

Quarrels between my parents awaited me daily when I came home. Often he would barely respond to my mechanical embrace and merely look at me either coldly or angrily, knowing that I had as little desire as Mother to follow him to France. The insight of one compassionate moment on a winter evening had left me, and only the fear of my father remained. Each moment in his presence grew more unbearable, and the house seemed too small when he was in it. Our home, I felt, had turned into a prison, and whenever I entered the front hall, I was repelled by the heavy smell of his cigars, which penetrated the remotest corners of the house.

At times I would run through the hall on tiptoe to avoid my parents, and shut myself in my room before my homecoming was noticed. I tried to study but was haunted by my father's suspicious expression, his hard, angry fist striking the table, his sonorous voice bursting through the walls with its angry explosions. If love for Dario had unnerved me before, it was fear that prevented me now from concentrating on my tasks. Bent over my books, I would often catch myself in the act of anxiously listening to real or imaginary sounds from the living room. My anguish increased with Father's suspiciousness and hostility. During our meals I could hardly swallow my food when I felt his eyes upon me.

Since he was included in this wave of enmity, Dario hardly dared enter our house. On those rare occasions when he did, I had to be careful not to betray my feelings to my father by a glance or gesture.

One day Father came to my room and asked me whether I had seen a great deal of Dario during his absence.

"No, just as usual," I said, without looking up from my book.

"Then tell me the real reason why you and your mother don't want to go to Paris."

I sighed impatiently. "Please, Father, I have quite a bit of studying to do for tomorrow," I said.

"I know you don't love your father, or else you would try to please me. And I also know that you and your mother are hiding something from me."

"Oh, please, leave me be! I can't stand this any more! You and Mother do whatever you want, but stop these arguments!"

"*You* can't stand it any more!" Father banged the door as he walked out furiously.

Unable to go on with my studying, I went over to the balcony doors and leaned my forehead against the windowpane. Unseasonal snow was covering court and garden. Winter had set in once more, matching my gloom. Storms came and went, the snow fell and

196

thawed, but this time it seemed to have come to stay. I thought sadly of the meadow of narcissi.

The next day I had to wear boots to school. By afternoon the snow reached to my ankles. My parents were not home when I returned, and I settled down in the guest room with my history book. Everything I tried to do seemed futile. After a while my parents returned; I heard them enter the living room. They were talking more quietly than usual, but quiet was perhaps more menacing than thunder.

"It must be Nicole!" I could hear my father say. I held my breath as I listened. There was a tremor in his voice. The door between the guest room and the living room stood slightly open. "In all these years, Clarisse, you have done nothing but set my own child against me. I love Nicole as much as you do. Do you think I'm a monster? Do you think I would chase my flesh and blood from my home? So tell me, yes, or no: Is she or isn't she going to have a baby?"

"But Richard, how absurd!" I heard Mother protest. Ah, that short, nervous laugh! "No, no, I assure you it's nothing of the kind."

"Then why is she evading me? And why your stubborn refusal to move?"

"But there is someone pregnant in this house," Mother said, ignoring his questions. "Our poor Zita confessed it to me the other day."

"I'm not in the least surprised!" Father replied. "You gave that girl too much freedom. There is no morality in this house. Everything is *laisser faire, laisser aller.*" Although he was grumbling, there was relief in his voice.

"Don't worry. Her corporal is going to marry her in the summer."

"Well, that solves all our problems," was my father's ironical reply.

197

I heard the living-room door open and close, then silence. The shocking news of Zita's condition struck me like a blow. In one moment our chatty, pretty maid had become a tragic figure in my eyes. My heart went out to her. I could not help connecting her fate with ours. In an indirect way she had to thank Dario for her lot. My father's remarks were not unfounded, I thought. Mother had constantly given Zita the evening off when Dario was at our house, and there she was, thrown into the arms of her corporal on cold winter evenings. What did Mother expect?

It could have been my baby. . . .

Mother stood on the threshold in the dusk. "Nicole!" she said. "Have you been here long?"

"Yes."

"What are you doing here in the dark?"

"Thinking."

She stepped into the room and sat down on the couch at my side.

"What are you thinking about?"

"Zita."

"Oh. So you heard."

"Yes."

"It's not so terrible. Merletti loves her and they are going to get married."

"I suppose that solves everything," I said. "Getting married."

"Not everything—maybe, for some people," Mother said meaningfully. We were silent. I felt that the air was filled with all the things that had never been said between us.

"So Father thought I was going to have a baby," I said after a while.

"You heard everything?"

"Yes."

"You can't blame him. After all, we have opposed him so much."

"Yes."

It was on my tongue to say, *You know my reason. What's yours?* But I swallowed my question, and again we fell silent. She put her arm around my shoulder. The gesture, our weariness, our bewilderment made us comrades-in-arms. For an instant I felt we were neither rivals nor enemies, nor friends nor mother and daughter —we were one and the same person in profound distress.

Later the three of us sat like a shipwrecked crew around the table. I hoped that Father would not notice that I kept my eyes fixed on my plate. I was oppressed by a vague sense of guilt. Mother and I dared not look at each other in the glare of the light. I was full of grief for us all: for my father, my mother, Zita, myself. We sat in silence, each of us a separate cell, once more hopelessly divided.

I withdrew early that night, poring over my schoolbooks without seeing the lines under my eyes. It was snowing when I went to bed and still snowing when I rose after a sleepless night. At lunchtime I found both my parents in what appeared a more peaceful mood. I went back to school through the thick soft whiteness. The whole world seemed suspended in a cloud of muffling snow that might never melt. It seemed to be my last protection. If it melted, I thought, my secret would be revealed with the naked earth, my heart exposed, and the tragedy would finally hurl us all into the abyss.

That afternoon I found Mother and Zita together in the kitchen, both of them weeping. Mother was holding Zita in her arms like a child, stroking her hair. I asked what was wrong, but Mother gave me a sign to leave. She came to me after a while and said Zita had just

199

found out from the doctor that her fiancé was stricken with leukemia and had only six months to live.

I turned away, unable to speak, to breathe. All the sorrow in the world was heaped on my shoulders along with the falling snow, and I broke down under its weight. Mother made dinner and told Zita to rest in her room. Later I washed the dishes and then went into Zita's room, where I sat on her bed and took her in my arms and wept with her.

"I knew it all along!" Zita sobbed. "The janitor's wife said that people with eyebrows growing together over their noses are doomed to die young!"

It had grown dark by the time I left her, and when I opened the balcony doors of my room for fresh air, I saw that it was still snowing. I put on coat and boots and went noiselessly through the hall and down the stairs. I wondered what Dario was doing. Probably playing games at the officers' club. The janitor's wife waved at me through the glass of her door as I passed. True or not, thank God Dario's eyebrows did not grow together over the bridge of his nose.

I walked swiftly to Corso Orbassano. As I crossed the street the bells were ringing seven times, then three quarter-hours. The snow sparkled crisp and starlike in the dim glow of the street lights. My head lowered, my hands in the pockets of my coat, I went on more slowly, along Corso Galileo, listening to the crisp sounds of the rubber of my boots in the snow.

The ghosts of chestnut trees stretched white on either side, their presence seeming to deepen the silence. There was no other sound but the rhythmic tread of my steps. I walked closer to the trees where the snow was fuller so that I would not disturb the stillness. The whole world seemed to sink into this white silence, and the soft, lovely snowflakes falling, falling unheard around and above me, whirled and whirled in a white shower about my head. Every now and then a streetcar, covered by a cap of snow, moved by with a sound so muffled that it seemed not to have passed at all.

As I walked slowly through the silence I felt as guilty as if I had had a taste of the forbidden apple—bitter-sweet and sour, not quite ripe. I looked back at the imprints of my feet in the snow and thought that they were like a trail dividing two silences: on one side was the stillness of the snow, white and pure as the days of my innocence; and on the other side I saw my secret wrong. I became aware of the sin of silence, of passive acquiescence, of the guilt I shared with my mother. Yes, I was a conspirator. All at once the burden of my father's eternal suitcases seemed to drag me down. They counterbalanced the bitterness of my guilt with the heaviness of his love, which had come too late. Would he still love me if he knew?

An almost physical pain at an imagined slap in my face accelerated my steps and brought a sense of relief. Oh, if only the soft, cool purity of the snow could cleanse me! Lorenzo's words came back to me, "Try not to judge your father, yourself, or anyone else," and the words now awakened an immense and all-including feeling of tenderness and compassion.

I thought of the young leaves of chestnut trees, of flowers cruelly exposed to the winter cold; of Zita's doomed young corporal, of her unborn child who was to be fatherless, and of Zita robbed of her love. I thought of my own father and the heartbreak he might yet have to face. All shelters, the shelter of childhood, security, delusion receded like walls beyond which I had never dared look, and the pain of all creatures, of human suffering, gaped red and sharp like an open wound against the white silence. This new revelation seemed to enter my body like a sacrament of love, and I yielded to it wholly, as though I were yielding to Dario's embrace.

I had walked on and on, unheeding; now, as I stopped near an intersection, I noticed I had reached a livelier part of town. At the corner, under a street light that cast a purple light and bluish shadows, people were waiting for trams, and behind them, against the wall of a building, a dwarflike chestnut vendor was rubbing his hands above the warmth of his stove.

It all seemed shadowy and unreal except for a tall man who stood at the dwarf's side, a paper bag filled with chestnuts in one hand, the fingers of the other hand swiftly cracking off skins. He was chewing chestnut after chestnut greedily, and when the bag was empty, he threw it into the gutter. Then he turned around and remained standing lost and hesitant under the lamp, the fine silhouette of his profile turned in my direction.

Unruly strands of hair had fallen over his forehead. With a pang I recognized Lorenzo. I watched him turn back to the dwarf after a moment, hand him some coins, and take another bag from his hand; and, in fascination, I saw him devour the second bag of chestnuts with the same avidity.

Lorenzo hungry? Lorenzo jealous? Lorenzo in need, as I was, as we all were? I stood trembling with the shock of the revelation that had come to me. At this moment I grew aware how I had idolized Lorenzo. As I took him off his pedestal I made him part of my deep love for all living creatures.

A tram stopped near the curb. I turned my head away for a moment, and when I looked again, Lorenzo was gone, and I saw the tram gliding through the lights and shadows of the street lamps and then dip into the darkness of a narrow street in the direction of Piazza Cavour.

The vendor was kindling the bluish flames under a

fresh batch of chestnuts. I remained leaning against a tree, and then I bent down and formed a snowball in my bare hands. I felt something close to joy as I flung it away as if it held all my outworn values and perspectives. I had never felt so free. For a moment I had been able to leap over my shadow. If only I could turn this moment into a continuity! Freedom could be found in one's own heart, I thought, and to reach out for it was even part of something like saying Yes, Father with a smile.

I went up to the corner, feeling for a coin in my pockets. The dwarf was just filling a bag. "How much?"

"*Cinquanta centesimi.*"

His head was grotesquely large, almost shaped like a square above his small, hunched body. As in a child's drawing, his features seemed unevenly spaced; his nose reminded me of a button. I gave him the money. His enormous black eyes looked up at me, shining with unexpected warmth.

"Keep the change," I said.

"*E grazie, signorina. Iddio la benedica.*"

"This isn't the chestnut season," I said. "What do you do when the weather gets back to normal?"

"I sell flowers, signorina. *Poveri fiori . . .*"

♣ ♣

Was it coincidence that prompted my mother to come to me later that evening and tell me of her decision before I could voice my own? She looked pale and determined as she entered my room and sat down beside me at the table.

"Nicole," she said, "I have just told your father that I am willing to move before the end of the school term." She paused, waiting to see my reaction.

"Oh, what made you change your mind?"

"Life is difficult enough. We mustn't complicate it further."

"Yes. I feel the same way about it."

"Really? Why?"

"For similar reasons," I said. "You were thinking of Zita, weren't you?"

"Yes. Why do you ask?"

"Because you thought, 'Death can't be avoided, but this is in our hands, and we still have the time to choose.' "

"How mature you are, Nicole." She looked at me as though seeing me for the first time, not as her daughter, but as a person with a separate identity. "I suppose you also know how difficult it is to follow reason, when . . ." She stopped short of a confession.

"Nicole," she said after a pause, "do you think you could ever turn against me?" As I did not answer at once, she added uneasily, "I mean, at your age so many daughters turn against their mothers in rebellion, and later . . ."

"Oh, Mammina!" I threw my arms about her. "No matter what I do or say, I shall always love you!"

She held me in a tight embrace. Her eyes filled with tears. "Thank God, for that, my darling! Ah, you are the only thing I have left in the world."

Those words! The memory of Maxine's funeral came to me like the completion of a circle: I was nothing more than the consolation, forever the consolation, the second choice! I freed myself of her embrace, got up, and went to the window.

"Nicole, what's the matter?" she asked almost in alarm.

"Nothing," I said. "I'm tired." Then, after a silence, "I think it has stopped snowing."

"I hope so," she said, quickly wiping her tears.

204

"Does Dario know we are leaving—soon, I mean?"

She shook her head. "Father said he will go to Paris, the day after tomorrow and look for a furnished apartment. In the meantime I shall start packing." She stared sadly at nothing at all. "He plans to come back in a couple of weeks and to send us ahead so that you can start school in Paris immediately."

"Who cares about school?"

"You seemed worried about it," she said.

"*Al diavolo.* So did you."

We avoided looking at each other. It was up to me to question her, and perhaps she was waiting for me to speak, hoping to redeem herself in my eyes, to free herself of the burden of her doubts, as though I were the judge and the jury that would pronounce her guilty or innocent. I could feel almost physically that I was a part of her, that on bearing me she had transmitted her conscience to me; and I rejoiced, not without cruelty, in her suspense, in her desperate need to have me say: *All right, all right. What you did was folly, but I understand because I share your love and your sorrow.* Yes, she might be waiting for something as simple as that.

She probably thought that I had decided to wait until Father had left, and I took advantage of the shield of this unspoken excuse by asking her if he had gone to bed. I kissed her good night and started undressing, and then went to wash and brush my teeth. When I returned to my room she was sitting on my bed, immobile, as if paralyzed.

I slipped under my covers, watching her stare at the future with my father, devoid of love or joy or hope for renewal. For the first time I realized that she dreaded retiring to her bedroom so full of memories, to lie at my father's side, tonight of all nights, after his hard-won victory. I began to understand that the agonies following deception must have been her worst expiation. But soon I was involved in my own problems again, in my last hope, in my anxious waiting to see Dario.

For on my way home in the snow, I had found the way out, through an arduous thicket perhaps, but the only way that seemed good and honest and right. First I must know whom Dario really loved. Whatever his decision, Mother and I would have to follow my father to Paris. If Dario chose her, it would be my undoing. Now or never he would have to make this choice.

Mother went to bed at last. Through the night I thought of the lonely years to come, if Dario chose me, years that would be endured serenely, if only he loved me and was willing to wait for me. We would seriously dedicate ourselves to our tasks. I would obey my father, comfort my mother, and try to help her forget, to help her find renewed interest in her music, in other people. We would never again get involved in subterfuges.

Oh, Dario, I thought, *I shall go to the end of the world for you. I could stand anything for the sake of your love!* Then, after five or six years, we would be able to meet in the open, there would be no more secrets, we would be free for each other. Surely there could be nothing wrong after so many years of patient waiting!

Yet the next moment I wondered, why make patterns out of hopes? Why make conditions to life since it went on regardless of my preposterous dreams? To try and mold the future to my needs was as futile as to touch the leaves of the mimosa bush. It was I who had to learn to abstain from the meddling touch, to grow and wait in silence, to learn how to accept life's intrinsic laws.

♣ ♣

The day after Father's departure for Paris most of the snow had melted under the hot spring sun and only a few hard, soiled patches remained. When I came home for lunch Zita told me that Mother had not yet come back from her shopping, and Dario was waiting for me in my room. We had not expected to see him before five in the afternoon.

He was pacing up and down when I entered, obviously worried. "There you are, *tesoro!*" He embraced me before I could set down the books I was carrying, and then he drew away and kissed my forehead absent-mindedly.

"What's the matter, Dario? Is anything wrong?"

"No, not really. Well—yes. No, it has nothing to do with us, or Mammina. I phoned—she wasn't home, so I've come here to ask you a special favor."

He took my books, put them on the table and helped me take off my coat. I remained standing at the table, waiting anxiously for him to speak.

"It's about my mother," he said to my astonishment. His hands clasped the back of a chair as he faced me across the table. "She's been ill in the hospital for some time." He did not look at me as he spoke.

"I'm so sorry! Here, in Turin?"

"Yes. It's one of her kidneys. She had an operation last winter; then she was fine for a while, and now . . ."

"You have never told me about your mother, and you don't see her much, though . . ."

"We haven't been on good terms," he said. "We are like strangers. She's managed pretty well for herself, but she has never done anything for me."

He spoke breathlessly, as if in a hurry either to come to the point or to discard this unpleasant subject, I thought. He looked disturbed and preoccupied, for what reason I could not tell.

"What about your father?"

"He left her when I was quite small," he said, "and then my uncle took over my education and sent me to" the priests. Not the Rimini uncle, my father's brother. My father is supposed to be somewhere in Libya. I never hear from him."

He had spoken like a child reciting a poem in class while fidgeting with a gold button on his olive-green uniform. Now his broad fingers were tapping a rhythm on it while the other hand was tilting back a chair. "Anyway," he went on nervously, "what I am trying to tell you is that my mother has managed so far, but the hospital bills have been piling up. I've helped her for a while . . ." He let go of the chair so that its front legs landed on the floor with a plop. "But now that she has to stay in a convalescent home for at least another month, I'm running out of funds."

During his rapid speech he had continued avoiding my eyes. I glanced in the oval mirror on the wall across from where I stood and then, using my hand for a comb, tried to adjust my wind-blown hair.

"Does Mother know about it? I'm sure she'll be happy to help you."

"Yes. She has helped me already." He hesitated. "Please, *piccola*, don't tell her why I came." He took his hand off the button and reached across the table to me with a pleading gesture. When he finally looked at me, I felt that he did not really see me. "I told Zita I brought over my things on the way to the officer's club, so I won't have to get them later."

"I wish I could help you, Dario," I said, "but all I have is a few lire. Let me get them for you."

"Darling, that won't do any good. I was thinking . . ."

"Yes?"

"Of your ruby and diamond ring. The one you inherited from your grandmother. That's pretty valuable, isn't it?"

"I suppose so."

208

It excited me to be able to help Dario in his need and to give him something that was precious to me. I went to my cupboard, opened a drawer, took out the small white box in which I kept the ring, and handed it to him. As he took the box from me, he held my hand and pulled it slowly toward him, as if trying to tell me that he wanted to take me along with the ring. Then he let go of me, opened the box, took out the band, and held it up against the light. I could see the crystal prism of the diamond embedded in its platinum casing above the drop of dark red wine, and I looked at the wrinkles around Dario's half-closed good eye as he inspected the stones with the air of a connoisseur.

"I hope it will be of real help," I said.

He closed the box, put it into his trouser pocket, turned back to me, put both hands on my shoulders, and said, "Sweet one, darling, I don't want to take your ring! I merely want to pawn it for a while, and then save up the money and give it back." He bent down and kissed me tenderly. "I'll never forget this, *piccola*. I know what your ring means to you. But each of your kisses is worth more to me than all the diamonds or rubies in the world.

"*Ciao, tesoro*," he whispered, "I'll see you later," then walked out swiftly. I heard him call good-bye to Zita, who was busy in the kitchen. In the confusion and sorrow before our departure, I felt sure Mother would never notice the absence of my ring.

The next afternoon as I was leaving school, I suddenly caught sight of Dario at the end of the block. He was heading toward the center of town. He had never come to pick me up at school before, and this unexpected appearance made me wonder if he had come to tell me something important. In order to avoid gossip, he probably meant for me to follow him unobtrusively, at a distance.

I found some excuse to leave my friend Oretta and ran after him toward Via Pietro Micca, bending against the wind as I ran. When I reached that street, I saw him walking briskly at a distance, his chin lifted and his officer's cap in one hand. His gait was swift and leisurely at the same time, and there was something carefree about the way his arms were swinging to the rhythm of his steps.

I called his name, but the wind blew my words back in the opposite direction, and when I called again more loudly, a streetcar came toward me, drowning his name beneath the busy clanging of its bell. Dario crossed the street, and then, about half a block before the intersection, he turned into a narrow lane. I ran over the gray cobblestones, along the cream-painted *palazzi*, and when I rounded the corner of the lane, I was just in time to see Dario disappear into a store.

I stopped for a moment in front of the quaint tobacco shop into which Dario had disappeared, holding my side, which had a stitch in it from running, and trying to catch my breath. There was a metal sign on top of the shop window: *"Sale e tabacchi."*

A bell rang as I opened the door, then rang again as I closed it. There was no trace of Dario inside the dark shop. An angular, gray-haired woman leaned over the counter, her arms folded under her breasts. She was talking to a fat black-haired woman in a raincoat who was putting a small blue package of salt into her shopping net. Besides the entrance door there was only the door behind the counter where the proprietress stood, and this probably led to her living quarters. The other two walls were lined with shelves.

I went over to a picture-postcard stand and looked at

the black-and-white reproductions of the Superga, the Po River, and a bird's-eye view of Turin.

"Is there anything else you'd like?" the proprietress asked; and the woman shook her head and said, "No, thank you, Signora Ventura." She put her change into her purse, fumbled with her shopping bag, and then asked, "So your son is going to be an economist? Will he go back to his studies after the military service?"

"Only God knows what Dario is going to do," Signora Ventura said, turning her eyes to the ceiling with a sigh, as I realized with a pang that her face looked exactly like Dario's in his black swimming cap.

I took the card from the stand, went over to the counter, and asked for a stamp.

"Anything else?" the woman asked.

"No, thank you." I pulled a five-lire piece from my purse and put it on the counter.

"*Grazie, signorina,*" she said, giving me the change.

As soon as I left the shop, I began to run aimlessly, unseeingly through the streets. Why on earth had Dario lied to me? I asked myself. It wasn't just a small white lie, but such an awful, elaborate story! The cobblestones made my feet hurt through the soles of my shoes, and those dark arcades, those heavy Victorian *palazzi* weighed oppressively on my chest. My side was aching again, and everything else ached inside me. I awoke to my surroundings only when I found myself near Piazza Solferino, waiting for a tram to take me home.

Dario came for lunch early the next day, and we had five minutes alone together before Mother returned from her errands. When he arrived, I was sitting on the living-room sofa, deciding how to confront him. As soon as he entered he called, "*Ciao, piccola!*" and walked over to me with a beaming face and tried to embrace me. I drew back from his touch.

"*Piccola*, what's the matter?" The smile left his face.

"You lied to me," I said. "Why?"

"I don't know what you are talking about," he said uneasily.

"You said you would always be truthful with me. Now I can never believe you again."

"You are talking in riddles," Dario said. "Would you please explain what you mean?" He sat down beside me on the sofa, waiting for me to speak.

"You didn't have to tell me that your mother has a tobacco shop in town," I said. "But you told me that big story about the hospital bills and the convalescent home so that I would give you my ring."

Dario frowned and remained silent for a moment. Two deep vertical lines appeared between his brows.

"A tobacco shop? But that's preposterous!" he said with a forced laugh. He sat staring at the fringe of the beige table cloth, then began to make pigtails out of it, taking three strands at a time.

"Please, Dario," I said, "don't deny it. I saw you go into the shop yesterday. I saw your mother. She looks like you. A woman addressed her as Signora Ventura and asked her about her son Dario."

"So you were spying on me, were you!"

"Yes. I sneak and I spy. That's all I ever do." I got up to leave the room, but he seized my arm, drew me back, made me sit down again, and asked me to forgive him.

"Try to understand, *piccola*." He put his hands on my shoulders, then turned me toward him until we faced each other. "I was ashamed to ask for your ring for such a trivial reason as losing money at cards."

He was looking directly at me at last. I saw an almost imploring expression in his eyes. "I was afraid you might feel contempt for me if you thought I had become a gambler." He let go of my shoulders, then took my hand and began to play with my fingers.

"Well, have you?" I looked down at my hand in his, then at his face again and at his thin lips that were like his mother's.

"No, darling. I was bored at the officers' club, so I started to play cards with the other fellows and kept losing. Mammina helped me in the past, and I gambled more to pay her back, but instead . . ."

"I don't understand why you didn't tell me. I would have gladly given you the ring, Dario. Now you have spoiled the best thing we had!"

"*Piccola*, will you believe me if I say I lied out of love and respect for you?" He squeezed my fingers tightly as he went on, "You think so highly of Lorenzo, and I desperately want you to think well of me, too!"

I saw that his eyes were filling with tears. "I don't know what to believe any more about anything, when it comes to you," I said. "But what I think of you matters little"—I pulled my hand out of his—"since I can't stop loving you." I looked straight into his eyes and then added softly, "If someone could give me a potion to free me of my love at this instant, I would drink it as quickly as possible."

"*Piccola!*" he cried, "how I wish to be given a chance to make up to you for everything!"

He drew me to him fiercely but let go of me at once and moved over to the far corner of the sofa as we heard Mother's voice in the hall.

NINE

That afternoon Dario had to leave town on military maneuvers. He was away for forty-eight hours, and when he came back, only two days remained before Father would return from Paris. When Dario joined us that evening, the three of us sat silent and oppressed in the living room, holding back the flood of emotions we had so little time left to express.

I was hoping Mother would go out and leave us alone for a moment so that Dario could tell me if he was coming to my room. Mother never moved. She kept secretly glancing at her watch, waiting for a plausible time to send me to bed. At last she broke the silence and began to talk about how much there was to do, saying that Zita was really no help in her condition.

"What's the matter with her?" Dario asked.

Mother told him. Dario said he was sorry for her, but that such a pretty and fickle girl would get over it soon enough. I looked at him, wondering how long it would take him to recover from losing us. He looked healthy and weather-beaten from his active life outdoors.

"I can't let you go!" he cried unexpectedly, looking first at me, then at Mother, then back at me again.

"It has to be," Mother said, sighing.

"It has to be if we let it be." Dario's voice was full of defiance. I was startled by the look of angry determination in his eyes.

After a silence, Mother asked if we would like some tea. I hoped she would go out and make it. Instead she said, "Nicole, would you put the kettle on?"

I went into the kitchen, shivering, and filled the teapot. I lit the gas under the kettle and stared mindlessly at the bluish flame.

Zita was spending every free minute with her corporal. At least she had him all to herself. Tonight they had gone to the movies at the flea theater, around the corner. Because of our willingness to move, Father had been in a generous mood, and he had provided her with a good sum of money to tide her and the baby over for a while. She and the corporal were going to get married as soon as we left. Mother had spoken to him and told him that Zita needed a home now. Merletti knew nothing about the seriousness of his illness, and although he had flinched a little, Mother had said, he was perfectly agreeable and had thanked her for her help.

When the water was boiling, I carried the cups in on a tray and asked Mother to fix the tea to her liking, then anxiously searched for traces of lipstick on Dario's face. Both of them looked just the way I had left them, thoughtful and sad. It seemed as if they had never budged.

Mother made me return to the kitchen with her so that she could show me, once and for all, how to rinse the teapot with hot water and then put in one teaspoonful of tea for each person and one for the pot. She poured the boiling water over the tea, and we went back into the living room together.

An hour later Mother sent me to bed. I lay in the dark

215

with a thudding heart, waiting for the door to open softly. Every now and then I slipped from my bed to check if I had missed the sound of the turning knob. But the door was closed. My hopes sank. I buried my head in my pillow.

It was past one o'clock when I heard Dario come in. The room was so dark that I could not see him at all. He sat down on my bed. I sat up, and we embraced in silence, my heart beating against his through the thin cloth of his pajamas.

"It's been such a long time," he whispered. The touch of his chest against my breasts made me feel faint with desire.

"It's been even longer than that," I whispered. "So much has happened—inside me."

"*Amor mio*, how I missed you!" He kissed me tenderly.

I took his face into my hands and pushed him away from me because I was afraid of my wild longing.

"What is it, *piccola*?"

"Dario, I must talk to you." Now I regretted my past hesitation, my cowardice. I should have spoken to him sooner, much sooner.

"Tonight, of all nights?"

"Yes. It's about you and Mammina." I was close to suffocation.

"What about her?"

"You know what I'm trying to say."

"No. You tell me."

"Do you love her?"

"We all love each other, *piccola*."

"That's not what I mean. Do you love her . . . as you love me . . . when we are alone, in the dark?"

"Come on, little one. This is much too complicated."

216

"It's true then that you are her—lover?" I tried to speak soberly.

"Let me explain."

"There is nothing to explain," I said. "I have known for a long time."

"Then why have you never asked me before?"

"Because I was a coward. If you and Mammina had known that I knew I would have lost you."

"When did you find out?"

"The day you told her that she looked like a fifty-year-old woman."

"That's monstrous! Did I really say that?"

"Yes. After you came back from the mole with Natalie."

"And you have kept it a secret ever since?"

"Yes."

"I've always suspected you knew."

"And Mammina?"

"She has never said anything to me," he said.

"Because she didn't want to know that I knew."

"She didn't want to lose me either," he said.

"And you? For the same reason you never mentioned your suspicion to her?"

"That makes us all cowards," he said.

"I am trying to understand, Dario. If you love Mammina, why pretend that you love me, too?" I could not keep my voice from trembling.

"*Tesoro*, please listen," he said. "I know how hard it must be for you. If I try to explain it to you, I may understand myself a little better, too."

As he began to speak, I felt the blood slowly ebbing away from my heart. "In the first place you must never say that I pretend to love you. You know that I do. When I think of the times I hurt you, *piccola* . . . Why

217

on earth should I have acted that way unless I felt you were tearing my heart out?"

"Was that the reason?"

"Yes, and also because we are both tempestuous and easily explode when we are together. I need peace. I must get away from myself. You, too, seek Mammina whenever you need rest. You see, darling, I feel so close to you that I rebel against you as if I were rebelling against myself. If I seemed to hate you at times, it was because a man can stand only so much ecstasy and so much hell."

"Go on," I said.

"Perhaps this is hard for you to understand, but I love you both together, as a family. You two are my family, the only one I have ever had."

He told me how as a child he had been pushed around from place to place, from school to school. His childhood had been spent among strangers. It was worse than being an orphan. "I told you that my parents were divorced when I was quite small," he said. "One day as I was playing on the floor my father threw a plate at my mother, but the plate hit me instead. I was lucky, for it could have killed me or made me lose an eye."

"Oh, Dario! So your scar . . ."

"Yes, that's what gave me the scar," he said. "Soon afterward my father went to Africa, and we never heard from him again. Then my uncle paid the priests to educate me. And educated I am . . . Educated! To know that the world is a cesspool of . . ."

He waited for a moment, and went on, "Anyway, that's the way I felt until I met you. And you know what I loved first? That indescribable tenderness you two had for each other. That's the one thing I was always terrified to destroy. That sincere, wonderful relationship I have never seen between two women, especially between mother and daughter. I know how jealous you have been of each other, but even the jealousy couldn't destroy it. This to me is the greatest kind of love."

"But you," I said. *Suppose you had to choose between us*, I thought in anguish. *You must know whom you really love.* The words were on my tongue, but I was too terrified of the verdict. Dario had fallen silent and his hands were groping for my face, my eyes, as though expecting to find tears on my cheeks. I felt parched. I was aware of the empty sockets of my eyes. "I can't stand thinking of you two together after I've gone to bed!"

"*Tesoro*, let me explain . . ."

"I don't want to hear any of it!" I said fiercely.

"Oh, I know how confusing and difficult it is," he said, after a pause. "I feel a tremendous gratitude to your mother, for all she has done for me. I have been cruel to her, too, Nicole, and I feel that somehow, somewhere, I must make up for it."

"Gratitude and remorse aren't love!"

"But they may have as much power," he said.

"Anyway, it's too late. And perhaps our going away is the right thing."

"You call being torn from each other the right thing, Nicole?"

"For me it's only torment! It's easier to be separated and to wait for each other . . . if you care, that is."

"What an optimist you are!" If I don't hold on to you now, at this moment, there won't be any future left us."

"I see."

"Nicole, I have wanted us to belong together completely. I have wanted it to madness . . . I may be guilty of many crimes, but you were always sacred to me."

"Oh," I said. How I hated being sacred!

"As to the future . . ." He paused. "Life is cruel," he then said, "and besides, there is the growing danger of

219

war. Your father is right, war is close now, and we don't know who will be fighting whom, right here in Italy. As an officer I can't even get a passport. I'm a plaything in the hands of the state!"

"We had better get some rest now," I said listlessly. "I have to go to school early in the morning."

"Let me hold you in my arms for a minute," he whispered.

"I'd rather sleep now," I said, turning from him.

When he left me, I lay motionless in my bed, which seemed to sink slowly into the ground. I felt as if I were being buried alive, with my eyes wide open.

♣ ♣

It was only the next afternoon on my way to say good-bye to the Manettis that I knew the reason for my deadly tiredness. I was like someone deported from a country he had lived in and loved and found was not his own. I could no longer be a citizen of Ventura—still, there was no other place that I could belong to as wholly, as unconditionally. I had repudiated my citizenship with my mind only, and I felt that wherever I went, Ventura would remain a part of me and I would feel like an exile.

"How I hate good-byes," Sandra said to me, as we sat down side by side on the black sofa in her music room. "Will you go on studying after you finish school in Paris?"

"Who knows?" I said. "I keep seeing chaos and destruction."

"It's true, the world does look grim," she said. "But you see everything through your unhappiness."

"Everything was in flower." I stared at the parquet floor. "Then the snow came back. . . ."

"If it's any consolation to you, Nicole, I've been

through it myself—the pains of first love, I mean. You are forced to go away, but I shall leave of my own accord."

"Are you going away, Sandra?" I was perplexed.

"Yes." There were green reflections in her amber eyes picked up by her grass-green sweater. "I have to tell you something." She paused. "I broke my engagement."

"What?"

"It wasn't an easy decision, Nicole. You see, I loved him—I used to love him. But after his return to Turin he had changed; he was no longer the man he used to be. There was wonder just in being near him, once—a soft expression in the corners of his lips that made me want to kiss him. Even the way he turned his head or helped me put on my coat . . ." she said, dreamily staring into space. "Maybe I have changed. Who knows? But he seems now just like a stuffy professor to me."

She took my hand and held it as she went on: "It was Alfredo who made me realize that I have always been playing the role of the meek Italian girl who does what is expected of her—and for this I am grateful to him. If I ever play that part again, Nicole," she added, "it will only be on the stage!"

"On the stage?"

"Yes. I've studied for the last two years—drama, ballet, elocution. I might even get a scholarship. I am planning to go to Rome next fall and study at the academy."

"But what about your mother and Lorenzo?"

"You know Lorenzo. He's delighted that I won't ever let anyone dictate my life to me again, and of course he has convinced Mamma that it's all for the best."

"But how is he going to manage without you?" I asked, concerned. "Is he so sure the operation . . . ?"

"He insists that I leave," Sandra interrupted me. "He says he can manage very well with Mamma's help. It's true he never was a hindrance to me, in spite of certain needs," she added thoughtfully. "He was, rather, some kind of liberating force. That's why I hoped some day you might . . ." For a moment she pressed my hand tightly in hers. "Well, it was foolish, I know."

"What was he like—before?" I asked quickly.

"Oh, he used to be full of fun," Sandra said. "Life with him was one great adventure. But since the accident he seems to have added another dimension to himself," she said, looking at the door as we heard steps in the hall.

"A shock like that often brings out some latent emotional illness in people," she went on softly, "but with him it was quite the opposite—the tragedy gave him a new strength of spirit."

"Yes, I've always felt that," I said.

"So remember, Nicole, no matter how unhappy you feel—if you can think of suffering in terms of Lorenzo's life, you may accept it from a different point of view."

"Yes, if you could be near me and remind me!"

"I shall be with you," she said in a firm voice. "Wherever you are, whatever happens, you may turn to me."

We embraced each other in silence. As if someone had given them a cue, Signora Manetti came in from the dining room at that moment, and Lorenzo entered from the hall.

Sandra and I smiled at each other amid our tears, and the three of them surrounded me and asked me to stay for a while, but I remembered I had promised my mother to help her pack our books. As I took leave of Signora Manetti, Sandra said that they would all come over in the next few days to say good-bye to my parents.

Lorenzo put on his coat in the hall. As we went down the steps together, memories overwhelmed me, the few memories that we shared, and when we passed the landing where we had first met, Lorenzo took my arm.

In silence we walked out into the warm spring sun-shine. Our steps moved together in a single slow rhythm, our steps, our breathing, our knowledge of each other.

"The operation . . ." I ventured at last. He said nothing. "Let me know how you are." He pressed my arm.

It struck me that the outcome of Lorenzo's operation was the only thing left to hope for. "Sandra told me about her plans," I said. "And you really want her to leave town, before your oper——?"

"Yes!" he said. "I am so glad about her decision. She is really coming into her own. Sandra has too much to give in every way. She needn't depend on anyone—least of all, me. We have come to the crossroads, she and I, and it's time for us to part."

"Are you writing these days?" I asked after a long pause.

"A new play. There are always new plays." He smiled grimly.

We passed gardens with magnolia trees, gardens full of flowers that had come into bloom too abruptly after the thawing of the snow. They were dream flowers to me, and I stared at them out of a dark cloud of dejection. They reminded me not of life's continuity, not of rebirth and renewal, but of life crushed before it could take roots. I looked at Lorenzo. His face was unshaven and the corners of his mouth were pulled down, the way his father's used to be. His neglected looks fitted my mood, creating a strong, unexpected intimacy.

As if guessing my thoughts, he said, "So we are back where we started. Let's pretend it's the beginning."

"But it *is* the beginning, Lorenzo!" I cried. "It always is, for me. There's a big dictator in my life who never lets me settle where I'd like to stay. 'Pack up,' he says, 'off with you, off, off, to Calabria!' "

"I can well imagine how painful it must be for you,

Nicole," he said softly. "If it's any comfort, it's not easy to let you go. It's not easy for the ones who stay behind."

"But you lose only one friend, while I . . . have to give up everything."

"Yes, I know. To grow is painful enough. This way it must feel unbearable. But couldn't you try, just to make it easier on yourself, to see some bitter advantage . . ."

"Try what?" I asked as he stopped.

"To remember that you are learning early to get ready for the great departure, the big leap. I don't mean it glibly, Nicole, and it's not sour grapes."

"Do you mean—death?" I asked, uncertain.

"Of course not," Lorenzo said, and I could see him smile. "No, not yet, Nicole. I mean freedom. So many people cling to their habits and little comforts, but you are way ahead of them. Some day you may turn your pain into work, into the writing you want to do. Then you can make your roots and your home in the mind."

"How, Lorenzo?" I asked. "By changing languages every few years?"

"Yes, you have that to contend with, too," he said. Then he was quiet for a while. We had stopped near Lorenzo's lilac bush. He broke off a small branch and gave it to me.

"Oh, you chose the fullest one!" I cried, burying my face in the dense, fragrant clusters of blooms, then lifting the branch to his face so he could inhale their subtle sweet scent.

"They are like a myriad of purple stars," I said, "and here, feel the sticky sap!" I lifted his hand and put his finger on a drop of resin. "It seems to be crying where you broke it off; the bark is all black, and the wood inside is creamy white and tender."

"My dear Nicole," he said, pressing the hand that was

224

holding the branch, "how will I go on seeing without your eyes?"

For a moment I thought he was going to take me into his arms, but he hesitated, stepped back, then went on. "You know the branch is torn and bleeding, but the tree is still whole and will bloom again." He was deeply moved. "If it's any comfort to you—you are that tree." His hand wandered to my face and he stroked my hair softly.

You have always been a comfort, I thought sadly, *dear, dear Lorenzo . . . but one is comforted only for a while, and then the darkness will close in again when you are no longer around.*

We walked on slowly. "I have a hunch that you will overcome your hurdles," he added, after a pause, "just as I have to get over mine. Because I know that you, too, can't bear the chaos without trying to make some order out of it, at least."

"If only I could do it in my own house," I said.

"We share the same house, all of us. You will see, Nicole. The future will tell you that the universe is a very private affair."

"I don't need the future to tell me," I said.

"*Perbacco!* How old you are!"

"As old as Methuselah," I said.

"You will be young again. In ten, twenty years from now."

"God save me from ever being young again!"

"Don't say that." His right hand groped for mine and covered it with a tender but wary pressure. "That's the good kind of youth. It will come to you, too—the one that we all love."

His warmth became part of me through his infinitely delicate touch. He stopped once more and released my hand. I knew he was about to turn around and walk out of my life. And as he did so, tapping his cane in his usual, wordless way, I stood motionless, aware in the midst of my sadness that his spirit had become one with me, like the spirit of someone beloved who had died.

♣ ♣

Numb as I was, after leaving Lorenzo, I felt no particular disappointment at finding Mother at home without Dario. She followed me to the kitchen, where I put the lilac branch into a vase, and then to my room.

I put down my books and set the vase on the table. She said she had something important to tell me. I sat down on Maxine's couch obediently, staring at a beam of sunshine on the floor, and waited for her to speak. *So here it comes at last,* I thought, *and what difference does it make? Except that now, when it's all over and finished, she needs to unburden herself and find justification in my eyes.*

"What I'm going to say, darling, will come as a shock to you." She hesitated, then sat down beside me.

To save her embarrassment, I said, "Mammina, you needn't say it. I know."

Instead of dismay, there was an expression of relief. "Ah, then it won't come as a surprise to you that Dario has asked me to marry him."

"Oh, has he?" I said tonelessly, in an effort to sound casual.

She interpreted my silence as if I were merely waiting for her to say more. "You take it so quietly, Nicole," she said.

"And . . . what have you decided?"

"I tried to talk him out of it. I told him that I am much too old for him, that I can't do it to you or your father."

"But you love him. Suppose I didn't exist—Would you go through with it, then?"

"Well . . . I might. But you do exist, and you are my first consideration." Mother took my hand and sighed. "I argued with Dario about it, and he said that in a year, after you finish high school, your father will send you to some university anyway, and then we could move close to wherever you are." She looked at me with an air of confusion and helplessness.

"Piccola, he had told me, *I can't even get a passport!*

"That's a good idea." It was as if someone else were borrowing my lips to speak.

"Do you really think so?" she said hopefully. "Of course, in a few years you will be of age, and then you will be able to live with whomever you choose."

"Of course." I said. I could tell she wanted me to encourage her to divorce my father and marry Dario.

"I am speaking from a realistic point of view," Mother went on. "In the case of a divorce, the law will be against me. But things might turn out better than we expect. Your father might let me keep you."

Let her keep me. *"What about the furniture, Richard?"* *"Keep it." "I give you back the jewels." "Nicole?" "You keep her. No, I want her." "All right, you may have her."*

"So what is your decision?" I heard my own voice asking.

"Nicole, darling, I'm so torn! I'll do what you say. You are the last person I want to hurt. Help me. Tell me what to do!"

"Do you think you will be happy with Dario?"

"Oh, yes! For a few years, certainly."

"And then?"

"Who knows when he'll tire of me?" she said candidly.

"But who can plan so far ahead? Look at Zita and Merletti."

"At least she'll have her six months with him," I said.

"That's exactly my way of reasoning."

"I want you two to be happy," I said.

"But you," she repeated. "And your father. I don't have the heart to make him lose us both."

"He has lost you already. Every day with him will make the lie grow bigger."

"Yes, but as long as he doesn't know. And once it's all over, he needn't be hurt. Don't ever judge us too harshly, Nicole. Some day you will understand that two worthwhile people can still be unhappy with each other."

"I do understand. Only tell me one thing: Why did you marry my father?"

"Oh, I was young and naïve . . . He was so imposing. I thought I was in love with him."

"The way you are in love with Dario now?"

"Ah, that is different!"

"Suppose Dario were sent to Siberia or Devil's Island," I said. "Would you go with him?"

"Of all places!" She laughed. "What an imagination you have!"

"Would you scrub floors for him and visit him once a week in prison for the rest of your life?" I insisted.

"Nicole," she said irritably, "what silly questions you ask!" She looked tired and worn out, and was obviously piqued with me for keeping her on tenterhooks.

We spoke no more until Zita called us to dinner a few minutes later. As I sat at the table without touching my food, I told Mother that the Manettis had stuffed me with cookies and cake. This wasn't true, but what difference did lies or truth make? It was all part of the same futile farce of living.

Mother looked at me from time to time with obvious

unease. "I wish I could read your thoughts," she said at last.

She had finished eating, and I asked if I could be excused. I told her I was tired since I hadn't slept well the night before. "Give my love to Dario when you see him," I managed to say as I kissed her good night.

She pressed me to her with a sudden passionate intensity and said, "Thank you, Nicole."

"For what?"

"For being so wonderfully understanding."

I went to my room, undressed in a hurry, and without washing, slipped into bed and turned off the light.

A few minutes later I heard Mother open the door softly. "Are you asleep?" she whispered. I did not answer.

& &

In the dark Dario silently entered my room. When he sat down on my bed, I did not withdraw from him since my body was merely an empty shell that I had left ages ago.

"*Piccola*," he whispered. "Forgive me for disturbing you so late." He took my hand, and I let him hold it. My hand was a frozen shrub that no warmth could bring back to life. "So Mammina has told you everything. I thank you for your wonderful reaction, but I don't want you to misunderstand me."

"What is there to misunderstand?" my lips were saying.

"I mean my motives. Remember what I told you last night? I haven't the strength to lose you! And I owe Mammina a great deal. I do want to make her happy."

"For how long?" I said.

"As long as it's humanly possible."

229

"Mammina has told me already. You have my blessing. Now, will you please let me go to sleep?"

"Nicole, dearest, don't be like this! Don't you understand?" His voice rose with excitement.

"*Sssh*," I said. "Do you want her to find you here?" The bitter irony of my own voice seemed to fill the dark.

"*Tesoro*, don't you see that for the first time we shall be free? We will be able to live openly, without secrets, without lies!"

"You mean you and Mammina."

"No, no, the three of us! You were the one who said last night that even if we are separated for a while, it's better to give up the moment for something good and lasting. I've thought about it a great deal."

"Yes?" My mind was still curious.

"It may be tough for a while, *piccola*. But I'm sure that your father won't force you to stay with him against your will."

"He won't," I said, knowing that he would.

"Oh? Have you thought of some way to join us then?" he asked anxiously.

"No," I said.

"Look, *piccola*. You are young and confused. Why don't you leave it to me and Mammina?"

"Has Mammina given you a definite answer?"

"Yes—since you took it so well."

"Then don't worry about me," I said. "You have both made your choice. I won't stand in your way."

"Oh, you silly darling. That's not what I worry about. Why must you be so damned heroic and calm?"

"I'm not. Just tired."

"I feel there is so much still left to say to you. And this is my last opportunity—for a while."

I had drawn the blanket up to my chin, and I lay on

230

my back staring into the darkness. The bell from the Corso rang three times. I felt as though it was ten years later and I was living in some distant land. But this was merely another futile thought. Dario bent down to kiss me. I turned my head away.

"Nicole," he begged. "Let me hold you just once more! Please, darling!"

I shook my head in the dark and reached out to shield myself from him. He rose in silence, as though the impact of unspoken laws had struck him only at that moment. His shadow vanished in the darkness; the door closed quietly. The wall between the guest room and mine grew thick and impenetrable, separating us forever. I lay still and determined, waiting for the first light of dawn.

♣ ♣

In the morning as I dressed mechanically for school, the darkness inside me did not alter. Mechanically my body performed all its usual habitual actions. I put on my brown pleated skirt, a tan sweater, and brown walking shoes. Then I opened the door to my room and remembered to take my books.

I crossed the hall on tiptoe. Passing the library, I saw Dario fully dressed and asleep in a chair. It was impossible to open the front door without some noise, and as the door gave, Dario opened his eyes. I pretended not to notice and slipped out.

"Nicole" I heard him call after me, "Wait, wait!" But I had already begun to run down the stairs; I hurried out of the building.

I escaped across the street, around the corner, and then waited for Dario to come out of the house and look for me in the opposite direction. A moment later I went up to the next corner and took the tram that was just heading for town.

I stood shivering in the morning crowd, heedless of time and movement, somewhat disturbed in my purpose by Dario's call. Did he expect me to waver again?

"Wait!" he had called. No, I was not going to wait. Had I not waited enough? I glanced at my school books pressed under my arm like a last memory of a former life. Anonymous faces swam through my unsteady sight.

At one point I was pushed out of the tram with a throng of workmen who were getting out near the river. I let myself become a part of the human wave, somehow carried along with its current, existing only as it existed. But as soon as the crowd dispersed and only single individuals with single purposes remained, I became sharply aware that my own existence had no purpose.

I must have come either too soon or too late into life; the doors had closed before I found my place; I felt that I had no function left. Those that I loved considered me little more than an obstacle. If I hindered them from going freely on their way, they resented my existence. If I gave them permission to ride over me, they accepted it without hesitation, perhaps even with a clear conscience. Consequently, there was nothing else for me to do but remove myself. It was as simple as that. I had been living with the thought of death a great deal, so it no longer frightened me, but I was afraid of what might come before—something vulgar, painful, abrupt, unnatural. I remembered how, on the other hand, I had swum out to sea that morning in Rimini, and it had seemed as easy as if it were going to happen by itself.

I went down the steps to the bank of the river and began to walk beside it. The day was as gray as the water, and everything was still and deserted at this hour. Occasionally a voice came faintly from the other side.

As I looked across the river, I remembered that somewhere in those hills the nuns of the Vergine Santa lived and prayed and taught young girls to become sisters or good mothers of families in the even stream of years that never rose or fell. The hair might turn gray on their covered heads, a voice grow rusty, a hand less secure. It was comforting to think of chiming bells, of softly closing doors, of tiptoed steps in felt shoes in the stony halls and rooms containing their simple lives. How happy the girls had seemed in their small communities, so warm and secure: rooted and belonging like those men heading for work a while ago who tonight, on coming home, would find their mothers, wives, or sweethearts. . . .

I had suffered, and yearned to become part of them, yet I felt proud to regard myself an outsider because I had believed that God had chosen to put me on this earth for some great revelation and future mission. To try and bring some order in my house. . . .

"What mission, what order?" I asked myself, chilled in the cool morning wind.

The answer seemed to come with a breeze from the river—scornful laughter, then the word *sacri-lege*, long drawn out, then torn to shreds and lost above the water. I covered my face with my hands and began to moan with a fear that was beyond the fear of death.

There was the river, but not the River Po. And there to my right was a door that led neither to Hell nor Heaven but into the Unknown, which was more frightening still, and like that other door bore the last verses of its famous inscription.

And again, again there came the laughter from the river. I could hear Zita's voice saying, "Do you know what happens in those tunnels, under the hills?"

My nuns, my white-clad nuns and days of purity! I could see Mother and Dario meeting in the tunnel and

233

then emerging to confront my father. . . . The vision choked me until I saw my father stab Mother and Dario both, and only this relieved me.

Yet here they were again: rising and smiling at me and pulling me down to their darkness. Choosing each other and discarding me. The second choice, the lesser alternative. Their smiles, so tender and sweet, made me die another death. . . .

The Po was a livid, monstrous stream, and the silence terrified me with its ghostly voices. Once I had meant to swim beyond the horizon of the sea that was life, but now I merely walked on and on and on. Instead of water, I would move through air. I could walk out of the city, close by the river. I had always felt that one could reach the beyond by any kind of motion, since life and death seemed like the wandering from one land to another through time and space. The strength of my suffering and the motion of my concentrated will would bring me out into the infinite, the nothingness that was equal to the all-embracing love of God. Rhythm would bring me back into His wholeness, not an ugly and violent act. *The great departure, the big leap, Lorenzo*, I thought, *may be the leap into freedom through death.* . . .

I heard a distant church bell strike. I was in a trance, unaware of time. There was the Valentino Garden. Mother and I used to take walks there, during our first year in Turin. I found myself crossing a wide green lawn edged by clumps of tall trees. The grass was short and damp, and I watched my brown shoes grow dark with wet as I walked. There were buttercups and forget-me-nots growing around the trees I passed while following a trail leading into a thicket.

The moss was young and tender at the roots of the trees, and on either side was a thicket of plants and bushes. I was tempted to walk on the deep carpet of moss

234

but forced myself to stay on the hard ground of the trail.

I hated no longer. In my dream I had stabbed Mother and Dario with the help of my father's hand. I had killed my hate. As I kept on wandering aimlessly about the paths, I shivered with cold. The earth turned into a huge balloon under my feet, moving and rolling under my unsteady steps while I tried to cling to its slippery surface. I kept walking and feeling like a ball tossed aimlessly about by fate: "That terrible humorist," as Dario had called it in his poem.

Dario. I could see the many Darios I had known: the Dario of the day of the narcissi, the Dario who had lain in the hospital, the Dario in the swimming cap, the jealous, the charming, the horrid, the cruel, the loving, the reckless, the considerate Dario, the Dario who had come to my room only the other night and said that he was cruel because he loved me too much. . . .

Above me the sun now tried to break through the clouds, but the wind blew them together again, pulling gray blankets over the patches of blue. I could hear no sound but that of my own steps on the path and the rustling of the wind in the trees. I was beyond all fear; I only wanted to forget earthly and finite things; I wanted to melt away and become one with the immensity of the universe.

I must have wandered around the park for hours. At last I stopped near an old beech tree and pressed my cheek against its smooth gray bark, then put my arms about its trunk, pressing myself against its firm and steady life as though I were leaving the last friend I had. It gave me a strength no human being was capable of giving me.

"*Oh, bella bimba,*" I suddenly heard a voice behind me, "I'm warm. Oh, so warm! Embrace me!"

I felt a hand on my arm, and my heart leaped to my

throat. Tearing myself away from his touch, I saw a bum's black-stubbled face, a black-toothed smile from slimy red lips, and dark needle-point eyes, naked and lewd.

As I ran from his greasy voice I could hear him following me, calling out words I did not understand but knew to be obscene. Feeling lighter than before, I realized that I had lost my books. The shock and fear seemed to give me wings, but still I felt my legs could not carry me fast enough.

I flew through the park in zigzags, followed by his loud, vulgar laughter, running and running, long after I had shed him, until I reached an avenue outside. The roaring laughter that was more like a jeer from the underworld resounded in my ears, mocking me as I ran through a maze of unknown streets toward the center of the city. God had forsaken me. Useless to life and rejected by death, I must continue to move in that never-never land between—not a proud outsider but the lowest of outcasts.

I held my side, which hurt painfully from running, and then continued more slowly, halting from time to time and gasping for breath. At last I reached a large square I vaguely recognized as Piazza San Carlo. Once more the city bustled with life. It must be afternoon. Trolleys stopped, spat out people, sucked others in. I went on, oblivious of direction.

It hardly occurred to me that Mother might worry where I was—how much could she care since she had made her final choice between me and Dario? Ah, the self-deceit of her talk! She would join me wherever my father would send me . . . Didn't she know how impossible this would be? "Oh Mammina! How could you let me down like this!" I sobbed. Ours was the greatest love, Dario had said. The mockery of it! The less people felt,

236

the more they used words to stuff the gaps of their emotions!

As I stopped at a busy corner, trying to see where I was, I found myself face to face with the dwarf who had been selling chestnuts last April. He was perched on a crate, a cap on his enormous square head, smiling at me.

"Buona sera, signorina!"

I nodded at him in the semidarkness. Tears stung my eyes. A basket of flowers swam across my vision. Then I saw his bloated hand rising toward my face, holding a tiny bouquet of violets.

"Signorina, gradisce? Spring has finally come, eh?"

Our hands touched for an instant as I took the flowers. *"Grazie."* I tried to smile, but couldn't.

I ran across the street, sobbing blindly. There was a strident stopping of wheels. A car honked furiously behind me. Someone was shouting. The violets fell out of my hand.

I kept running and sobbing, running aimlessly through a blue world of violets and a sky screaming red into my ears.

TEN

It was only when the door opened and I stood before Signora Manetti that I awoke to my surroundings.

"Signorina Nicole!" she cried. "I am so glad to see you!"

"*Buona sera, signora*," I managed to say. Her reception vaguely surprised me. "Is Sandra at home?" She shook her head.

A door opened and I saw Lorenzo on the threshold. "So it's you, Nicole!" he exclaimed. "*Grazie a Dio!*"

My legs gave away. The two last sleepless nights, my endless wandering without hope, rest, or sustenance had taken their toll. The dark hall turned into a gray vortex as I leaned against the wardrobe, but then the wardrobe grew soft like my legs and melted under my touch. I sank. The water closed above my head. Like bubbles, vague and distant, voices and words caressed the rippling surface above me. I stretched out my hand in vain to reach for the hieroglyphic sounds of another world.

The *moscone* was like a dark spot in the distance. The tiny white parasol was turning and turning. They were rowing farther and farther away from me, leaving me alone, to drown. I cried for help; then I opened my eyes and found myself clinging to Lorenzo with the shadow of his mother scurrying about.

It was no dream, and with his arms around me, he led me firmly into the music room and there made me stretch out on the black leather chaise longue. He pulled the piano bench close to my side and sat down. He took my hands into his and said, "Rest now. La Mamma is making some hot *caffé-latte* for you."

"Lorenzo, I'm sorry . . . sorry to . . ."

"*Sssh,*" he said.

"And Sandra?"

"Don't talk. Sandra's taking her ballet. Listen to me. Your mother called about three hours ago. She said you hadn't come home for lunch. She called the school, and they told her you hadn't been there at all." His voice rose sharply. "Do you know what you are doing to her?"

I said nothing.

"Nicole, we have been frantic with worry about you. What are you trying to prove?"

I remained silent.

"Lie still. I'm going to call your mother and tell her you are all right." He got up and left the room. I remained motionless in the dusk, filled with the angry and anxious ring of his voice.

The door opened again. Signora Manetti came in with a tray. She set it down on the bench, turned on the lamp above the piano, and put a pillow behind my head.

"This will make you feel better, *cara,*" she said. "Let me hold it for you while you drink."

I lifted my head and took a sip of coffee. "*Grazie, signora,*" I said.

Her hands were still supple though worn, with calluses and lines deeply engraved in their palms and the backs showing veins running like streams on a map.

My mother's hands were soft and white. I suppressed

239

a sob. Mother's image rose like the memory of another beloved country from which I had been expelled. I was ready to break down, but took a deep breath and swallowed some more coffee instead.

Lorenzo came back. His mother rose. He resumed his place. She put the cup into his hands and said, "You make her drink this, *figlio mio*. Make sure she eats the brioche."

"*Tante grazie*," I said again. She left the room.

"Your mother is very happy to know you are safely with us," Lorenzo said. "She wanted to take a cab and come right over. I told her you should rest here for a while. I'll take you home later."

Now I saw how pale he looked. He put the cup into my hands. I felt very thirsty and avidly drank down the hot sweet milk and coffee.

"Where were you all day?"

I put the cup back on the tray. "Walking," I said.

He pondered for a while. "And what made you decide to come back to us?" I said nothing. "So you were running away, hoping to die, perhaps, just to get even with them, is that it?" he asked sharply.

"No!"

"Then why did you?"

"Because I have nothing left to live for," I said.

"Then eat your brioche."

His remark struck me with a humorous grimness. I began to laugh helplessly, hysterically, and then my grief welled up, dispersing the bubble of laughter. My body was an empty shell holding nothing but a flood of sorrow. I began to shake. My teeth chattered. Lorenzo groped for my hand and sat down at the edge of the chaise longue, firmly holding me by the shoulders. He said nothing, but the gentle pressure of his hands gradually soothed me.

"I'm sorry," I finally managed to say.

240

"Is your mother nothing to live for?" he asked. "Or your father?"

"They don't need me."

"Perhaps you wouldn't say that if you had heard your mother's voice this afternoon." I shrugged with his hands on my shoulders. "What you were about to do is the most cruel act of hate, Nicole. You had a sister once, didn't you?"

"Yes."

"And now you want to make orphans of your parents!"

"They made me an orphan long ago," I said bitterly.

"Pity, pity, pity!" he cried. "All for yourself! Give them a little, too! They are helpless and confused—parents aren't all wise and perfect, you know!"

"I found that out long ago!"

"And you can't forgive them."

"I am not accusing them," I said. "There is nothing to forgive."

"That's where you are wrong, Nicole! You have a whole book of memories in that little brain of yours! Instead of facing them, of accusing them, of being honest with yourself, you retaliate in silence."

"Lorenzo," I said, "please don't turn against me. You and Sandra are the only friends I have."

His fingers glided along my arm until they found my hand. "I must say what I have to say. It's all I can do to help you. You understand that, don't you?"

"Yes."

"I'm not saying this because I'm against you, but because I . . ." He stopped short and let go of my hand. Then he moved from the chaise longue and sat again on the bench. The sight of his suffering face made me forget myself abruptly. His lids, fallen more than halfway over his eyes, usually left some of the white exposed. Now his

241

eyes had closed completely, and tears shimmered on his lashes.

He turned his head aside and wiped them off with the back of his hand. "Anyway, who are you," he said clearing his throat, "that you think you can pull all the strings? God Almighty?"

"No," I said, mortified.

"Then try to act as wisely as you talk! Use your power where you should use it, instead of dramatizing yourself and pulling everyone down with you!"

"Lorenzo, what am I to do? Can you tell me? Help me, please help me!"

"I wish I could! There are things you may understand some day . . . I can't make you bleed with my blood, can I?"

"No," I murmured. "It was foolish of me to ask."

"All I can say is, try to live through this by forgetting yourself a little. Try to help those about you. It will teach you to see that you and your sorrows aren't more important than those of the next fellow. Some day you will be ready to grasp the meaning of it all—and then you will be strong."

I wondered how much he had really guessed about us. I was grateful he had asked me no questions.

I said, "Lorenzo, and if I won't ever understand it, then what for . . . ?"

"But you will," he said, finding my hair and stroking it gently. "That's the risk we have to take with any operation, don't you think?"

"I wish I were as wise as you."

"You are. We are all born wise. All our lives we try to recapture the wisdom we lose with experience. That loss was my undoing."

"What do you mean?" I asked, not understanding.

He took my face into his hands, then touched my temple with his index finger, and said huskily, "Right there I pulled the trigger. To make an end to it all. Because of one moment of despair." He took his hands from my face, straightened himself, then went on, "Take a good look at me. Perhaps it will help you to know what you must never do. Like a madman, out of one season I made eternal darkness."

"Oh, Lorenzo!" I cried, forgetting all my own sorrows.

"So now you'll understand. Now you see why you gave me such a fright," he said.

"I am sorry. I didn't know."

"Didn't know what, Nicole?"

"That you would really care—that much," I said softly.

"Now you know it. Does that change anything?"

"Yes," I said. "Let me stay with you! We could go to Greece together after your operation."

"There can't be any operation," he said. "The optical nerve is severed."

"Oh, no, Lorenzo!" I sobbed. "And you are letting Sandra go to Rome!"

"No," he said quietly, "I'm sending her. I spread the news about the operation for her benefit. I want her to live her own life and stop worrying about me. I can't stand Good Samaritans," he added, groping for a handkerchief, and putting it into my hand, "and I hate blubbering."

"I'm not a Good Samaritan!" I protested. "I want to be of use. I want to be needed," I went on stubbornly, blowing my nose and wiping my tears, "and besides— I have nowhere to turn but to you!"

"Come, I'll take you home before you think of another solution," he said. "No, wait, you haven't eaten your brioche."

I reached for the sweet roll soberly, then chewed and

243

swallowed in silence. Lorenzo left the room to call for a cab. *So he doesn't want me either*, I thought. How could I tell what anyone really felt? It was easy to reject me with the excuse of not wanting my "sacrifice."

I got up slowly and went to say good-bye to Signora Manetti. Lorenzo and I put on our coats in silence. I could not remember where I had lost my schoolbooks—near the river perhaps, or in the park, or maybe I had dropped them when I ran from the bum.

"You needn't come down with me," I said. "I can ride home by myself."

"I'll be right back, Mamma," Lorenzo said, paying no attention to my remark.

As soon as we stepped outside, the cab came to a halt in front of the apartment building. We sat down in the back, close to each other, stiff and silent.

"Nicole, you fool," he said unexpectedly, "don't misread the signs now—don't judge me by the habit of your pain. If anything, I want to soothe it, not add to it. Don't you see?"

"Forgive me," I said. I took his hand and bent over it and kissed it. "How do you do it," I whispered, "how did you learn to live without hope?"

"But I don't know how," he said, drawing me into his arms, "since I am now hoping for you. . . ."

As the car pulled up at the curb near our house, he kissed my lips, then groped for the door, opened it, and smiling his touching smile, said in a whisper, "To think of all the things that could have been. . . ."

Before I could answer, he had gently pushed me out. I stood on the sidewalk and he called, "*Ciao*, Nicole! Be brave!" and closed the door. The car began to drive slowly around the corner.

"*Addio*, Lorenzo!" I cried in silence. The touch of his

244

lips was still on mine as I faced the house and reluctantly walked past the nodding head of the concierge.

❧ ❧

Mother had never looked so disheveled and pale and old as at the moment she opened the door and took me in her arms. She must have been waiting in the library, for she was at the door almost before I put the key into the lock.

"Oh, thank heaven, Nicole," she whispered, "thank heaven you are back!"

No, I had never seen her like this, not even after Maxine's death. So I really mattered to her after all. It surprised me, though it failed to make me happy. She had almost had to lose me in order to find out what I meant to her. I could think about this without bitterness because I felt I was a different person now, older, less anxious about what others thought of me, but preoccupied with a new purpose. As I was haunted by Lorenzo's tragic revelation I knew I must act at once in order to avert a final tragedy for us all.

I waited quietly for Mother to grow calmer, and then asked her to come to my room. There I immediately lay down on the bed, exhausted. She seated herself at my side, without letting go of my hand.

"Oh, Nicole, will you ever forgive me?" she burst out, sobbing. For answer I pressed her hand.

"Why have you changed your mind?" I asked.

Before she could say anything, the telephone rang, and she leapt from the bed and hurried into the guest room. As she had left the doors open, I could hear her conversation.

"*Pronto, sì, è quì.* She came back a few minutes ago. Dario, I don't feel like talking now." Silence. "No, you

245

had better not come over. She is very tired. We must let her rest." Silence. "Please don't. You know she is safe. For the moment, nothing else matters." Silence. "Yes, I'll tell her. Good-bye."

She came back and said, "Dario sends his love. He called me all day. He, too, was awfully worried."

"Did he want to see me?" I asked.

"Yes. You heard what I told him."

"How come Father hasn't come back?" I asked in alarm, all at once remembering that his train had been due earlier that afternoon.

"He cabled that he would be home tomorrow. It took him longer than he thought."

"Where's Zita?"

"With Merletti."

"So, are you going to tell Father right away?"

"Tell him what, Nicole?"

"About you and Dario."

"There is nothing to tell, darling," she said. "I thought I made it clear to you that I can't go through with the divorce."

"No, you didn't!" I cried. "And how do I know you won't change your mind again?" In my excitement I had sat up in bed and now was watching her wan face.

"Don't worry, I won't," she said with an air of quiet determination. "Because now I am sure that I love you more than anyone in the world."

"Oh, Mother!" I hid my face on her breast, and we held each other for a long time in silence.

Later I asked, "What about Dario? Did you tell him?"

"Yes. He came over in the early afternoon."

"And he didn't try to get you over to his side again?" I propped myself up on my elbow; I wanted to see her face.

She looked at me sadly and said, "Whatever his side

is. . . . No, he seemed relieved. He told me that he, too, is much too fond of you to hurt you."

"Is that what he said? Fond?"

Mother gave me a meaningful look and replied, "That's what he told *me*."

"Dario isn't afraid of hurting," I said. "He's afraid of losing."

"So I am learning."

"Aren't we all?" I looked at her sideways.

"I suppose so, Nicole." She sighed.

Only a moment ago, before Dario's call had interrupted our conversation, I had decided to tell Mother the whole truth about myself and Dario in order to make her come to her senses, to make her revise her decision of divorcing my father for his sake. But now, what need was there to say more?

Another silence, I thought, not of innocence, not of acquiescence, but of love. Truth, Lorenzo had taught me, even when hard and cruel, could be kindness if it was given as a bitter potion to cure a disease. But what was the purpose of truth once the crisis had passed, except to inflict unnecessary pain? And then, what was the truth? I asked myself, puzzled. All the things that were never said? Statements were facts, yet as soon as it was stated, the truth like the leaves of the mimosa bush withdrew from the touch of the uttered word. Who was I to say what Dario's intentions were?

I lay down quietly again, and as I caressed my mother's hand, I felt that she and Dario were my children, that I had grown to accept them as they were, to love them in spite of their weaknesses, just as I was learning to accept my own. It meant embracing life, instead of trying to mold it to my vision.

As I looked at Mother I saw her face pucker, so that it resembled the face of a small child or a very old

247

woman, and then the tears gathered and silently rolled down her cheeks.

Cry for both of us, I thought. *I have no tears left.* I took her into my arms, and this time she leaned her head against my breast and wept bitterly.

"Do you know what I would do if I were you?" I said to distract her when she had grown calmer.

"What?" She lifted her head, found her purse at the foot of my bed, took a handkerchief, and vigorously blew her nose. "Tell me."

"I would break away from everything."

"How, Nicole?"

"By going to Paris with us and helping Father get settled in his new work first. Then I would try to stand on my own feet."

"How?" she said again.

"You were a fashion designer once. You could try that, for one thing."

"That was twenty years ago! Paris is very difficult."

"Then let's go to America! Uncle Raymond asked us so often to come back. We could both earn a living as soon as I finish school."

"Do you want us to leave your father?"

"It would be the honest thing to do," I said. "Unless —we could all live in peace together. . . ."

"Nicole," she said, "you will finish school, and then I shall see that you choose any profession you like. No more conflicts and upheavals, please."

Here I was again, playing God Almighty. . . . "Whatever you say, Mammina. It was just a thought."

"It's a good thought," Mother said. "I shall try to stand on my own feet as you say. As for your father— he may need us—and now that Dario won't be there any longer . . ."

248

We can make believe we have never betrayed him, I
finished the sentence for her in my mind.

Mother took a deep breath, and then said, "Some day,
Nicole, you will understand that kindness may be better
than honesty."

♣ ♣

The ordeal of those last few days, those days that I
had hoped to spend at least in outer calm, seemed more
than I could endure.

Dario called me as we were getting ready to meet my
father at the station. Mother remained in the room during our conversation, and Dario at the other end of the
line kept saying desperately, "*Piccola,* I must see you.
I simply must talk to you alone once more."

"It's no use."

"Please, Nicole!"

"But why?" I asked in a low voice.

"There is something I want to tell you."

"I understand. There's no need to say anything more."

"You understand, but you don't even know what I'm
going to tell you."

"Dario, I must go to the station. Father is coming
back. Did you want to speak to Mammina? She's right
here."

"Not now. I said good-bye to her this morning."

"Oh. I see. Well, *ciao,* Dario," I said quickly, and
hung up.

I turned to Mother feeling the old terrible pain. "Why
didn't you tell me he came to see you this morning?"

"What difference does it make? Mother said. "He just
wanted to say good-bye."

Going to the station to get my father, who had already found an apartment for us in Paris, was like
meeting the future together: the resignation to life

with him, which Mother and I shared. Yet when Father alighted from the train, my heart instantly surged with love as I kissed him. *God save him the pain*, I thought, trembling. He, perhaps sensing a feeling I had failed to convey to him before, embraced me more warmly than usual.

"How are you, my child?" he asked, and before I could answer he went on, "I have good news for you. You both will like the apartment. It's within walking distance of the Quartier Latin and the Seine and an excellent school. After that, the Sorbonne. You may study anything you like."

"Thank you, Father."

"How pale and thin you are, Nicole!" he said later, at home. "Are you ill?"

"No," I said.

"Do you get enough food and sleep? Is something ailing you, Nicole? Tell me!"

"No, don't worry. I'm all right."

"I have never before seen you look like this. I'll have you thoroughly checked as soon as we get to Paris."

It was good that we were all busy preparing and organizing our departure. Zita wept a great deal as she helped Mother pack. I could not tell whether she was crying for herself or because she would miss us. There was something odd and forced about her behavior. Whenever she had a moment alone with me I felt she had something on her mind she wished to tell me, but she could not bring herself to say it.

We went to see the small furnished apartment that she was going to share with Merletti as soon as Father followed us to France. It smelled of chlorine, and all the dresses my mother had passed on to her were neatly arranged in the closet. Corporal Merletti came over to say good-bye, and we all sat stiffly in the parlor, sipping the port wine Zita poured for us. We drank to their happiness and wished them luck. Zita could hardly control herself and ran from the room in order not to cry in front of her fiancé. When she came back, her eyes were red and swollen. She explained to Merletti that she could not bear to see us go.

The next morning she came into my room, sat down on my bed, and waited for me to wake. She was patting the pink blanket with her pudgy hand. I glanced at her bulging stomach under the white apron. Her condition was beginning to show.

"When is the baby due?" I asked sleepily.

"November fourteenth."

"Maybe it will get here on my birthday."

"Maybe." She continued patting the blanket. "After all, my child belongs a bit in your family, too."

She looked down at me with that sly, familiar air of hers, and I opened my eyes fully and asked, "What do you mean?"

"Oh, nothing, nothing." She looked out the window at the dismal, cloudy morning, as she went on: "I was wondering if you could put in a good word for me, so *la Mamma* will help me out a bit—if things should get rough, I mean."

"Do you want her to send you money?" I asked.

"Well—hmm, yes. Whatever she can spare."

"But Zita, my parents have done a lot for you already. I'm sure Mother will be glad to help you again later on. Why don't you ask her yourself?"

"That's just it. You are still a gullible girl, after all—you don't understand."

I knew she was waiting for me to ask, "Understand what, Zita?" but I had no desire to make her tell me what she wanted to say because in a flash I understood only too well. I sat up in bed and said that I had better get ready, since I did not wish to be late for school on my last day, but she remained glued to her seat. Then, whispering, as she tried to work on me with her old superiority, she poured out a torrent of words, "I can't ask her, see, because she will think . . . After all, she let me go out with Merletti all the time so I wouldn't be around when that Ventura was here. So maybe she's afraid that I'm going to tell your Papa all about *that*. Poor thing, your mother is just crazy about him, a young man who could almost be her son! What a scandal that would make! So you see why I can't ask her for money? And all this has gone on right under your nose for years, you poor innocent thing!"

I pushed her away in a fury, got out of bed, and reached for my underwear.

"You still don't believe me, *nè?*" Zita stood beside me, arms akimbo. I had to keep myself from striking her face, which at this moment was full of a peasant woman's cunning.

I concentrated on getting dressed—put on my socks and panties, pulled off my nightgown, and shivering, slipped my arms through the straps of my brassiere. She tried to fasten the hooks in the back, but I shrank from her touch, and flared up angrily, "So what, if you tell my father, it will be your word against hers!"

"But I have proof!" she cried in a whisper.

I turned around to her triumphant face, asking, "What proof?" hiding cold fear under my show of defiant innocence. "You are just bragging and lying, and I won't believe you unless you show it to me!"

"All right," she said, "just a minute!" And she ran out of the room.

I began to count as I finished dressing, and continued counting while I combed my hair, so I would not lose my

252

temper or panic. Zita came back waving a letter in front of my eyes. At once I recognized Dario's straight handwriting.

"How dare you take letters that don't belong to you!" I said icily. "And that's all you have?"

She fell into my trap and answered, "Yes, but that's more than I need to prove it to you!"

"Let me see." Before she knew what was happening, I had snatched the letter from her hand. I ran into the bathroom and locked the door. I was about to tear up the letter, but could not fight the temptation to look at it for a moment. From the date I saw that it had been written about two years ago. So Zita had kept it all this time.

I read only the last sentence: "My darling Mammina, how I long to be inside you again and again and again. . . ."

I tore the letter into shreds and flushed it down the toilet. As I listened to the water's brawl, a darkness came over me. I closed my eyes, and saw nuns and monks, and Mother and Dario and myself in the tunnel.

I unlocked the door and came out to face Zita.

"Now it's only your word against hers," I said. Then I went out to the kitchen for my *caffé-latte*. She followed me slowly with a meek and mortified air.

"I wonder what Merletti would think of you now," I said, heating some milk on the stove. "Do you think he would still love you?"

"But I didn't mean to . . . Nicole! I've been so desperate," she added, bursting into tears, "and there will be all those hospital bills. . . ."

Her words made me think of the ring Dario had not returned to me. "I thought the army was taking care of all his medical expense," I said. In spite of my jealousy

I plotted to prevent Zita from ever telling my father what she knew about Mother and Dario, and I was prepared to do this relentlessly until I felt sure she would not talk. As the milk came to a boil, I turned off the gas and then faced the sobbing Zita, who had followed me like a help-less child, and said as quietly and firmly as I could—for already her wretchedness had moved me to pity—"If you breathe one word to my father, I shall put a curse on you and your baby, a terrible curse, do you hear me?"

"Never, never, I promise, Nicole!" She looked terrified. "Oh, please, forgive me! I didn't mean to. Really, I didn't! Your mamma has always been good to me."

"So you won't tell my father?" Ashamed of exploiting her superstitiousness, I now felt truly grown-up; I, too, had learned to play their games.

"Of course not!" she sobbed.

"Cross your heart and hope to die?"

"Cross my heart, Nicole, and hope to die!"

I poured the coffee Zita had prepared earlier into two cups, added the milk, lifted one of the cups to her lips, and said, "Here, drink! It's good for the baby." She sobbed, then sipped, then took the cup and thanked me, then sobbed and sipped some more. I raised my own cup and gulped down the hot *caffé-latte.*

"I'm so very fond of you, Nicole. Really, I am."

"You fool," I said. "Then why did you try to hurt me? If you are in need, just write to Mother in Paris. I'm sure she'll help you, *vabbene?*"

She nodded. "And you won't tell her what I said?"

"Cross my heart, Zita."

♣ ♣

Later, in school, I had to comfort my classmates. Oretta cried all through the morning. During recess my

254

friends surrounded me and made me promise to keep in touch with them. I accepted their affection with gratitude, for each sign of love was precious to me, as is the song of a bird, the tiny face of a flower, to someone confined to a prison cell.

The air felt sultry, and I saw black clouds gathering above the heavy sand-colored buildings when I left school. I felt like a haunted figure in a dream, unable to voice the cry in my heart.

On rounding the corner, stung by the rays of a hot sun that was trying to break through the dense clouds, I saw Dario leap out of a cab. He took me by the hand and drew me toward the car. I climbed in, my head turning.

The taxi drove on again as Dario gave directions to the driver. We sat in a rigid silence. I vaguely remembered that Mother expected me home for lunch. We turned to look at each other. The car drove on and on.

At last we stopped and got out. Dario dismissed the cab. I realized that we were in a deserted part of the park. The black clouds now hung over the trees. A thunderstorm threatened to break at any moment. We ran along the paths as aimlessly as I had run only a few days before. At last we found a bench and sat down under a large beech tree.

I could feel the darkness of my own eyes as I looked into his, black with the reflection of the clouds above us. Slowly he took my hand, then pressed it until it hurt. His jaws were tightly locked against the pain he suffered, and as I gazed at him, it was as if the world ended there, in his eyes. In the silence of that moment we engraved on our memories each feature, color, quiver of expression, of the other's face.

As I looked at the tiny wrinkles around his eyes, I asked myself, *Why is it that among the million faces on*

*earth this face is so beloved, these hands alone have a
magic touch for me, this head and body and soul are
dearer to me than life? What witchery is love?*

Then Dario spoke. "Why didn't you wait for me that
morning when I called to you from the library?"

"Because there was nothing left to wait for," I said
softly.

"I couldn't go to sleep at all that night. That's what I
wanted to tell you—that I was unable to go through with
it. I mean marrying Mammina."

"Why? Did you tell her that?"

"Of course not! But when you acted so strangely,
when you became so distant, I simply couldn't bear it!"

"Dario, what did you expect?"

"The impossible, I suppose. *Piccola*, oh, *piccola* . . ."
The knuckles of his hand turned white as he pressed
mine.

"We can't do violence to the laws of life," I said.

"Life!" he cried.

"It was nothing reasoned out. Don't you know what
I'm trying to say?"

He shook his head.

"We might have destroyed everything . . . in the end."

"I don't know," he said.

"Yes, Dario, you do! But let's not think back on that.
What's the use of talking about it?"

"Oh, my little one!" he cried, sinking against me.

"Let's not think at all," I whispered. "You are here
now, and there is no past and no future. I can see the
hills across the river. No, don't say anything. You are
here. It's now. Now. I close my eyes, and it's not a
dream. Nothing has ever existed but this now. Nothing
will ever be—afterward."

"Nicole—there is nothing more wonderful and more
terrible than a love that remains unfulfilled, like ours.

256

. . . For its passion is not borne in the flesh but through a hunger that comes from the self."

"Yes," I whispered.

"But it's unbearably painful. If you had been a grown woman, I would have tried to kill my love for you by consuming it, by tearing you to pieces until there was nothing left of you. But I would never have succeeded. . . . Oh God, what makes me say this . . . I have no right!" He almost pushed me away, then hid his face in his arm.

"Why," I asked, shuddering, "why would you do that?"

"I don't know what made me say it. Perhaps I want to free myself from the chains by which you hold me. You are the yardstick against which I have failed in measuring myself." He drew me back into his arms and kissed me with desperate fierceness.

"Dario, we mustn't," I protested faintly, clinging to him with my lips and eyes and arms as if I could never let go of him again.

"*Piccola*, I don't know what makes me talk to you as if you were still a child. You are a woman. But you are so different from anyone I've known. It's as I said, even the passion in your blood is nothing but an expression of the hunger in your heart!"

He bent over me and added in a whisper, "I shouldn't do this to you now, I have hurt you enough, forgive me. When I kiss your lips, I always feel I am kissing your very soul. . . . This never happened to me before."

"What about Mammina?"

"You can be sure that when I kissed her lips, I kissed her lips."

He put his hand into his trouser pocket and drew out the small box in which I kept my grandmother's ring. "Here," he said, "I almost forgot. And here"—he dropped a gold bracelet into my hand as he gave me the box—"a small token of my love. I wanted it to be as unobtrusive as possible," he said. "Almost invisible—a part of your skin."

"Oh, Dario!" I whispered. I did not want to ask him how he had earned the money to redeem the ring and to add the bracelet as well. It was enough that he should have remembered. He fastened the smooth, wafer-thin chain of the bracelet about my wrist and put the ring on my finger.

"I wish it were my engagement gift for you," he said, holding my hand. "*Amor mio*, listen carefully. A few days ago you suggested we should wait for each other. I have thought about it ever since. This is why I had to speak to you, to see you once more."

"Yes, Dario?" I said faintly, waiting for him to go on.

"I am taking you up on it. In three or four years you'll be of age, and then we can get married."

"Oh, Dario, Dario!" I burst into tears, burying my face in my hands. "Don't you see it's too late?"

"Why too late? If I promise to wait for you?"

"Don't you see? I can't do this to Mammina, not any more, after she's given you up for my sake! Do you think I would put a dagger in her heart?"

"Time is a great healer, Nicole. It may no longer hurt her three years from now."

"Never, never, never!" I cried, shaking all over. Now I could hear the storm raging above the river.

"Nicole, *anima mia*, what is to become of us!" He pulled my hands from my face, then turned away, sobbing helplessly. I could see flashes of lightning that were followed by the hollow boom of thunder. We rose, hand in hand, and began to run aimlessly again. The rain poured down in torrents.

"Nicole, where do we go from here?" Dario stopped under a tree and pulled me to him.

258

"I don't know," I said.

"Oh, where, where are we going!" he cried out in agony. I could not tell whether his face was wet with tears or rain. He kissed me furiously, holding me close and whispering, "Where, where, where?" between each kiss. I could taste the salt of his tears as I clung to him, and I was consumed by the same terror and passion.

"I don't know," I sobbed, "I don't know!"

"You were always right not to know. Oh, what do we know, Nicole . . ."

"But I, too, can send you to Rome!" I whispered unexpectedly.

"What? What did you say?"

"Dario!" The rain whipped against our brows as I bit into his lip in a frenzy. I could taste blood and tears. Then I tore myself away and, turning my head, ran toward the street, sobbing wildly.

♣ ♣

Our departure was like a flight in its furtive abruptness. The street at that early hour was deserted as we stepped into the cab. But as I looked out of the taxi at the house I was leaving forever, I became aware of a solitary figure standing at the corner. It was Dario, in his officer's uniform, watching us go.

For an instant it was as though he were reaching out his arms toward us, but blinded as I was by my tears, I might have confused a gesture from outside with the cry that rose in my heart. As we began to drive away, the street separating us became a deep sea. All the way to the station Mother held my hand, turning her head from time to time, as if watching for a car that might be following us. Once, in the crowd at Porta Susa, I was certain I saw Dario's eyes.

We said good-bye to Father and got on the train. From

the window of our compartment we saw an officer in a field-green uniform among the civilians on the platform beyond other tracks. Mother and I looked at each other, our hands clasped together like one. As the officer walked searchingly up and down the platform, I thought I recognized the sweep of Dario's dark hair. Before I could see his face, the black monster of a train blocked our view.

Our train began to move. Sunbeams passed over our faces, then shadow; then sunbeams again, then shadow. As we came out of the station and saw the city of Turin spread in symmetrical lights and shades, the sun wandered to the other side of our compartment and painted a dazzling triangle of light across an empty seat.

Mother leaned forward and pulled down the blind.